# THE FAN LETTER

THE FAN LETTER IS A ROMANTIC STORY OF A TELEVISION SERIES FAN WHO WRITES TO HER FAVORITE ACTOR. SHE SENDS A SHORT STORY, A PHOTO OF HERSELF, AND COMMENDATION FOR HIS ACTING ABILITIES. THEIR LIVES SOON INTERTWINE WHEN HER LETTER SETS OFF A CHAIN OF EVENTS THAT AFFECT BOTH HER LIFE, AS WELL AS THIS ACTOR'S LIFE AND CAREER.

LESLIE NELSON, RIGHT AFTER A FAILED MARRIAGE, FINDS HERSELF ALONE BUT WITH PLENTY OF SPARE TIME ON HER HANDS. HOOKED ON A POPULAR FUTURISTIC TELEVISION SHOW, "THE TIME POLICE", SHE DECIDES TO WRITE HER OWN EPISODES JUST FOR THE FUN OF IT. BEST FRIEND JANICE URGES HER TO SEND THE MANUSCRIPT ALONG WITH A FAN LETTER TO THE ACTORS ON THE SHOW. LITTLE DID SHE IMAGINE THE CHAIN OF EVENTS THAT FAN LETTER WOULD SET IN MOTION!

GUEST STAR ON "THE TIME POLICE", PHILLIP BECK, RECEIVES LESLIE'S LETTER AND MANUSCRIPT DURING A FILMING. RECOGNIZING HE HAD ALWAYS BEEN A SECOND-BILLING ACTOR AND THAT HIS PERSONAL LIFE SEEMED TO BE FALLING APART, HE SEES AN OPPORTUNITY TO BETTER HIMSELF WITH A GREAT ROLE.

AFTER HE EXTENDS ENCOURAGEMENT TO THIS MYSTERIOUS FAN HE ALSO FINDS HIMSELF BEING DRAWN IN. HOWEVER, HIS WIFE, WORLD-FAMOUS MODEL SARAH BECK, SEES THE FAN AS A THREAT AND TAKES MATTERS INTO HER OWN HANDS BY HIRING PRIVATE INVESTIGATOR WAYNE FIELDS TO SPY ON LESLIE.

ONCE LESLIE'S NOVELS ARE PUBLISHED AND EVENTUALLY TURNED INTO SCRIPTS, SHE FINDS HER WHOLE WORLD IS CHANGED. HER LIFE IS NOW BECOMING INTERMINGLED WITH FAVORITE TELEVISION STARS SHE HAD ONLY ADMIRED FROM THE SAFETY OF HER LIVING ROOM. WHEN AN UNEXPECTED, EXCITING OFFER COMES HER WAY, WHICH LIFE WILL SHE CHOOSE? WHAT WILL SHE DO WHEN SHE LEARNS THAT HER EVERY ACTION IS BEING REPORTED BY A PI?

FOLLOW THE ACTION AND ROMANCE AS THE FAN LETTER FOLLOWS THIS "OUTSIDER" AS SHE BECOMES AN "INSIDER" IN THE FASCINATING WORLD OF HOLLYWOOD. SEE HOW LESLIE COPES AS HER FICTION BECOMES HER REALITY AND SHE FACES SITUATIONS THAT HAD PREVIOUSLY EXISTED ONLY IN HER WILDEST DREAMS.

# THE FAN LETTER

BY

NANCY TEMPLE RODRIGUE

2011
DOUBLE-R BOOKS

**DOUBLE-R BOOKS** ARE PUBLISHED BY
RODRIGUE & SONS COMPANY
244 FIFTH AVENUE, SUITE 1457
NEW YORK, NY 10001
WWW.DOUBLE-RBOOKS.COM

# THE FAN LETTER
1ST EDITION - 2011

PAPERBACK ISBN 13: 978-0-9833975-2-6
PAPERBACK ISBN: 0-9833975-2-X
EBOOK ISBN 13: 978-0-9833975-3-3
EBOOK ISBN: 0-9833975-3-8

COVER DESIGN BY DOUBLE-R BOOKS
WWW.DOUBLE-RBOOKS.COM

PRINTED IN THE UNITED STATES OF AMERICA

*I would like to dedicate this novel to two special people.*

*First is my husband Russ Rodrigue who has been the source of encouragement and support in everything I have done. I really couldn't have done any of it without him!*

*The second person is my friend Anne E-T in Modesto. Anne was my "Janice" and my cheering section when I first came up with the idea to write for my favorite TV show. And, yes, she was with me when I went to my first Sci-Fi convention. She didn't even blink when I gave her wrong directions to the Golden Gate Bridge!*

**Nancy Temple Rodrigue**

## Disclaimer

All references to television shows and/or episodes, movies, businesses, persons named, and/or events described are purely fictional and a product of the Author's imagination. Any resemblance to television shows and/or episodes, movies, businesses, people, and/or events are purely coincidental. The actions depicted within the book are a result of fiction and imagination and are not to be attempted, reproduced or duplicated by the readers of this book.

Dear Readers,

I took a break from the Wonderful World of Mickey and my *Hidden Mickey* action/adventure series to share with you a story I wrote a little over 20 years ago.

This story is a fantasy I created when I attempted to write novels for an extremely popular television series during the late 1980's and early 1990's. My novels never came to fruition at that time, but I envisioned what it might have been like if they had. As you read, you might wonder: Have I really been on the working set of a television series or to a huge Hollywood party? Let's just say a quick No, and move on. The wonderful thing about a fantasy is that is doesn't have to be grounded in too many things, like facts!

One similarity that I do share with the heroine Leslie is that I did receive an encouraging phone call from one of the guest stars on that aforementioned television show. I really did send him copies of the short stories I had written, and he really did call me to offer encouragement as well as to extend his appreciation for the effort I had put into my manuscript (and, yes, I do still have the tape recording that he left on my answering machine). After that uplifting incident, the similarities within *The Fan Letter* end.

Two decades later, within the writing of my second Hidden Mickey novel, *Hidden Mickey 2: It All Started…*, I came back to fantasy writing with a special character I named Wolf and a mysterious pendant tied to him. I liked Wolf so much that I gave him his own book titled *Hidden Mickey 3 Wolf! The Legend of Tom Sawyer's Island* where his background and special, unique abilities are more thoroughly investigated. I am now in the midst of writing Wolf's continuing story in the novel titled *Hidden Mickey 4 Wolf! Happily Ever After?*, scheduled for release in 2012.

So, for now, sit back and relax as I bring you this romantic fantasy *The Fan Letter*. As I prepared it for publication, it was as enjoyable for me to read again twenty years later as it was to pretend it was all going to come true the first time around!

I hope you enjoy it as well.

Sincerely,

Nancy Temple Rodrigue

# CHAPTER 1

# 1988

"Hey, Bob, have you seen....Oh, never mind. There he is. Mr. Beck? Mr. Beck, wait a minute!" The aide hurried across the noisy set to the actor who was now turning to see who had just called him. The aide was smiling. The actor was not.

"Mr. Beck? These papers came for you. The Fan Club asked me to bring them down. They knew you were shooting today," he hurriedly explained as he handed the bundle to Phillip Beck. The aide then turned to go, and he added with a smile, "Cute bunny!"

A confused expression crossed Phillip's face at this comment. "Bunny?...Er, thanks, uhm...Andy," he mumbled after reading the security I.D. badge hanging off the young man's lanyard. Phillip looked down at the photograph clipped on the top of a letter and what looked like a script. There was a six-foot tall amusement park rabbit hugging a brown-haired woman. The rabbit he could identify. The woman he could not.

Still staring at the rabbit, he slowly shook his head. "Now what do *they* want?" he asked himself with a sigh. "They" referred to John Q. Public. Always wanting something from him.

Always asking favors of him.

Phillip glanced at his watch and realized he was due in Make-Up in fifteen minutes. As he hurried off to his dressing room he was somewhat irritated that he was now behind schedule. He hadn't even looked at his script changes for that day's shoot or changed into his costume.

"Thanks, bunny," he grumbled as he quickly tossed the papers onto the one over-stuffed chair in his dressing room and got into costume. He grabbed up the daily changes that were waiting for him on the mirrored dresser. Reading as he walked, he headed for Make-Up. So far nothing major had been changed, he noticed.

One of the regular stars of "The Time Police" was already seated and being worked on by one of the make-up artists. Eddie Chase, who played the romantic lead and rated second billing, smiled his greeting. "Hey, Phillip, you're late! This is a first. Thought we'd have to replace you!" he kidded, as Jill, the make-up gal, smiled but stayed silent.

Phillip eased his six-foot-one frame into the comfortable make-up chair and replied straight-faced to Eddie's reflection in the brightly-lit mirror. "Some aide brought down a letter from the fan club. *He* seemed to think it was humorous." He automatically lifted his chin as a make-up cape was draped over his costume and snapped into place at the back of his neck.

"Thanks, Jill," Eddie said as she finished with him. He swung his chair around to face Phillip, a look of interest on his ruggedly handsome face. "A fan letter, huh? We usually never see ours. What'd it say?"

"I have no idea." Phillip's attention was back on the change sheets. "I guess I should look it over during the lunch break.... Now why in the world did they change scene four? It was fine the way it was," as he slapped the papers with the back of his hand.

Eddie shrugged as he rose from his seat and checked his hair. "They said it ran too long. Don't worry," he grinned with the small charming type of grin that was plastered all over his publicity photos, "they just cut out most of your lines!"

Phillip didn't return the smile. He didn't even take note of Eddie's humorous comment. "No kidding," as he flipped through the rest of the pages. "All I have to do now is just lie there and react.... Edward," he called offhandedly, as his co-worker headed for the set. "You said you usually don't see your mail. None of it? How come?"

Already out the door when he heard his name—or rather, Phillip's formal use of his name—his head peered around the doorframe. His shrug went unseen. "Too many letters, too much legality, I guess," he answered. "The volume is overwhelming. Especially Tom. They tell us his Loner character gets more mail than any of us. See you on the set. Don't forget your lines now!" he laughed as he headed out again.

Phillip Beck didn't respond. He didn't even hear that last crack of Eddie's. He was thinking back on his run with the popular television series. "The Time Police" had been on the air for three years now and was consistently in the Top Ten. He had guest-starred as Professor Rex Farrell five times in those three years. This would be his sixth show. How many letters had he received? Ten? Twelve? Fifteen from the fans of the show? They were always the same. "I want an autograph." "I want a picture." "What is Tom Young really like?" "Will you give Eddie Chase my phone number?" "Are you at all like the Professor?"

The make-up artist was startled when Phillip suddenly laughed dryly to himself and shook his head. His eyes looked a million miles away. She quietly finished her work, removed the cape, and left the room.

Phillip hadn't noticed any of this. He was thinking back to that Friday three years ago when his agent, Bill Michaels, had told him about a new television show that was being developed.

"Phil, you're going to love it! It's called "The Time Police" and it's about a group of special police officers who travel back and forth in time with this time machine. The Professor who invents the machine starts off as one of them, but an accident affects his brain, you see? He becomes super intelligent and a little demented. Now he disappears into time and causes problems that the squad has to correct. The lead, Sir Charles, is the time expert and squad leaded. The brains of the group is Jack

"The Loner" Newby. Then there's two more stars in the plot, a guy and a girl for the romantic parts. What an idea! The squad goes wherever they are needed to fix all the wrongs—like correcting serial killers, or to help prepare people before major disasters! This Professor guy starts fooling around with established events. It becomes a game to him!"

Bill finished out of breath. He could tell this would be big and he wanted his long-time client and friend to be part of it. He waited patiently as Phillip mulled over the plot in his mind. Phillip never did anything quickly.

Looking over the pilot script that Bill had handed him, he eventually nodded. "I could do this," he murmured more to himself than to Bill. "I could put a little grey in my hair for Sir Charles. A little age, a little more dignity."

"No, no," Bill broke in. "Maxwell Marlowe has already signed for Sir Charles. Majestic Studio has been after him for months."

Phillip glanced up briefly. Maxwell Marlowe. Big guns. "Good casting," he nodded. Changing gears, he weighed the other option. "The Loner. Jack Newby," as he mulled over the name as if feeling them out.

"Tom Young," Bill cut in again. "He contracted last week. We want you for the Professor."

Phillip noticed the omission of the other male lead character, Andrew Fox, the romantic adventurer. "I'm not sure I want to commit to a full-time series. I had enough of that off-Broadway. I'd like to keep my options open."

"You didn't read the fine print. The Professor is a recurring character. You'd be in the first two shows to establish what happened and set it up. Then, probably two, three episodes a season. It's a great part, Phil," the agent added unnecessarily. "Think of the possibilities for the character! He can go anywhere and do anything!"

"Yeah, yeah, I know." The actor looked away from the script and out the window that overlooked the heart of Los Angeles. He had wanted the lead. Badly. He'd been in the business for fifteen years and never once.... "When do you need an answer?" he asked as he stood to go, still holding onto the pilot.

"Wednesday," was the reply. Bill wasn't worried. He knew

that, once Phillip read the entire script, he'd get a call. Probably Monday.

Phillip hesitated at the door, his hand on the doorknob. "Where is this "Time Police" based?"

"The Silicon Valley about one hundred years in the future. Apparently our future isn't very pretty and the squad works on things like corrupt politicians, polluting industrialists, land grabbers, stuff like that as well as established historical events."

The spark of interest had grown. The actor raised a hand good-bye and shut the door quietly behind him. Bill Michaels sat back in his chair and put his hands behind his head. "Naw. He'll call me Sunday at home!"


Phillip did indeed call Bill at home on Sunday just as Bill had predicted. He had been irritated, however, when Bill told him the contract was already drawn and just needed his signature. He liked to make his own decisions.

Sarah, Phillip's wife, had urged him to accept the role. "It's a great opportunity for exposure," she had said. But, she always said that. Sarah felt every two-bit part that came along was right for him, he reflected. As a much sought-after model, she seemed a lot more selective with the commercials she was offered than she was with *his* career. But, then, every major company was clamoring for the beautiful model. Cosmetics. Appliances. Cars. Travel companies. Food. Even foreign companies had been contacting her agent lately.

All it takes is hard work and the right part for that great break-out role...and Phillip knew that this really entails careful deliberation...not snapping up everything thrown in your face. And Bill Michaels sent him almost every new series and small movie part that appeared on his desk. Phillip spent days pouring through the scripts Bill sent him looking for that one prime role. He found good leads—but they were always filled by "names." The lead's wife's girlfriend's uncle was available, though. "It's a small part, Phillip, but it is vital for the scene."

*Okay*, Phillip argued with himself, the *Professor was quite different from his other roles.* It had become an enjoyable character to play. And the writers were giving him more to do as the series progressed. The shows he had previously appeared in were some of the highest rated. But, still….

Fifteen letters in three years. "I should have gotten Sir Charles," he groused.

The sound of Phillip's own deep voice startled him out of his reflective mood. He hadn't even realized he had just spoken aloud. Quickly glancing around the room, he was relieved to see that he was alone. Looking back to the mirror, he experienced a shock. His face was a ghastly shade of white with red blotches…. Oh, right. The Professor had been injured in a blast meant for the squad. He was supposed to look like he could die at any minute. He did.

Leaning closer to the mirror to study the bleeding gashes, he saw the face of a seventeen-year-old boy peer around the door-frame. He was the producer's nephew. "Mr. Beck? You're wanted on the sound stage. They're finished with the lighting tests."

*I'll be there when I'm good and ready*, he said in his mind as his voice calmly replied, "On my way."

It was a private joke on the set of "The Time Police" that the director got his name because he always got his five-cents worth into whatever was going on. Ron Nickles, however, was unaware of the pun and wouldn't have been interested anyway. His joy in living was his job and it quickly became obvious to onlookers that he knew what he was doing. Ron had just turned fifty and was actually proud of the fact that his hair had turned grey twenty years earlier. He blamed the phenomenon on his job and the stress level under which he worked and thrived.

At this point in the day, he was in his glory—behind sched-ule, over budget, and understaffed because of a flu epidemic. The whole crew respected and admired his on-the-edge-of-a-breakdown methods and now they awaited their first shot for the day's filming.

Glasses pushed on top of his head, Ron was putting the actors through their lines and actions and showing them their marks.

"Okay, people, listen up. We're already behind schedule today, so let's not have to do too many takes. Eddie. The scenes are quiet, the action shots have already taken place—nice you could join us, Mr. Beck—and you are all now working over the injured Professor.

"Places. Eddie and Cindy, over by the mark for the time portal. Eddie, your hands off Cindy and folded over your chest. Look disgusted. Cindy, you're worried. Maxwell, further to the left. Where's the computer prop? Good. Just keep working calculations. Phillip, Tom, on the floor center stage. Cameras two and three, both get the shots. Three, you come in closer. We need some more smoke coming out of the rubble!

"Are we ready? Tom, down on both knees, please, not one. You look like you are going to propose in that position.... Quiet! Slate.... Roll...."

*Professor Rex Farrell opened his eyes slowly. They were showing the pain his body was feeling. He focused into the face of his ex-colleague, Jack Newby. He had given Jack the nickname The Loner. It had stuck all these years since the split. The Loner was working over him to see how badly he was hurt. The Professor saw the others and noted the scowl on Andrew's face. "Why are you helping me? Why don't you just let me die...cough...."*

"Cut!" yelled Nickles' voice. "Phillip, you're giving me too much energy. You're half dead, remember. Begin again. Slate it.... Action."

*Quieter, "Why are you helping me? Why don't you just let me die...cough.... I do believe that would be Andrew's recommendation."*

*The Loner placed his fingers on the artery in the Professor's neck. "I cannot let the second greatest scientific mind perish as long as I have the capacity to help."*

*"Second greatest?" A sickly laugh rattled his chest, then a wheeze. "Don't flatter yourself. Your intelligence nowhere near matches mine." Eyes closed, a groan came from the slightly parted lips.*

*"An intelligence used for evil and mischief cannot be measured against one being used for the good of the people. Plus, there is always the chance I can reverse the damage done to your mind."*

*The Professor's eyes opened and a faint smile came to his white lips. "Wasted effort...Moan....I enjoy my...my...." He fainted and his body relaxed.*

*The Loner gently set the Professor's head down on the ground and stood. "You may enjoy your mischief, but you are hurting innocent people who have already suffered enough. Sir Charles, he's ready for transport. Andrew, help me get him to the portal. Let's get back to the lab!"*

*Andrew and The Loner bent down to pick up the motionless Professor and supported him to the spot where Maggie Rush stood by the portal that would take them back to their time period. The five of them froze in their motions. Two, three, four, five and "Cut!"*

Tom and Eddie glanced at each other and, on a silent signal, let go of Phillip. Without their support and caught unawares, he banged heavily against the set that rocked precariously. Tom and Eddie held back their grins as they turned to face the director.

Ron was used to their antics and ignored Phillip as he wiped white make-up from his face off of the set. "Perfect," Ron told them. "Now I need Cindy and Eddie back to their places for some reaction shots. The rest of you relax. We'll do the laboratory scene next. Phillip, your face is smeared. Where's Jill?"

Phillip looked accusingly over at Tom who smiled innocently back at him. He couldn't understand how those two could clown around so much on the set. Neither one had been in the business as long as he, so they probably hadn't yet learned the seriousness of good acting manners, he decided. It amazed him that they were so popular on the set and that they showed up on late-night interview shows so often. Their shenanigans made them regulars on the television goof-and-bleep shows. Even the respected Maxwell Marlowe was affected by their antics now and again. The favorite clip of all was the three of them, in full costume and mid-scene, breaking into a three-part harmony song of questionable taste. They had received the expected tongue-lashing from the director and then had to battle a fit of giggles led by Cindy Sanders for the rest of the day.

The filming of the medical scenes on the laboratory set took the rest of the morning. Since Phillip's lines had been cut, he was required only to lie on the examination table as the others worked over and around him and react to what they were doing as he supposedly drifted in and out of consciousness.

The medical terminology slipped up Tom a few times and Cindy missed a mark and dropped a tray of instruments. All were relieved when Ron called for the lunch break. "Keep in costume," he reminded them as they prepared to scatter. "We'll pick up here in an hour."

Outside of the sound stages on the Majestic lot were rows of vendors allowed on the site for lunch. Here Phillip picked up his customary ham and cheese sandwich and a coffee and headed back to his dressing room. He preferred eating lunch alone as he didn't like surprises in his coffee when his attention was diverted. The laxative incident a year ago was still fresh in his mind.

Setting his coffee on the small table, Phillip dropped into the easy chair. The sound of papers being crushed and the feel of a plastic spiral binding startled him at he sat. Thinking he had just ruined the script they were filming, he quickly pulled the papers out from beneath him. A handwritten letter was now badly crumpled. The fan letter. He had completely forgotten about it. So much for the idea of a quiet, relaxing lunch. "Thanks, bunny," he mumbled as he unwrapped his sandwich and smoothed out the letter.

There were two pages to the letter written in an easy, looping handwriting. The paper was a plain ivory color with no heading or borders, no perfume or hearts or animals. Phillip noticed the paper matched the color of the included script paper as he started both the letter and the sandwich.

*"Hello, Phillip."*

He reread that. Not "Dear Phillip." Just "Hello Phillip."

*"You probably noticed a book attached to this letter. I figured you received so much mail that I'd at least get points for originality!*

*I enjoy watching "The Time Police" and I enjoy your character of Rex Farrell. I admit, though, that I didn't know your real name until just recently when I started writing my own stories for the show.*

*The Professor is a lot of fun to write as he can do and say anything and get away with it! Who could stop him? You must really enjoy portraying him. It looks like you are having a good time with him.*

*This is the second story I have written. The first, called THE LONER FINDS LOVE, I sent to Tom Young as it concerns his character. I thought you might be more interested than he would be since this story concerns the Professor more than The Loner. (That is, if the first story interested Tom or even got to him!)*

*For a little background, the new character I introduce is Jane Barrett. The squad rescued her from sixteenth-century Scotland where she had been injured in a clan raid. Knowing she would die and not affect history, the squad brings her back with them to their time. As she recovers and learns about modern life, she and The Loner fall in love and get married to the surprise of everyone and to the disgust of Andrew who had taken an unexplained dislike to her. The Commissioner of the Time Police makes her a full member of the squad in the end of the first book.*

*I hope you enjoy reading this story. I really enjoyed writing it. I also think it would make a terrific episode for the show. And, in case you need a brown-haired, blue-eyed co-star, I happen to know of someone who is quite familiar with Jane! She can be reached at 555-4029.*

*I'm sure you get a lot of mail and I'm sorry all of this is so long. I'm one of those rare individuals who enjoy writing letters.*

*The picture was taken a couple of years ago. I'm sure you can identify where it was taken. (I'm on the right!)*

*May the series have a long run and may the next episode you shoot be a Western!*

*Take care,*

*Leslie Nelson"*


Phillip sat there with the letter in one hand and his sandwich with only one bite out of it in the other. He must have read it wrong or skipped something. Where was the request for a picture or an autograph? Where were all the personal questions? Where was the mush about Tom or Eddie? "They" don't send letters that don't demand something.

He reread the entire letter. It sounded the same. He looked again at the picture. Short brown hair swept back from the face. Probably messy from the roller coaster behind her. Her eyes were red dots from the flash. Big smile on a friendly face. Certainly not beautiful, hardly even pretty, but, still, a pleasant face. Compared to the size of the rabbit next to her, she was short in stature, slender frame, casual clothes. She looked like she was having fun. Twenty-four years old? Twenty-eight? He couldn't tell.

With an interested snort, he clipped the picture back onto the letter and took another bite of his sandwich. The forgotten coffee remained untouched and would now be an undrinkable lukewarm. His attention moved to the story. It had all the appearances of a script, but was printed on a heavy, grained paper. The cover was blank. The title page read WESTWARD REX.


### Chapter One

The Commissioner's face was stern as he was finishing the instructions for the squad's next assignment. "The computer indicates the Plague of '98 could have been averted if Dr. Marian Jones had gotten the grant from the government in 1996. You are to go back to early 1996, to Washington, and see that that happens. Among the victims of the Plague was a young man who had been working on a solution to the ozone depletions. You can all see the necessity of his surviving.

Maggie Rush looked up from her desk in the laboratory. "Commissioner? Couldn't we just rescue the man and see that his work continues?"

"No, Maggie," he responded. "The doctor is important as well. Her studies in immunology must be developed, also. Her further contributions could be vital. Are there any other questions?"

The squad glanced at each other. They were ready.

Sir Charles stepped forward. "We're set, Commissioner. Has the portal been programmed?"

"Yes. All is ready. I know I don't need to stress the importance of your mission. Not only will that generation be helped, but our entire future as well. Success," he concluded and the view screen went blank.

As preparations for the journey were underway, the door to the portal opened. Professor Rex Farrell emerged dressed as a riverboat gambler from the late 1800's.

Jane Newby gasped and dropped her handheld computer link-up. At the sound, the rest of the squad turned and saw the intruder. Jane was stunned. No one else was supposed to have access to the portal.

"Rex!" shouted Sir Charles, losing his usually cool countenance. "Leave this lab at once! We don't have time to fool with you!"

"Good to see you, too, Sir Charles," smiled the unperturbed Professor. "I'm sorry to break in like this, but I was caught cheating at poker and an unruly group of gentlemen had some rather unpleasant plans for my neck.... Who's this, now?" he asked, wickedly smiling as he went over to Jane.

She backed away from this tall, strange, handsome man as he approached her. She grabbed her husband's arm as she moved behind Jack.

"Leave my wife alone, Rex," The Loner warned the advancing Professor.

A big grin suddenly broke over the Professor's face. "Wife, you say? Someone actually broke through The Loner? Well done, ma'am," as he took off his black wool top hat and bowed low to her.

Andrew broke in, not liking the attention to Jane, and shortly said, "We have to be going. You and Jane can exchange recipes later. We have an assignment to do."

Maggie threw him a disgusted look as she went to the portal with the others. She couldn't understand Andrew's continued irritation towards Jane. Maybe she would talk to him when they returned.

The Professor watched as they entered the portal and said nothing when he was told to be gone before they returned. As the door closed, he took out of his brocade vest pocket a small computer remote and pushed the red button. Waiting five seconds, he smiled, opened the portal, entered the empty room, and again, pushed the red button."

A loud knocking noise disturbed Phillip. He looked up, mid-sentence, at the interruption.

"Mr. Beck? The director is looking for you. Are you awake?" the aide was asking, almost pleading. He knew the morning shots had to be redone and Ron was tense.

Phillip glanced at the clock on the wall. An hour and a half had passed. He hadn't realized it. Stifling a curse, he quickly finished his sandwich and grabbed up the coffee. He knew it would certainly be cold by now.

"Coming," he called as he threw down the story and went for the door. He was late again. Grumbling, "Thanks, bunny," he headed for the set.

Ron was pacing the set of the lab when Phillip strode in. Eddie and Cindy gave each other a worried glance. They knew how Phillip hated to be counseled in front of everyone.

"Sorry," was all Phillip muttered as he was motioned to resume his place on the examination table.

As Jill repaired the actor's make-up, Ron filled everyone in on the afternoon's plans.

"We're not happy with the quality of the medical shots. I want less energy from Mr. Beck and more from Miss Sanders and Mr. Young. As you Mr. Chase, we decided to remove you from the scene entirely. Andrew will say, 'Why don't you just let him die. That would solve everything,' and then you leave the room...out that door," he pointed and glanced at Eddie, expecting an argument.

Eddie had moved over to the table where Phillip was now sitting. He knew Ron would love an argument to release his tension, but, instead, he merely shrugged his acceptance. In a low voice to Phillip, he smiled, "That must have been some hot letter you received. I figured that's why you were late."

His one-track mind reverting from the scene at hand to that last remark from Eddie, Phillip was momentarily stumped. "Hot?" His mind quickly went over the gist of the letter. That word didn't apply. He shook his head, frowning. "No, it wasn't at all like that. I don't get...." He left the rest unsaid and turned to see if anyone else was close enough to be listening. All were still being instructed by the director.

Eddie slapped him affably on the leg. "Don't let it worry you, old man," he kidded. "Everyone gets dog letters now and then!" as he moved off to take his mark.

When Ron was ready, all went to their places and awaited his cue. Phillip was prone on the table, shirt off, eyes closed, as Tom waited with his hands in midair.

As the scene commenced, Phillip thought on Eddie's remarks. Both "old man" and "dog letter" stuck in his mind. He didn't understand "old man" as a joke as Eddie was age thirty-seven to his forty years. He then remembered to open his eyes briefly and move his head as if in pain. He frowned to himself. This hardly qualified as a "dog letter" —one that was negative in content or from an unattractive person.

He heard Tom say, "Ah, that's it! He's going to live. Sir Charles, I volunteer to stay with him. He'll need constant monitoring until he is well."

Maxwell's voice replied, "All right, Jack. He'll be assigned to you. Keep an eye on him. We still don't know about the blast. I've sent Maggie and Andrew to investigate."

Phillip knew Tom was now nodding to the camera and he felt a sheet being pulled up his chest. All held their places for three, four, five, and.... "Cut."

Phillip threw back the sheet and sat up, looking for Eddie. The other actor was sitting off the stage watching the scene. Phillip headed over to him, pulling on the shirt he had left draped over his own chair—the one that read "Guest."

The director called Maxwell and Cindy over for some close-ups. Tom wandered over to his chair and leaned over the back of it with no specific goal in mind other than waiting to see if Ron called him back.

Phillip turned to Eddie. "It hardly qualified as a 'dog letter'," he abruptly stated.

"What?" Eddie had no idea what he was talking about. He was thinking about his next scene.

"My letter," Phillip doggedly explained. "You were unfair. The script Bunny sent is actually very interesting."

Finally remembering the fan letter, he was surprised that it had elicited *any* response from Phillip. Now it seemed as though Phillip was defending the writer. Trying to hide his amusement, Eddie assumed it was all because Phillip wasn't used to getting much fan mail. But, he was still unsure of something. "Did you say script? What script?" he asked.

"I haven't read very much so far, but it looks like a Western," explained Phillip.

Eddie's look of amusement changed. "Really? We've never done a Western."

Ron called for Phillip to redo one of his shots. As he removed his shirt, he remarked to Eddie, "See? When something is creative like that, you can hardly refer to it as a 'dog'."

When Phillip had returned to the table, Eddie glanced over at Tom, who had remained silent. "You know?" he drawled, "We should all chip in a few bucks and buy Phillip a sense of humor!"

"**D**addy! Daddy! Daddy!" The four-year old threw himself at Phillip's long legs when he entered his house at seven o'clock that evening.

With a warm smile, Phillip bent down and picked up his son. "Hello, Davey. How's my boy? Where's your mom?"

Davey held out a drawing he had done with his crayons. It was a bright assortment of lines and circles.

"Well, what's this? You're getting to be quite the artist." Phillip looked at the paper as he sat himself down comfortable on the sofa.

Davey kept his arms locked around his daddy's neck as he explained, "That's you, daddy! And that's Uncle Tom and Uncle Eddie," he pointed.

Phillip smiled. So the circles were heads and the lines were legs and arms. He immediately distinguished that *his* lines were the longest. He was the tallest on the set, measuring out at six feet two inches, whereas "Uncle" Eddie was only six feet one.

"When can I go back on the set?" Davey eagerly asked— again. Ever since Phillip had taken him last season Davey had been asking for another visit. Eddie had given him a "Time Police" badge and Tom had taken him into the time portal. It was all very exciting for a four-year old.

"Maybe next time, son. We're going to be finished in a couple of days. Eddie mentioned a party at his place after we're done. You're invited!"

That prospect wasn't as exciting as a visit to the set, but it was better than nothing. "Okay, I guess. Will Eddie Junior be there?" He sounded wary and not at all happy about the possibility.

"Of course. I thought you like Eddie Junior."

Davey rolled off Phillip's lap and sat next to him, his expression becoming very serious. "Well, I did. But then he got to be on the show and I didn't."

Phillip turned his head away and briefly rolled his eyes. They had had this conversation before. "Eddie's son is older than you. And you know there aren't that many parts for young boys on the show. You were in a commercial with your mom, remember?" he pointed out.

"It's not the same," was the pouty reply.

Phillip gave him a hug. "Just be patient until you grow some. Where's your mom?" he repeated.

"Looking over Japan."

Phillip reminded himself he should never ask a four-year old anything that required a definite answer. He then noticed the door to Sarah's study was closed.

Going over, he knocked and opened the door a crack. "Sarah? Want to go out for dinner?"

"We're going to the Matsui's for a get-together. Did you forget?"

He swallowed his groan. *Wonderful. Another long evening with her potential employers and her scummy agent.* This job would take her to Japan for a month. With Davey. Without him. An excellent career move. For her.

Davey came over and wrapped himself around Phillip's leg again. "I'm going to Japan!" he announced. "Is that near your studio, Daddy?"

"*Maybe* you're going, Davey," Phillip corrected. He pushed the door open. "It hasn't been decided yet," he said a little louder so he would be heard.

Sarah looked up from the contract and some sample ads of the product she would be representing. Her long blond hair was artfully arranged on top of her head for the party and dangling diamond earrings caught the light. She heard what Phillip had said just fine..

"Can I go to the party, Mommy?" asked Davey, taking the opportunity to come into her private study where he was usually forbidden.

"No, honey," as she kissed his upturned, hopeful face. "It's just for grown-ups. Mrs. Clark will be here soon.... You'd better hurry, Phillip. We have to leave in half an hour."

Eyes narrowed, her husband just stood by the door. She had already decided to take the job. He could tell.

"Oh, Phillip? I forgot to tell you. The Matsui's also invited Bob Carlson. I hear he's divorced again," she casually commented as her attention was once again focused on her contract.

*Bob Carlson. Head of Zenith Pictures. Second largest stu-*

*dio in the world*, ran through Phillip's mind as he stood there looking at her.

Realizing he hadn't moved, Sarah glanced around at the severe look on Phillip's face. "It's a wonderful chance for you, Phillip. He's doing a movie-of-the-week and doesn't have the full cast yet. He offered me a role, but I don't want to do television movies just yet," her beautiful face momentarily betraying how beneath her she felt television work was. "Besides, I'll...." She broke off, thinking it best not to pursue that matter right then.

With forced civility, Phillip finished her sentence for her. "Besides, you'll be in Japan."

She gracefully stood and took Davey by the hand. "Come on, honey. You can talk to me while I finish getting ready." They walked past Phillip as he stood in the doorway. He could smell the subtle fragrance of her perfume.

His eyes searched out the photograph on the wall behind her antique desk that showed her modeling for that perfume. Low cut black velvet dress trimmed in gold braid, slit up the leg. Her intense blue eyes looking over the perfume bottle. His glance fell on her awards that lined her beautiful Laotian Black and White Ebony burlwood built-in bookcase. Her beauty and poise and business sense had gotten her far. Too far? No, he admitted with a sigh, not yet. She was still his wife and mother of his son. And she was trying to be helpful in his career. She just needed to trust his judgment and allow him to make his own decisions. Like she was making her own decisions. And succeeding. At age twenty-eight, her face, if not her name, was known across the country. Soon it would be known around the world.

Next to the polished hardwood staircase leading upstairs was an etched Italian glass mirror. Phillip paused and considered his reflection. Dark wavy hair. Hazel eyes. Firm mouth. Dimpled chin. He had modeled some when he was in college, but he had wanted to be an actor. That had been his aim since his thespian days in high school. He had previously married his high school sweetheart and she left him high and dry when acting jobs were few and far between. She wanted stability, not an actor. Then, eight years ago, after a play, he met Sarah. She had been with a group who came backstage to see the star of the play. He had literally bumped into her by accident and immediately fell in love with the most beautiful face he had ever seen. She was twenty-years old at the time and had already done a few minor modeling jobs for a few different catalogs. Sarah was charmed by the tall, handsome actor who, at age thirty-two, was close to appearing on Broadway. When it was time for him to leave for the West Coast, he took her with him, stopping en route in Las Vegas to get married. Four years later they had a son named after Sarah's father. She still had the most beautiful face he had ever seen.

Just then, the doorbell chimed and brought him back to the present. It was just who was expecting it to be. Mrs. Clark had arrived, so Phillip greeted her and excused himself to go change clothes. He knew his tuxedo would have been laid out on the bed for him by now.

*Maggie Rush ran into the police headquarters where Sir Charles was talking to a Lieutenant.*

*"Sir Charles! We have to get back to the lab. The Professor has gotten away from The Loner. We believe he will use the portal to escape. Andrew is on him way now."*

*"Where's Jack?"*

*Maggie looked worried. "We don't know. We haven't heard from his all day. He might have bee hurt."*

*Sir Charles took her arm. "Come. We must hurry. He mustn't use the portal."*

*The two rushed out of the room.*

"Cut," Ron called. "That was good. Are we set for the lab scene? Is everyone here? Good. Looks like we'll finish early today.

"Phillip," he continued, "you just knocked out Tom and are to rush to the portal. When you get to the door, stop, look back once, and then return to Tom for your final words. Eddie, you run in just as the door closes and then go to Tom and help him up.

"Camera one and three, go to opposite ends, and two, follow in close," Ron directed. "Places. Slate.... Ready.... Action!"

*The Professor stood from his evil deed and ran to the portal door. He hesitated with his hand outstretched and looked back at the figure prone on the floor. He returned to The Loner and gently lifted one of his hands.*

*"Forgive me, Jack. You were getting too close to the truth. We're a lot alike, you know. Someday, perhaps, we can be friends again. I won't forget the kindness you showed when I was hurt. But, now is not the time."*

*He looked up suddenly and ran into the portal. He slammed the door and vanished.*

*Andrew Fox rushed into the lab and found The Loner on the floor. He saw the portal was closed and knew it was already empty.*

*He pulled The Loner into a sitting position and began firmly patting his face to bring him to consciousness. "Jack! Jack! Wake up. Are you all right?"*

*The Loner felt the bump on his head and groaned. "Where's...."*

*"He's gone, Jack. I was too late."*

*Jack looked sadly at the portal door. "I almost got through to him, Andrew. I almost got through."*

*Andrew nodded. "I know. Next time we meet, Professor, we'll be ready," he finished, looking intently at the portal door.*

"Cut," Ron declared triumphantly. "Beautiful, people. That is probably a wrap. Hang around an hour while we preview this and then, if it looks good, you can go."

While the four regulars discussed next week's show, Phillip quietly headed for his dressing room. It was only twelve o'clock and he figured he had two hours to go.

He propped himself up on the oversized sofa and picked up the ivory-colored paper.

*Jane struggled valiantly against the drunken cowboy who kept asking her for a kiss. She thought about the knife in the top of her boot. The saloon singer dress she was wearing had effectively hidden the handle of the knife, but she had been warned about hurting anyone. She would have to use some other way to get out of this mess.*

*She remembered her training with Jack and brought her knee up sharply. The cowboy suddenly quit groping her and emitted a startled grunt. As he fell back, she made a fist and swung it into his stomach with all her might. The cowboy now collapsed onto the floor of the saloon.*

*Jane backed slowly away from the inert form. She was still scared and shaking violently. A body stood in the way of her escape. Screaming as hands touched her shoulders, it was too much for Jane as the world tilted around her and she fainted.*

*The Professor looked down at her and felt remorse for what he had put her through. Gently picking her up, he carried her into the deserted office and placed her on the couch. He could hear the stagecoach go by and knew it was time for them to go back. He hadn't expected Jane to be mauled like that.*

*Gently, he patted her hands and she slowly opened her eyes. Startled, she looked away from his handsome face and tried to find the cowboy. She sat up, not knowing what was going on.*

*"You're all right now," he softly said. "You handled yourself just fine. Jack taught you well."*

*Jane was shaking again. "He tried to…. I couldn't…. Please hold me," she whispered, holding out trembling hands.*

*The Professor didn't protest but held her close until she stopped shaking. He experienced a strange feeling in his heart and looked down at her head leaning against his chest.*

*"I'm sorry," he told her. "I'm sorry you all proved me wrong….and I am sorry you were hurt. It's time for you to go." He placed his fingers briefly against her cheek. "Jack is fortunate," was the last thing he said to her as he rushed out the back door of the saloon.*

*Andrew and Jack burst through the swinging doors, guns in hand. "Jane?" Jack called out, frightened by the sight of an unconscious cowboy on the floor.*

*"Jack!" Jane rushed into his arms.*

*"It's time to go home," Andrew said in a softer tone, finally affected by the tender reunion before him. "I'm glad you're all right, Jane. You'll make a good squad member yet!"*

*The End*


Phillip gathered all his personal effects and took one last glance around the dressing room to make sure he had everything. Then he threw his costume over the sofa and headed for the offices.

He found Maxwell, Cindy and Eddie near the door that read 'Ron Nickles—Director.' The threesome were discussing Eddie's party the next night.

"You'll be there? You and the family?" he was asked as he joined them.

Phillip nodded. "Yes. Davey is looking forward to it. He wants to tell Eddie Junior about his upcoming trip to Japan."

Cindy and Maxwell exchanged a private look. This would be big for Sarah. Phillip betrayed no emotion on his face. Sometimes it was helpful to be an actor.

Ron came out of his office just then and confirmed the party time.

"Say, Ron," Phillip cut in. "Can I use the phone in your office? It will just take a minute."

"Sure thing. Leave a quarter on the desk. Good job as usual, group. See you at the party. I have to see about some script changes. Some of these writers are so touchy about their work," and off he rushed without waiting for replies, comments, or good-byes.

Phillip waved a hand as he went into the office and sat in the big leather chair. The window looked over the back lot of Majestic Studio. But Phillip wasn't looking at the familiar sight. He was looking for a phone number on a crumpled letter.

He had no idea where the call was going. It was normal procedure for all mail to be read before forwarding and so he had no outer envelope. Only a name, a photo, and a script.

He held the letter in one hand as the phone rang on the other end. Two rings. Three rings.

"Hello. Leslie here. I can't answer. Please leave your message. Beep."

"Leslie, this Phillip Beck. I wanted to tell you I received your script and I enjoyed reading it. I was going to write you, but the envelope was thrown away, so I have no address. Sorry for the phone message.

"What I wanted to tell you was that your story was interesting and enjoyable. But since it isn't exactly a script or a novel, you should decide one way or the other.

"I suggest you go novel form and submit it for publication. There is a lot of interest in 'The Time Police' and the books do well. You have no chance as a script because there are too many legal problems for an outsider.

"Thank you for thinking of me. I have found the regulars are overwhelmed with mail and never see it. But I was handed your letter and script when I came onto the set.

"I just finished taping another episode called 'Hexed Rex.' Tell your friends.

"Thanks again for writing to me and the picture is great. Bye now."

Phillip hung up the phone and then took out his wallet. He placed a quarter in the middle of Ron's desk and put the bent photo inside the wallet.

Gathering up the letter pages that he had just clipped to the story, he headed for the door.

"Thanks, bunny."

# CHAPTER 2

Three hundred miles away, as a weary boutique clerk climbed the stairs leading to her apartment, she counted out loud as she went. "One thousand twelve. One thousand thirteen. One thousand fourteen. I swear they add more steps every night," she muttered to herself as her key slipped into the lock.

Since it was mid-December and after six o'clock in the evening, the rooms were dark and cold. Leslie Nelson shrugged off her warm coat, dropping it along with her purse and the mail onto one end of her handy white sofa and turned on the lamp. A half-read newspaper still sat waiting on the small, round kitchen table. The weights on her cuckoo clock were close to touching the floor. Stacks of binder paper filled with her handwriting were systematically piled on a small lap desk and also covering most of the sofa.

Leslie looked around the small living room and shook her head with a sigh. "Oh, good. The maid's been here. She's really doing a bang-up job."

According to her usual evening ritual, she now went towards the kitchen, pausing long enough to turn on the wall heater and turn off her answering machine. This evening, however, the red light on the answering machine was flashing.

Hitting the replay button, she was faintly surprised at how long it took the machine to rewind. If the light flashed at all, there were usually just hang-ups with no message. She sometimes wondered if the machine worked at all….

Taking a pen and scratch pad in hand, she let out a sigh. "Now what's wrong?" she wondered as the machine clicked and the first playback began.

There was a long pause, and then an obviously confused woman said something in a foreign language. As the sound of the phone being slammed down, Leslie rolled her eyes, pen still poised. "C'mon, people, I'm hungry," she muttered.

*Beep.* Click. "Leslie, this is Phillip Beck…."

Leslie dutifully wrote down the name Phillip Beck on the scratch pad and continued to listen to the message. Suddenly she froze mid-word as the deep, oddly-familiar voice continued and she recognized the name.

"…I wanted to tell you I received your script…."

Her tiredness flew away and her heart began pounding in her chest. A shrill "EEEK!" more than likely startled the people living in the apartments next to her.

Fumbling with shaking hands, Leslie turned up the volume and a wide, silly grin spread over her face as she stared at the answering machine.

"…suggest you go novel form and…."

"Novel? How!?" she found herself yelling at the machine.

"…and the books do well…."

"Where? Wait!"

"…the picture was great. Bye now."

Listening to his phone hang up, she just stood there, motionless, as static continued coming from the machine. All of a sudden she sprang into motion. "Oh, I don't believe it! He called! Phillip Beck read it! I have to call Janice! I have to call Anne! I have to call Renee! EEEK!"

Quickly dialing, her best friend Janice answered and was confused at the half elated, half hysterical Leslie on the other end. "Jan, guess who called! You'll never guess. Listen!" she demanded to her now-amused friend.

The message replayed and now Leslie heard a shrill "Oh my god!" come through the phone.

They both began chattering excitedly and neither could hear

or care what the other was trying to say. Finally running out of steam and laughing now, they both came to the same conclusion: This was an exciting event in their humdrum lives. A movie star, a television celebrity, someone famous had called Leslie!

Leslie was on the phone for another two hours replaying the tape for her different friends who had known about her writing as well as those she knew were fans of "The Time Police" television show. She came to realize that she was being asked the same question by all of them: "What are you going to do now?"

At first that stumped her. She wrote the stories. They were sent to the show. The actors read and liked them. That was it. She hadn't thought it out past that. What was she going to do next?

"I guess I'm going to rewrite my stories after I finish CHATEAU REX. What's novel form, anyway?" she asked all of them.

"I dunno."

"Me, either," Leslie responded, becoming a little more deflated each time she asked the question.

She had told Janice she hated rewriting.

"Get used to it," blunt Janice had advised.

Even though Leslie and her friends didn't know exactly what would come next, they were all unanimous about one thing: Phillip Beck was one terrific guy. He was now endeared to them. He took some of his valuable time and contacted one of the outsiders. To the fans of "The Time Police," he had now become their favorite actor. To them, he was now being referred to as "Leslie's Actor/Friend."

In the days that followed, after Leslie came back down to earth, she started doing research on novel writing at the library. The only difference she could see between a novel and what she had already written was, basically, the length. That meant one thing: Rewrite everything.

She hurriedly finished her favorite story so far, CHATEAU REX, in which the Professor abducts Jane and falls in love with her. It was short—way too short—but now she had plans for it later. Leslie made a duplicate copy for "her actor" the next day at an office supply store, and then sat down to compose a thank-you letter to Phillip Beck. Realizing he would probably no longer be at the studio, she called Majestic Studio and was surprised to be given the name and address of Mr. Beck's agent, a Bill Michaels. They were "sure she could reach him that way."

*"Hello, again, Phillip,*

*I wanted to tell you how much I appreciated your phone call. It was nice of you to take the time to read my story and to let me know your thoughts. It was an unexpected bonus.*

*Majestic Studio gave me your agent's name and address. I wasn't sure this letter would reach you the same way as the last time. I hope you don't mind. I really wanted to thank you for your call and also to send you this story.*

*I know your life doesn't revolve around "The Time Police." (Neither does mine.) It is a job in your business as an actor. But, you do such a good job with the Professor that I, in turn, enjoy writing about him!*

*Your call did raise some questions. Basically, how and where? How would I turn my stories into novels and where would they be sent? Script form doesn't seem wise at this point for me. I have a general, vague idea what a script might look like. (I'd love to see a page.)*

*I know. I know. I am runnething over with questions. Your business is fascinating to an outsider like myself. I have so many questions. For example, how long does it take to shoot an episode? Do you memorize all your lines or do you do piece-work? Things of this nature.*

*After a year of writing, it is exciting to have someone say 'I took the time. I enjoyed what you did.' So, I appreciate that you did contact me.*

*Tell you what. I'll get an agent and then my agent will call your agent and we'll do lunch. It will be on me. And, the way I eat, it probably will be!*

*Thank you for making my day and giving me something constructive to think about. Next time you're in Amherst, I'll show you my chateau.*

*Best wishes,*
*Leslie Nelson"*

Two years earlier, Leslie Nelson, suddenly having a lot of free time on her hands, found herself in a bit of a predicament. Her husband of two and a half years abruptly decided he didn't like married life any more, so why didn't she move out and he could have his house back to himself? She waited patiently for six months to see if things could be corrected, but the inevitable happened and they were able to reach an amicable settlement agreement. Irreconcilable Differences is what he listed as his reason, but only she knew the *real* reason. After those six months of hearing what an awful wife and lover she had been, her self-confidence plummeted to its lowest depth, Leslie left weak-kneed for her own apartment with the furniture she had had before her marriage. She couldn't help but feel disappointed, even when she knew in her heart that she had tried her hardest.

"Freedom!" might be the rallying cry from some quarters. However, what kind of freedom was it? Leslie did indeed have more free time, but she now found herself in an awkward position socially. All her married friends did things as couples. All her single friends were many years younger. She basically didn't fit in well any longer. More of this newfound free time was spent with her parents and more time was spent in front of the television to fill in the quiet evenings after her job in the upscale clothing shop.

As Leslie flipped through the dial, night after night, looking for that one great new show, she finally landed on a series called "The Time Police." Hers was not a scientific mind, so some of the plots were a little over her head. But, the program became part of her routine and slowly she came to appreciate the unique show and developed a sort of sympathy and liking for the characters.

One of the characters she especially liked was The Loner. As the weeks went by, she began to notice a pattern...the writers always killed off his romantic partners. Leslie liked happy-ever-after endings—even though she well knew real life wasn't that way.

On one particular foggy morning in the valley, an idea planted itself in her brain as she got ready for work. It was a vague idea, but nevertheless an idea just the same. *Why not write an episode for The Loner where he gets to keep the girl?* she thought to herself. She had written down fantasies and dreams she had had over the years, embellishing them into short stories. She knew how to carry a story through to the end. This couldn't be much different, could it? She was quite familiar with the characters of the show. Why not?

Far different from her other off-the-wall ideas, she just couldn't get this one out of her mind. Soon a plot was forming and new characters were taking shape and getting named. As all this started to come together, she knew she had to run out and buy a large notebook and a supply of pens. Still, it wasn't until two weeks later that Leslie sat on her sofa with the first blank sheet of paper waiting on her lap desk. The title of her story had been chosen five days earlier: THE LONER FINDS LOVE. That part was easy.

The opening paragraph was not.

But once she committed the opening words to paper, she was amazed how easily the words and ideas flowed out onto the paper. Hours flew by. She made notes while she was at work when an idea came or a chance remark by a customer sparked an inspiration.

Her parents started seeing less of her and her television became dark and quiet. Her mother would call to see if she wanted to do something and Leslie would say she was busy in her apartment. She still hadn't yet told anyone what she was doing. At eight o'clock on Friday night, however, the pen would be put down and Leslie would take a one-hour break to watch and record on her VCR "The Time Police."

When her best friend Janice would stop by on a Saturday afternoon, Leslie would quickly stuff the notebook under the sofa. She was amused when she realized she was actually saving a lot of money by not going to the mall so often with Janice or her mom.

In twenty-eight days, she had written ninety pages into the spiral notebook and wrote with an elaborate flourish "The End." It took Leslie a little over two hours to reread her story, adding a word here and correcting spelling there, but, liking what she read, she made no significant changes.

The next morning, before they started working out front in the boutique, Leslie approached Janice and quietly held out a blue notebook. "Will you read something I wrote and give me your honest opinion?"

Janice took the spiral book and a look of amazement crossed her face as she thumbed through the many pages. "What is it?" Janice had read some of Leslie's stories before. One had centered on a vacation the two of them had taken together. Another had been a love story about a boy Leslie had had a crush on seven years earlier. Those were just short, cute stories. Janice wasn't expecting something like this. This looked serious.

Looking around to make sure their boss wasn't nearby to overhear, Leslie lowered her voice. "It's a story about the T.V. show 'The Time Police.' I…I had some time to kill," was her only explanation as she blushed and walked away.

The notebook was returned the next morning and Janice was very enthusiastic. She, too, was a fan of The Loner. "Now that is more like it! Why can't they do an episode like that on the show!?"

Her reaction pleased Leslie. "You really like it?"

"Yes! Even though I didn't like how mean you made Andrew. That's not like him on the show."

Leslie thought for a minute and shrugged. "I guess somebody had to be antagonistic. Not everyone gets along with everyone else. It's not all la-de-da."

"I guess. What are you going to do with your story?"

"Do with it?" Leslie echoed with a frown. "I don't know. I just concentrated on writing the thing." A mischievous grin came across her face. "Maybe I'll type it up and send it to Tom Young. Who knows? Maybe they'll use it on the show."

Their boss's good-natured voice came to them from her office. "Hey, you two. I don't pay you to talk to each other. Get out there and sell some dresses to someone who doesn't need them!"

Janice and Leslie grinned at each other. "Aye, aye, Cap'n," Leslie saluted as they went out front and opened the shop for the day.

**A** bundle of one hundred forty carefully typed pages was nervously handed to the clerk at the print shop.

"I need two copies of this," Leslie told her, one hand still on the title page.

She was asked, "What kind of paper do you have in mind?"

"I...I don't know." Stumped by yet another problem she had not anticipated, Leslie lowered her voice. "It's going to Majestic Studio. What would you recommend?"

The clerk glanced up at this explanation, but Leslie's eyes were still on the story on the counter between them. She seemed afraid to let go of the papers.

A book of sample paper was brought out and Leslie chose a high-quality ivory-colored paper and a black spiral binding. The price quote made her groan, but she told the clerk to go ahead, and quickly left the store before she lost her nerve and changed her mind.

Impressed by the look of the finished product, Leslie slipped the small manuscript and a letter of introduction into a padded envelope addressed to Tom Young in care of the studio. She also included a copy of a photo of herself that Janice had taken in which she was being hugged by a large rabbit. "The Time Police" Fan Club of Los Angeles had supplied Leslie with the address of the studio and she managed to relax once it was actually mailed.

Her disappointment in not receiving a quick reply was offset by her involvement in the next story she decided to write. This one was set six months later and would be a Western highlighting the talents of the Professor Rex Farrell. He had appeared recently on the series and Leslie liked his witty dialogue and mischievousness. She could use all the sarcasm her mother had tried to eradicate in her all these years. Plus, the actor himself was tall, dark and handsome. Not a bad combination.

For this story, to help keep it all straight, she drew maps of towns and counties. There were character sheets and plot outlines as this story, WESTWARD REX, took the squad into a time period filled with new people and places. The squad's lives intermixed more than in her other story. This time they would actually have to live in that time period longer than usual, so Leslie felt more people were required to fill it out.

Leslie was thoroughly enjoying the writing process and Janice was soon converted into a fan of the Western. In the time span of thirty-one days, the story was written, typed out on her electric typewriter, and mailed off to Phillip Beck.

Exactly twelve days later, on a tired Monday evening when she arrived home to her apartment, there it was—the red light on Leslie's answering machine was blinking on and off.

"Oh, I hate rewriting," Leslie grumbled to herself as she struggled with her first story. "I hate rewrites. I hate typing. I hate correction fluid. I hate blue ink!"

She paused in her tirade and looked at the yellow and white striped stuffed cat sitting on the sofa next to her. It smiled complacently off into space. "Well, I feel better," Leslie declared with a self-conscious laugh. "I need a word processor," she decided, looking at the sheets of paper covering the coffee table in front of her. "And a secretary. I need a secretary. And I *really* need to stop talking to myself."

Leslie concentrated on adding new enemies and plot twists and made Andrew meaner towards the newcomer Jane. The story slowly expanded to one hundred ninety pages. It took her as long to add those fifty pages as it had to write the original story.

The Western took another month to expand. She enlarged the Professor's role and put her heroine Jane a little more into the background. The regular actors were profiled more and given more action.

Her co-workers at the boutique noticed her preoccupation. Janice, always the enthusiastic supporter, had not remained idle. She had been busy dropping names and hints around the shop to indicate something big was in the making.

She would ask Leslie, "Has Majestic Studio called you again?"

Or, "What do you hear from Phillip Beck?"

Or, "How's your second novel coming along?"

No longer being able to ignore the neon-bright hints from Janice, Leslie had to tell them about her little stories and her plan to send them to Adventure Novels Publications to see about getting them published.

The reactions were mixed. "I didn't know you were creative." "How much are they paying you?" "Why 'The Time Police'?" "Can I have a copy?" "Are you going to move to Los Angeles?" "You didn't go to college...."

Leslie smiled to herself. She didn't know what would happen. Plus, she had no knowledge of the publishing world. Again she had done a lot of research at the library, only to thoroughly confuse her. Three hours were spent reading over submission tips, and she decided to do the one thing that was not highly recommended: She was planning on submitting directly to the publisher. She would use Phillip's name on the introduction letter and hope it would sneak through the system.



After three weeks of part-time typing, Leslie was finished with THE LONER FINDS LOVE and was halfway through WESTWARD REX. She had used two hundred eighty-four sheets of typing paper, three bottles of correction fluid, and six typewriter ribbons. She needed a break. She unplugged her typewriter, turned off her apartment's lights, and went to the mall.

When she returned, she found a plastic container on her coffee table and a note.

Mom.

Leslie groaned and looked at the clutter of papers on her kitchen table where she did her typing. The top few sheets had been moved. At this point in time she still hadn't told her parents about her writing. They didn't like the television show and wouldn't understand why she was writing about it. She really didn't want to hear about wasted time and money and shutting herself up in her apartment instead of seeing her friends....

The phone rang.

Leslie stared at it. She knew who it was. With a sigh, she answered. "Hello?"

"Oh, good. You're home. I was by an hour ago, but you

were gone."

"Hi, Mom.  Yeah, I just ran an errand.  What's up?" Leslie asked, hoping something else was on her mother's mind.

But, no.  "Nothing's up with me.  Say, what are you doing?  Writing a book?" Bonnie Nelson asked with a laugh, indicating the absurdity of the notion.

Leslie silently drew in a deep breath.  Why not tell her?  "Yeah, I am.  This one's about half typed."

"No, really, what are you doing?"

Leslie thought to herself, I've *got to get my key back from her*....  Out loud, she tried to answer pleasantly, "Really, that's what I'm doing.  I've already written three stories.  I've lengthened the first two and plan on submitting them for publication."

There was a significant pause.  "Honey, if you don't want to tell me, fine.  I understand...."

"Mom! That's the truth.  I sent a copy to an actor at the Majestic Studio and he called and recommended I make it into a novel." Leslie was almost laughing.  She could just picture her mother's confused expression.  She could also hear Bonnie's muffled talking to her dad.

"Lou, she says she's writing a novel...I don't know....  Some actor called her....  I don't know....  What actor?" Leslie was asked as her mother's hand was removed from the mouthpiece.

Leslie knew what her mom's response would be to "Phillip Beck."

"Who?"

Right-o.  "He guest-stars on the television show "The Time Police."

The voice on the other end of the phone sounded disgusted.  "You mean those cops and robbers and mad scientists and stuff?"

"More or less.  There's a lot of time travel.  My story is a Western," Leslie explained, hoping the idea of something familiar would placate her.

Her dad, Lou, now came on the line.  "Les, if you need some money, just ask."

"I'm doing fine, Dad.  This is for fun."

"Oh, okay.  Here's your mother."

"Mom," Leslie spoke quickly, "I've got to get back to work.  I have a lot of typing to do."

"Okay. If there's anything we can do to help, just ask. Bye, dear."

When the phone clicked and the dial tone sounded in her ear, Leslie leaned her head against the counter, smacking her forehead lightly on the cool surface. "Well, that went well."

The clerk at the printers came to know Leslie on a first-name basis. Leslie would hand her the typed pages and say, "Two copies. The usual."

The books and an introduction letter were mailed to Adventure Novels. Leslie knew it took three days for the mail to reach New York. She figured she'd get a response within two weeks.

In six days the novels were back in Amherst. Leslie received her first rejection notice. The publishing company dealt only with agents. They were kind enough to enclose a list of literary agents. They were sorry they could not recommend a certain one.

The list was seven pages long, printed front and back, four columns to a page, twelve to fourteen agencies to a column. Leslie stared at the pages. Over six hundred names all across the country. She rubbed her forehead as a dull throbbing started behind her left eye.

Saturday was spent back at the library comparing her list to the list in the most current writer's guide. Most agencies were crossed off. Some were circled. A few received an arrow which Leslie used to indicate agents willing to work with new authors and who also accepted adventure novels.

She then copied an example of a submission letter and silently wondered why she was doing all of this. The throbbing had resumed behind her left eye.

The printer was visited again to get sets of sample pages and chapters out of her books. The typewriter was drug out of her small closet to type the first six letters to six different agencies.

Within three weeks, the rejection letters began coming in. For some reason, Leslie assumed they would be pink, but they looked like regular business correspondence. All six were worded differently with six different reasons for the rejection: They didn't handle that type of work; They only handled established authors; They didn't want any more "Time Police" authors. Regardless of how it was worded, it all meant the same thing—No.

Six more letters and copies were mailed out. As the rejects came back, Leslie's outlook sagged.

Her parents told her, "You've don't your best. Be proud of your books and just let it be."

When the fifth letter arrived, Leslie opened it to see if this agency had come up with a new reason to refuse her work.

*"Dear Ms. Nelson,*

*Thank you so much for submitting your sample chapters. We are interested in seeing the completed manuscript of THE LONER FINDS LOVE. If your work meets our requirements, we will forward the manuscript to Adventure Novels. Here's hoping for a long, successful relationship.*

*Sincerely,*
*Wallace Quimby*
*Literary Agent"*

Leslie spent the next two hours on the phone. Janice was thrilled. Anne "just knew this would happen." Mom was pleased. Dad wasn't home.

Leslie also dropped a letter in the mail to Phillip Beck to tell him the latest happening. She again sent it through his agent. In ten days a typed letter came back.

*"Dear Leslie,*

*I'm pleased your good work is being sent on. Remember that to succeed you must keep trying.*

*As I am overwhelmed with my own scripts and books and such, I cannot read your other books.*

*Best wishes for success.*
*Sincerely,*
*Phillip Beck"*

With renewed zeal, Leslie concentrated on rewriting her third book, CHATEAU REX. With growing appreciation and fondness for "her actor," she was determined to make this her best work. And if her work was published, she was also determined to see it sent to Majestic Studio. This would be a role worthy of Phillip Beck!

She kept the envelope from Phillip on the coffee table in front of her work area. She now had his home address.


It took another month to receive word from her agent. The letter from Wallace Quimby was short and to the point:

"*Dear Ms. Nelson,*

*This week I sent your manuscript and the outlines of your "Rex" works on to the editor of Adventure Novels. I felt it was strong enough as is for the market.*

*These things take time. Usually two or three months. Sometimes longer.*

*I will contact you to let you know of their decision. We will draw up the necessary contracts when they are required.*

*Sincerely,*
*Wallace Quimby*
*The Publisher's Agency.*"


Time never drug so slowly for Leslie as it did when she awaited to hear from her agent. Weekly she was asked if she had heard yet. Then, slowly, her friends' enthusiasm began to dull and a protective suggestion was added: They might say no. Be prepared.

As the three months turned into four, the queries became fewer and fewer and Leslie experienced a keen disappointment every time the mailbox was empty or her answering machine was silent.

Only Janice, dear, loyal Janice, kept up the full amount of spirit. She had no doubts. There was no way the response would be negative. This was her friend who knew an actor and had an agent. How could anything possibly go wrong? When she and Leslie went out to lunch, Janice would loudly talk of book contracts and trips to New York and meeting with the actors of the show as they prepared to tape Leslie's episodes.

Leslie smiled to herself through all of this. She secretly admitted that all of that would be just fine with her. She even let Janice take some photos of her that could be used on the back cover of her first novel. Yes, it was exciting. Yes, she would like to meet all the actors. But, yes, she knew the answer could be negative.

It was five months before she heard from the agent. That made it a full year since she had sent the short copy of the novel to Phillip Beck and two years since she had written the first word on a blank sheet of paper.

# CHAPTER 3

**S**tretched out comfortably on a floating lounge in his pool, a pile of scripts bobbing next to him on a small, inflatable drink table, Phillip Beck was still disgusted. The sky above was a cloudless blue. A motion out of the corner of his eye caught his attention as a squirrel from the nearby foothills ran across his terraced backyard and disappeared up the nearest tree. It was peaceful and quiet. Davey was down for a nap and Sarah was learning Japanese from a private tutor to ready her for her trip next month.

It wasn't his wife's sojourn that was bothering him this time. It was these blasted scripts that his agent Bill kept sending him. He had just finished filming a movie where he played a cheerleader's stodgy father. All the part consisted of was five scenes, twelve lines, and was gone before the second half of the film. Next week he would play a grandfather who dies in the first half hour. And these scripts next to him were more of the same. He felt like pushing them all into the pool.

Sarah had urged him to consider switching to her agent, Martin Thomas. That is, she *again* urged him to switch agents. After all, look what wonders Marty had done for her career in just a few short years. Why, Phillip was still just.... She hadn't finished her sentence, but Phillip had done it for her. Many times since, as well. Just where he had been for six long years. Still playing the same types of roles. Still had to audition. Still rela-

49

tively unknown.

The big opportunity Sarah had pushed and hoped for through Zenith Pictures and Bob Carlson had resulted in a role as a luxury liner captain that began filming next month. He would be required to stroll among the big-name stars tipping his white hat, break up a fight in the lounge, and dance with the dowagers. *My, what a stretch*, he thought.

"It could lead to other offers," Sarah had perkily told him, the falseness of her tone obvious to both of them. He had seen the disappointment in her eyes after she read his script. She had worked on Carlson all evening at the party—a point that had greatly bothered Phillip then and now. He was quite capable of landing his own roles, thank you very much.

Phillip knew what he needed. A role that was different, unique, fresh. These scripts were from the same writers turning out the same ideas for the same producers. He glanced over at the pile of scripts and shook his head, disgusted. He would call Bill later and demand some improvement in the quality of what he was being sent.

The sound of the patio door sliding open interrupted his sour line of thought and he glanced over to see Sarah come clicking over the patio. She was dressed to go out. Always the model, she could have been going anywhere from a photo shoot to dinner at Maxim's. "Phillip? I've been called downtown. Marty says there's some problem with Davey's passport. I need to take in his records."

"Why don't you just leave him with me while you're gone? Then there would be no problem," was his pointed, yet hopeful reply.

Sarah flashed him a smile. He still hadn't given up. "You know this is a wonderful opportunity for him. And Marty can help watch him when I'm on assignment."

Phillip felt his stomach tighten as he unconsciously made a fist. Her skuzzy agent would be with his son. He wouldn't trust that man with a wad of used chewing gum and now he has to turn over his son.

Sarah saw the muscles in his jaw tighten and knew how he felt. She didn't agree at all, but she knew. Marty's cut-throat business practices had benefited her greatly and had taught her a lot. She followed his every word. "You can't let people walk all over you. Do it to them first," was Marty's motto.

Not wanting to get into it again and to change the charged atmosphere, she held up some letters. "The mail came. Usual stuff. Who do we know in Amherst?" she asked as she paused flipping through the mail to look at an ivory-colored envelope.

"Amherst?" he repeated, allowing her to change the topic. He didn't feel like arguing again. Now. "I don't know. Where the heck is Amherst?"

Again glancing at the return address, she answered, "Apparently somewhere in California. It's addressed to you," as she stood by the edge of the pool, holding out the envelope. Her curiosity overcame her need to leave. As he paddled over to take the letter as he knew was expected of him, she waited and was rewarded when a look of recognition came over his face.

"Ah, Bunny!" he declared with a small smile as he opened the envelope and began reading, momentarily forgetting his hovering wife.

"Bunny?" echoed Sarah, her smile frozen unnaturally on her face. "I don't know any Bunny."

Phillip's eyes darted across the lines. "Hmm? No, that's just a nickname some aide at Majestic gave to her. I guess it stuck," he frowned, thinking back. Glancing up at Sarah, who was on the verge of tapping her foot in impatience, he continued, "Remember that Western script I was sent on the set? That's her. Linda.... No, that's not right.... Leslie," as he turned slightly soggy letter over to the signature.

Sarah's smile was still frozen. "That was a fairly interesting storyline, if I remember it correctly. Incomplete, but interesting. Why is she still writing you? How'd she get this address?" Her business downtown was pushed aside. That could wait. This was getting more interesting and worrisome by the minute.

He noticed she had sat down on one of the patio chairs near the edge of the pool. "What about the passport?"

"That can wait five minutes," she snapped. "Do you think it was a good idea for that idiot agent of yours to give out our home address like that? There're a lot of nuts roaming the streets. Anything can happen. Doesn't he read the papers?" The more she thought about it, the more worried she became. Sarah felt her heart start pounding in her chest. Security had always been an important issue for her—all the more so when her career had taken off. She wondered how Phillip could be so lax.

Having drifted with the gentle waves in the pool, he turned his lounge to face her. His pleasant smile was gone. "First, Bill isn't an idiot and he didn't send the address. I did. And, second, Leslie isn't like that. She has her own agent now and is trying to get published. I don't know why she is still writing me. Probably because she is grateful for the advice and encouragement I gave her before."

Eyes narrowed, she tersely asked, "Advice and encouragement for what?"

He looked away briefly and took a breath. This was turning into another needless argument. "I told you months ago about her two manuscripts. You read them both," he quietly reminded her. "I suggested she expand them into novel length and submit them to be published. I thought she had wanted them viewed as scripts. Now she has done just that and they are apparently being considered. This letter concerns a convention she attended last week. She didn't seem to have a very good time," he concluded, glancing back at the letter with a ghost of a smile playing over his face.

Silent, Sarah now recalled both stories and had liked them. With a little work they would have made excellent episodes for Phillip's character on that television show. *Leave it to Phillip to recommend something else.* That knowledge did little to allay her fears or to extinguish a small spark of jealousy deep within her. Outsiders can be totally unpredictable. Some had turned deadly. This one had their home address and was using it. And, she and Davey would be gone for at least a month.

Since her questions had stopped, Phillip returned to the letter and started reading the second page. "Hmm," he muttered out loud, "sounds like she's done some stage work herself."

Sarah sounded nonchalant. "Oh? How nice. Can I see the first page?"

"Sure," as the letter was handed back, two wet blotches

where Phillip had held it.

"*Hello, Phillip,*

*Just when you thought it was safe to go back to the mailbox....*

*I wasn't planning on writing you again until I had some word or other from the publishing company. Does time drag this slowly for you when you are waiting to hear whether or not you were chosen for a role you really wanted?*

*I do have just three words for you: You owe me! Big! Okay, four words. Let me explain. Since your kind encouragement I have paid more attention to "The Time Police" shows to help me with my writing. I was taken, almost by force, to a Time Convention last weekend in Rancho Blanco. I really didn't want to go. My best friend, Janice, forced, begged, and arranged the whole thing, and hey, let's take my car! No problem.*

*The day was hot, the hotel impossible to locate, and we waited in line for forty-five minutes to be admitted into a room filled with "Time Police" merchandise! Be still my heart.*

*Okay, I admit I bought a "Police" badge and some pictures (why weren't there any of you? That's want I wanted), and a couple of magazines....*"

The rest of the letter rambled on and on about the convention activities and her continued work on her third book. Sarah had trouble with a few of the lines: "You owe me." The one about wanting Phillip's picture. Her impatience and ambition. Her desire to see a page from an actual script. There were no outright words of admiration or love or anger. It was the familiarity that bothered her and possible subtle meanings that could be hidden within those lines.

"Phillip? How many letters have you received?"

His eyes were closed as if he planned on taking a nap. Hmm? I don't know. Four or five."

"This one is sure friendly," she offered pleasantly. "What were the others like?"

"I don't know," he yawned. "You can read them if you like."

Her lips parted into a silent "O". *He kept them? Seriously?*

Her mind visualized his private study. They would be in his desk. Third drawer on the right. That's where he kept his correspondence. She looked back at her husband who was now asleep, hands folded in his lap, shoulders starting to burn from the bright sun. Walking quietly so as not to awaken him, she went back into the house and called Marty. She would be about an hour late.

The letters were surprisingly easy to find. Phillip had made no effort to hide them. Ignoring the wrinkles it would cause in her meticulous outfit, she sank down on the floor behind his desk and read every word. A search for a mentioned photograph was fruitless. The only pictures on his desk or in the room were of Davey and her.

In her uneasy state of mind, she read words that weren't there—much like a frightened child sees dangers in shadows dancing on a wall in a darkened room. She focused phrases like "we'll do lunch", "handsome face", "next time you are in Amherst", "fill in the empty evenings", "555-4029", "your last call", and "I *really* wanted to thank you." In themselves, these words had meant nothing to Phillip. He was probably too flattered to recognize the potential powder keg. As usual, she would have to take matters into her own hands—even if it meant a solution neither Phillip nor Marty would like.

After writing down Leslie's address and phone number, Sarah carefully returned the letters to their original place in the desk. Going back outside, she awakened Phillip and remarked sweetly, "Honey, I've been thinking. Why don't you come to Japan with us?"

The irritation and grogginess at being abruptly awakened left Phillip. The possibility of him traveling with them to Japan never been broached. It was always assumed he would stay at home, out of the way.

"That's impossible," as he rubbed his eyes and flinched when he touched his red shoulder. "I have commitments coming up."

She waved a dismissive hand. "Oh, those two movies don't amount to anything," she replied airily and missed seeing the hurt look in his eyes. "Bill could get you more of those when we got back."

Having gotten out of the pool, he put a protective towel over his shoulders. With a wave of his own hand towards the scripts now piled on a chair, his eyes narrowed. "Might I remind you that one of those movies *you* helped arrange. And now you want me to back out of a contract? That doesn't do well for one's name in this business," he pointed out angrily.

Sarah dismissed that objection. "Oh, I'll have Marty fix that with Bob Carlson. I just think we should all be together in Japan."

Phillip looked away from her carefully arranged face. She was trying hard to look sincere. "This job of yours has been planned for months now. For weeks you have been learning Japanese. Now all of a sudden it is imperative that I come along. The heck with my career and promises—just as long as you are happy." He turned back to face her, his eyes showing the hurt and the anger. "If our family life is so important to you all of a sudden, then stay home! My jobs are just as important to me as yours are to you! They might not be as major as *you* would like, but you know I am waiting to find that one role that will do it."

Her anger, never far from the surface, flared to match his. "You've been waiting for eight years for that one role! Why don't you have your little novelist write one for you!" Sarah twirled around on her heels and stormed into the house. Grabbing up her purse and papers, she left for her belated appointment.

Silently cursing, Phillip gathered up the scripts and the mail unsure of what just happened. One thing he did know—he wasn't going to Japan.

Sarah's slam of the front door had awakened Davey. He now came slowly downstairs, his eyes puffy and his hair sticking up on one side. "Daddy? Where's Mommy?"

He picked his son up from the stairs and then winced as Davey poked his shoulders. "Your mom had an errand. I don't know when she'll be back."

Question forgotten, Davey's attention was on Phillip. "Why are you a funny color?"

Smiling as he climbed the stairs to his bedroom, Phillip explained, "Because I did what I am always telling you not to do. I was out in the pool too long."

"Do you want to see what I am going to take to Japan?" was the next eager question.

"Not now, son. Perhaps another time."

**A**fter the passport problem was straightened out, Sarah stood on the sidewalk with her agent, Martin Thomas, or Marty, as everyone except Phillip called him. Her anger and worry had returned.

"Can you believe it, Marty? He said he wouldn't go with us to Japan!"

Marty looked disgusted. "Why in the world did you even ask him to go? He'd just be in the way. Who wants some out-of-work actor hanging around? All you need is me. Am I right?" he asked, putting a familiar hand on her shoulder.

Sarah sniffed. "He isn't out of work and you know it. It isn't great work, but its work. It's just...." She broke off, unsure of voicing her fear.

The hand on her shoulder moved so it now encircled her small waist. "Come on, you can tell me. You always tell me everything."

Sarah lowered her voice even though there was no one else around. "It's these letters Phillip has been getting. You know, fan letters from one woman. Apparently he has replied to at least two and...well, I'm worried."

Marty smirked to himself. "So, the old man has a devoted follower. 'Oh, Phillip'," he joked in a squeaky, high voice. "'You are the greatest actor in the whole wide world'."

Sarah rolled her eyes and pulled away from him a step. "Oh, stop it," she almost smiled. "They weren't like that. Well, not yet, anyway. You know how dangerous outsiders can get. We don't know anything about this little person he calls 'Bunny'," she almost spat out the nickname.

Her agent studied her face. This was getting more and more interesting. "Are you worried or jealous?"

Her face jerked towards him, her blue eyes flashing. "Jealous?" she demanded with a questionable laugh. "Oh. Right.... I don't want some demented lunatic at my front door! Do you know he sent her our address! We might as well hang a sign out front that reads 'Sarah Beck lives here. Harass us'."

Marty still smirked. "So you want Phillip to tag along with us to Japan. To protect him, right?" he asked.

Sarah turned and strode to her white Jaguar. "Fine, Marty, make jokes. We don't know anything about this…this little 'Bunny' person," as she slammed the door shut.

Marty tapped on her passenger window until she lowered it. Leaning in, he cocked his head. "Do you want to find out about her? There are ways, you know," he said in a low voice.

She frowned and was silent for a moment as she studied the sly look on his face. "I didn't say I wanted her knocked off, Marty. I just want her to keep away from my husband. Some of the things she said bothered me."

Marty motioned for her to lean closer. He gave her a quick kiss on her cheek. "Don't worry. I'll have a friend of mine stop over to see you. When is Grandpa Beck going to be gone?"

"He's taking Davey to Majestic Wednesday around ten o'-clock to see Uncle Eddie."

Marty stood away from the car. "Good. A Mr. Fields will be over at eleven. Try to look pretty for him."

Sarah flashed him a brilliant smile. "I always look pretty," she shot back as she slammed the car into gear and sped away.


When Sarah returned home, she surprised Phillip by putting her arms around him and kissing him on the lips. "I'm sorry for what I said earlier," she explained. "I know your career is important. I shouldn't have asked you to renege on your contracts."

"You're in a good mood," he carefully observed as he returned the caress. "I take it the passport is no longer a problem?"

She pulled away and headed for her study, smiling. "Oh, yes. That, too."


The doorbell rang at exactly eleven on Wednesday morning. Sarah opened the door to see an average man of average height, brown eyes, brown hair, average build, who appeared to be around the same age as Marty—thirty. There was nothing out-standing about his appearance. He looked like the average guy in average guy clothes. Only his eyes showed something differ-ent, something extraordinary within. They were intense and ob-servant, always moving, always appraising. Eyes that would miss nothing. Those eyes now darted quickly over the beautiful model and then moved on to appraise the inside of their house.

Sarah smiled to herself as she motioned him to enter. *This man would do just fine*, she told herself as she led him into her study.

After his silent assessment of her room, he broke the silence with a quiet voice. "So, Mrs. Beck, who do you want me to blow away?"

At her startled, white-faced gasp, he chuckled, revealing even, white teeth. "Sorry. Just a little private investigator humor," he smiled.

"Very little," Sarah replied dryly as her heartbeat returned to normal. "I just want this Leslie person checked out to see whether or not she's harmless. Here are all the letters we have received," handing him copies of the letters. "In three weeks my son and I leave for Japan...."

"You will actually be gone for at least five weeks," he broke in, studying her face. "During that time Mr. Beck will be filming a new movie and probably signing for another. Did I miss any-thing?"

Sarah did another appraisal and smiled back. "You do your work well, Mr. Fields."

"Call me Wayne and don't try flattering me. I read the trade papers like everyone else. Plus, Marty filled me in on a little of the details. I'd like some time to read these," Wayne told her, in-dicating the letters.

"Now?" She had stood to show him to the door.

"You want me to leave? I was told I would have two hours."

"Oh. I thought you would take the copies and read them later."

Wayne shrugged. "Once I read them, if there are any specifics you want to go over, then would be the time."

"Oh," she repeated. This was all new territory for her. "I see.

Would you like some coffee, Wayne?"

He settled back on her white leather sofa. "Naw. I'm fine. Give me an hour." She was dismissed.

In thirty minutes Wayne was through with the letters. He combined what he had read with what Marty had told him. Grinning as he strolled along the white paneled walls of her study, he looked over the pictures of Sarah that filled the wall. This would be the easiest fee he had ever collected. How long should he drag it out? Two weeks? Three? Or should he have to send her reports over to Japan? Yeah, that would be a nice touch.

Wayne Field was making notations of the copies of the letters when Sarah knocked. She looked anxious and determined.

"Well?" she demanded as she sat behind her desk, trying to take back control of the situation. "Do you see now why I want to hire you?"

Wayne smiled to himself. "Yes, I know exactly why you want to hire me. Are you prepared for what I might uncover?" he queried, leaning forward, hands on his knees. "Have you considered what steps you might have to take?"

Sarah nodded. "You mean legal steps like police protection or restraining orders?"

This Leslie was already tried and condemned in Sarah's mind, Wayne thought. *Three weeks*, he decided. "That could be necessary in the most severe scenario. But the possibility exists that my investigation will reveal nothing of dangerous intent. Have you considered that?"

Sarah now looked annoyed. "I assumed you read the letters and weren't in here taking a nap. Am I the only one who can see this problem?" she demanded. "If you don't want the job, Mr. Fields, I'm sure there is another investigator who would."

"Oh, I'll take the assignment, Mrs. Beck," he countered as their relationship became all business. "These profiles can take time." After mentally doubling it, he wrote down a figure on a piece of paper. "This is my daily fee."

She didn't even look at it. "Fine. I'll want weekly reports while I'm gone. Marty will give you the phone numbers and addresses."

"When do you want me to start, Mrs. Beck?"

"Why, immediately, of course. I want to know everything about this woman before I leave. If she gets anywhere near an airplane, I want to know and I want the proper authorities alerted. Do I make myself clear, Mr. Fields?" Sarah demanded quietly, her blue eyes flashing. "I don't want her near my house!"

Wayne regarded her coolly. "Oh, I understand you perfectly." His eyes strayed to a photo near her head. It was a shot of Phillip and Sarah apparently on some vacation years ago. They looked relaxed and happy. "Say, Mrs. Beck? Are you sure there isn't anything else you'd like watched while you're gone?"

His question confused her. She followed his eyes to the picture on the wall. Her tone was icy. "You read too many tabloids."

Wayne returned her look. "I don't read them, lady. I write them."

"Well, you're out of line, Mr. Fields. I trust my husband implicitly. How else would I be able to go off and leave him for weeks at a time?"

"Fine. You trust him. I'll turn in my reports. All right? I'll keep these copies with me. I assume the originals are in their proper place?" At her curt nod, he stood to go. "I also assume you know not to report our little conversation to Mr. Beck. Have a pleasant trip."

"Same to you, Mr. Fields. Enjoy Amherst," she said from her desk with a cutting laugh, viciously tearing his retainer check out of her private account book.

"One last question, Mrs. Beck. Where the heck is Amherst?"


That evening, two men sat together in a posh nightclub having a drink.

"Man, Marty, you should have seen the look in those blue eyes of hers when she talked about the Evil One of Amherst!" Wayne was snickering.

Marty finished his bourbon and signaled for another. "I did. Last week. Gave me the willies," he shuddered. "It came out of the blue, too. This Leslie chick sent her story to Beck, I don't know, eight, nine months ago. Now, all of a sudden, boom!, Sarah is calling out the artillery," he gestured with his empty glass.

Wayne thought a moment. "How do you figure Phillip in all of this?"

Marty chuckled dryly. "The old man? He's probably flattered. He's forty and still a nobody. I doubt he's noticed anything different with Sarah. His mind is pretty one-tracked. I do wish Sarah would give in and leave the brat home, though."

"How do you stand being around them all the time? You didn't like women like that when we were in college."

Marty took a sip from his new drink and shook his head. "No, no. Women like that didn't like me when we were in college," he corrected. "Now, make them a famous millionaire, plaster their face over everything, and they're friends for life. It's a dirty job but someone has to do it," he sighed and then grinned, raising his drink to Fields in a mock salute.

Wayne made circles on the table with his glass. "Say, Marty, why are *you* going to Japan? Sarah's pretty sharp on her own. I've never heard of an agent tagging along. A posse, maybe, but not an agent."

The look on Marty's face was pure innocence. "Gosh, Wayne, you first have to convince them they can't do a thing without you. Then you sit back and enjoy the fringe benefits."

"Hmph," Wayne groused. "Fringe benefits. You get to go to Japan with one the most beautiful women in the world and I'm heading for Amherst to check out some plain, brown-haired store clerk."

"Where exactly is Amherst? Do you know?"

"Within driving distance of Rancho Blanco."

"Well, Wayne, that really clears it up. Thanks. Probably some one-horse town out in the sticks."

The investigator thought back to the letters he had read. "I don't know. Leslie didn't sound like a hick. She must have something on the ball if her work is seriously being considered."

"Yeah—if," Marty stressed. "You don't really know what you'll find."

Wayne just shrugged, unconcerned really. For what he was being paid he would agree to be staked out naked on an anthill. "I've got to pack. And find a map," he grinned as he stood to leave.

"One thing, Wayne," his friend said, stopping him. "I don't want my little lady upset while we're in Japan. You do your job however. Just tell her what she wants to hear while she's gone. She *wants* to hear that this person is a threat. If she doesn't get that from your reports, she will get tense. And a tense Sarah doesn't make for a very compatible traveling companion. I want her compatible. Agreed?"

"I'm way ahead of you, pard. The Evil One of Amherst will come through for both of us. Rest easy."

**W**ayne stepped back from his cluttered bed and took inventory. "Okay, figure five weeks tops. Shirts, slacks, socks, towels, tape recorder, camera, long-range microphone, addresses, phone numbers, sheets, silverware, blank tapes, film, bugs, swimsuit. Wonder if I'll need more than one good suit. Might as well. I'm taking everything else," he grumbled to himself.

The clothes were more or less crammed into suitcases. The surveillance equipment was handled with more care as it was packed into customized black bags to be stowed carefully in the back of the trunk of his nondescript car. The household items and then the suitcases were placed in the front of the trunk. He'd throw the bedding in the back seat in the morning.

He rechecked the map of California to trace the route he would drive. Six hours and he would be in Amherst. Middle of the San Joaquin Valley. Farmers. Ninety miles from the state capitol. Ninety miles from the coast. Ninety miles from Yosemite. Ninety miles in the middle of nowhere. If it weren't for the incredible amount of money he was going to make, he'd tell that neurotic model to take a flying leap.

Wayne already had a motel reservation for the first night or two. That way he would have time to get a bearing on the town, locate Leslie's address, secure his own apartment nearby, and arrange with a furniture rental store for the basic necessities. He had done this so many times before that it was second nature to him. His landlady knew when she saw those mysterious black bags go into his trunk that he would be gone for some time and she would collect his mail. Her monthly bonus assured that she would ask no questions or give out any answers.

After resetting his answering machine, he went to bed and wondered, as he fell asleep, what it was like in Japan.

# CHAPTER 4

*Jack Newby wandered through his silent house. The irony of his nickname The Loner, given to him by the Professor, struck home. He was alone. Jane was gone and he didn't know where she was. He knew the Professor was involved. There had been no proof, no sign, but he knew, deep down, that Rex had taken Jane away from him.*

*He hadn't known it was possible to miss someone so deeply. He, who had been alone for most of his life, had finally found love and happiness. It had taken him by complete surprise, but he had welcomed the new sensation. And now she was gone.*

*All the little noises she made as she worked around the house were absent and the silence echoed off the walls. Jack looked at their wedding portrait on the mantle and gently touched the yellow porcelain rose beside it. She loved flowers, especially roses.*

*He gave a sad smile as he remembered that foggy day in February when he....*

"Leslie? I said to take a break, not take the afternoon off. Leslie?" her boss Mona repeated as she stuck her head into the lounge in the back of the boutique.

*....in February when he had gone all over town to find*

*a yellow rose for….*

Leslie's pen froze over the page and her head jerked up. She turned an unseeing face towards the voice that had interrupted her.

Mona looked a little surprised at the expression on Leslie's face. "What's wrong? You look like you're going to cry."

Leslie blushed and put down her pen, her eyes coming back into focus. "Sorry, Mona. I had an idea for my story and wanted to get it down on paper before I forgot it. I'll be right out."

Her boss leaned against the doorframe. "That's fine. You were so quiet I thought you had fallen asleep. You have been dragging lately," she pointed out, not unkindly.

Leslie nodded as she folded up the paper and put it next to her purse. "I know. I've been staying up too late writing. My ideas are coming easily right now and once I get going, I forget to stop."

"So, it is going well now? I heard you tell Janice that you were having some trouble."

Leslie smiled as she stretched her back. "No, I'm coming right along. I'm jazzed about it *now*."

Mona Green gave her a smug smile. Still preoccupied with the scene she had been formulating, Leslie missed the warning. "Good. Glad to hear you're in a good mood. The high school just called. It's retailing project time again. We can expect some students today or tomorrow."

A loud groan was heard. "I got them last semester! It's Janice's turn. Or your's!"

Pushing off from the doorframe with a laugh, Mona told her, "Oh, but you do such a good job with the eager students. They're all yours." The boss returned to her office, still laughing, as Leslie went back out front, rolling her eyes at Janice.

Le Petite Boutique was small but a well-stocked dress salon that catered mostly to the social circle. Every dress they sold had a full range of accessories available. Having a profile on all their regular customers, they could bring to their homes a display in the correct size to meet any occasion. There was a seamstress, Paula, in the store at all times. They even had an errand boy on call to rush to the wholesalers in San Francisco if they happened to be out of a desired item. Their clientele was growing and faithful. Customers were willing to pay a higher price for the quality of goods and services they received.

The boutique was on the first floor of a Victorian mansion that once belonged to the founding family of Amherst. Located in what was now the Old Downtown District, the entire ground floor had been refurbished to accommodate the shop, but Mona kept with the Victorian theme. A beautiful copper and crystal chandelier that had always hung in the entryway of the mansion now held light bulbs instead of flickering candles. The original dark walnut hardwood floors were covered here and there with pastel Oriental rugs in elaborate floral patterns. Victorian Queen Anne chairs that sat waiting for customers had lovely tapestry seats. Four large dressing rooms were draped with velvet panels held back with gold braided cords. Gourmet coffee in an antique silver decanter sat waiting on an etched tray with delicate Petit Fours on lace doilies to spoil the best of customers. Highly polished mahogany display cases showed off the jewelry, as well as the purses. An open armoire held scarves, hankies, and linen. Dresses, wraps, and lingerie hung in recessed, lighted nooks. Then there were the beveled, etched, and leaded Italian mirrors: the accent lights hung with prisms or tassels. The pastel oil paintings on the walls of the boutique were copies of Monet and Renoir in floral-edged gold leaf frames.

The second and third floors were the private living areas of Mona Green and her family. Her husband, Patrick, owned and operated a small local dealership, and their two pre-teen children, Mike and Mary, attended school nearby.

It was in this surrounding that Wayne Fields first met the Evil One of Amherst. Within the first two days of his moving into the conveniently empty apartment directly below hers, he had learned much of her schedule and some of her habits. He had followed her to work the first day and entered her apartment the second. Now he was curious.

He entered the boutique and was momentarily taken aback. The size of the city with its two hundred thousand residents had already surprised him, but this shop was incredible. He could hear the soft strains of classical music playing lightly in the background and almost expected a maid to ask for his calling card! Instead, four well-dressed women glanced up from their various tasks of rearranging, dusting and ordering garments. He recognized Leslie immediately from the pictures he had seen with her curly brown hair, trim figure and friendly smile. After her first glance at the newcomer, however, she went back to organizing the armoire she had already dusted.

A tall, attractive redhead dressed in a fashionable white suit approached as he now self-consciously advanced further into the shop. He had been expecting the usual racks of dresses behind which he could stall and observe.

"May I be of assistance?" Janice asked, silently wondering why in the world this man was in their shop looking as if he wanted to disappear into a crack.

"Yes, I was…I mean…," he stammered as he searched for the excuse he had planned on using. The redhead was very pretty. "I wanted to find a present for my mother. I'm new in town and wasn't sure where to find something for her." *Yeah, that sounded good*, he thought, refraining from wiping his forehead. *Steady, man, you know what you're doing*.

Janice was now sorry she had rushed forward. She had liked the way his hair fell messily over his forehead. Her first reaction was to want to push it back with her fingertips. But, his eyes seemed to be returning to Leslie…. "All right. Did you have anything particular in mind?" she hoped, backing off and getting down to business.

"No. Maybe a nice dress," was the vague reply. *That should allow me plenty of time to observe*.

"Do you know what size she wears?"

Wayne looked her over and then Leslie. "Somewhere around the size of you two."

Leslie, a petite size six, bit her lip as she glanced at Mona who hurried to her office. Janice, a tall size ten, tried another approach.

"Well, maybe a nice scarf or some jewelry would do as well. That way we wouldn't have to worry about sizes."

That was fine with Wayne as it took him over to where Leslie was busy working. He saw the amusement in her eyes as she stood back. He pretended to study her face which immediately made her blush and become nervous.

"I've seen you somewhere before," he stated before she could bolt and retreat.

"I'm sorry. I don't recall." She was torn between being polite to this customer and getting away from his intense, rude stare.

Wayne looked like he was thinking hard. "I know! Don't you live in the Brighton Apartments? That's where I've seen you. I'm your new neighbor, Wayne Fields. I just moved in below you."

Leslie looked relieved. She didn't like conversations that started that way. "Oh, really? I didn't even know someone had moved in. Shows how much I pay attention," she replied, giving a small self-conscious laugh and then falling silent.

"I'm Wayne Fields," he repeated, making it obvious he wanted formal introductions.

When her friend remained silent and blushed again, Janice turned to the armoire and pretended to look through the scarves, intentionally bumping Leslie in the process. She got the point. "I...I'm Leslie. This is my friend Janice."

"Good to meet both of you. I hate being the new one in town!" Wayne said with a self-deprecating grin that, on a handsome man, would have been charming. It just made him look self-conscious. He added as if an afterthought, "You know, you're pretty quiet yourself. It's like I don't even have neighbors in that complex."

Now that they had talked a little longer, Leslie felt more at ease and her eyes gave a mischievous twinkle. "That's because I haven't given my weekly mambo party!" Her attention was suddenly drawn to the front door, her smile froze on her face, and an almost inaudible, "Oh, goody," was heard.

Three giggly high school girls armed with notebooks and pink feathered pens entered. They attempted to straighten their faces and become sophisticated, but failed in a chorus of nervous giggles.

Leslie muttered to Janice, "Muffy, Buffy and Fluffy are here. No. No. Let me get them. I insist," as she left to do her inflicted duty.

Janice hid her mouth with her hand and saw Mona grinning off to the side. Wayne was forgotten for the moment as they all watched and listened. He didn't mind because buying a scarf wouldn't have taken very long and he wanted to stay and observe his target in her natural surroundings.

Leslie fixed her smile. "Ladies?" she said in a way that would cut butter. "May I help you?"

The one pushed forward first became the spokesperson for the trio. "Um, like, see? We didn't want to buy anything. Like, we're from Amherst High, you know? And, see, we're doing this project, like, in retailing, you know, and wondered if we could, umm, ask a few questions. 'Kay?" she finished brightly as the other nodded in agreement.

"'Kay," Leslie responded just as brightly. "Like, what did you, like, want to know?"

"Okay, like, okay. What's your most expensive item?" Buffy asked looking around eagerly as the other two held their pens ready to write.

That was always the first question. "If you'll come here, like, I'll show you." Leslie shot a glance back to Mona who, in turn, pulled the corners of her mouth into a smile. Leslie batted her eyes at her boss and gave a rather silly smile. She dropped it before turning back to the girls.

Janice's shoulders were shaking at her friend's antics and she had to turn away. She then remembered the customer, Wayne Something. "Oh! I'm sorry. You wanted a scarf or some other thing?"

Wayne's eyes still followed Leslie. "What's the show about?" he quietly asked, indicating the girls with his chin.

"Every semester the seniors in the retail management classes are sent out to talk to shop owners about their businesses. It's like a term paper," she explained and then shook her head with a smile. "The ones who come here usually just want to see the 'neat stuff' as they call it."

Wayne indicated Leslie. "She's the owner, then?"

"Oh, no. That would be Mona Green, back there by the piano. Leslie is the senior clerk. We all know how much she enjoys these interviews," Janice grinned wickedly.

"I can tell.... I'll take this scarf," he said, picking up the closest one. "Do you have gift wrap?"

They moved over to the cash register which brought them closer to Leslie. She was holding up a beautiful black velvet evening dress appliquéd with gold and silver beads.

"This lovely creation is $4,500," she told the gaping girls.

They all wrote down $4,500 in their notebooks and added three exclamation points.

Muffy asked, "So, like, how much would it have cost wholesale?"

"A little less," was her reply as they wrote down 'a little less.' "The beadwork is hand sewn and the velvet is imported from France. We captured some runaway grandmothers to sew the beads on. We keep them in the cellar."

"Can we see them?" Fluffy asked eagerly.

"No."

""Kay, like, what do you call these little, you know, these little buttons that you can't get off?" Buffy took over the interview again, indicating the security tag attached to the label inside the gown.

Leslie fought to keep her face straight. "That would be a Detonating Untheft Monitoring Instrument, or a D. U. M. I," she spelled, "as it is known in the business."

"How do you spell that?"

Leslie slowly repeated, "D. U. M. I."

Paula and Mona were nowhere to be seen.

"Like, where do you get all this neat stuff?"

"We have wholesalers in San Francisco, and contacts in New York and Paris."

Buffy wrote that under her D. U. M. I. and wondered if this place ever had clearance sales.

The others could see Leslie visibly cringe at the thought. She answered slowly, "No. You see, nothing here really goes out of style. That's one of the keys to good buying."

The girls wrote down "No" and asked what the cheapest thing in the store was.

*Probably your earrings*, Leslie thought, but answered, "Some of the lingerie begins around twenty dollars."

"Oooh!" Fluffy squealed. "Twenty dollars just for underwear?"

"We don't carry underwear. That would be a satin camisole." Leslie gave the returning Mona a glazed look that the owner knew meant "Get me out of this <u>now</u>!"

The girls closed their notebooks and headed back to the dresses. As one of the girls reached for a shimmering pink gown, Leslie warned, "No, no. Don't touch. Hand oil on silk doesn't come off."

"You touched them," Muffy obstinately pointed out.

Leslie held up her hands for them to see. "My hands are specially treated."

"Oooh! Cool!"

"Any other questions, answers, comments, observations, queries, statements?" as Leslie herded them towards the door.

"No, like, that's all, I'm sure," Buffy replied, still cheerful. "Thanks ever so much. Do you carry prom dresses?"

Leslie's smile froze again. "Oh, sorry, no. We don't have the room. Nuts."

"Bummer! Maybe, if, like, you got rid of that old piano you could in a neat circle rack," Muffy offered, pointing at the baby grand.

"I'll mention it to the owner. Thanks for coming. Bye, bye," as she closed the door and turned to face her co-workers. "Not one word," she warned as she walked past them and into the lounge where she put her head on the table.

All of the other women stood outside the door and shrilly shrieked, "Ooooooooooh!" before they returned to their duties.

Wayne had sat unnoticed by the armoire throughout all this. He had already paid for the silk scarf he had no use for and had it wrapped. Now he arose and left, likewise unnoticed. He tossed the carefully wrapped package into his trunk and decided he wanted another look at Leslie's apartment tomorrow. It was too close to closing time to carry this out tonight.

He sat there, just for a moment, behind the wheel of his car. He had conflicting information and was trying to sort it all out in his mind. She had been both gushy teenager-like and all business in her letters to Phillip Beck. She had blushed and gotten nervous when a stranger got overly familiar with her. Then she had sweetly made a group of silly girls look like, well, silly girls without their knowing what she was doing to them.

The investigator chuckled to himself. "I'd like to see her get good and mad at someone! Wow!"

He headed back to his apartment to make some notes for his first report to Sarah Beck.

At ten minutes after six, he rolled his newspaper back into a bundle and put it outside on his door mat. At six fifteen, from the corner of his front window, he watched Leslie walk past their building to the mailboxes. At six eighteen, he opened his door to retrieve the paper he had just set there and startled the disappointed look off Leslie's face as she headed for the stairs leading up to her apartment.

"Hello, again," he said cheerfully. "That was some performance you gave."

Leslie was looking at him as if he were a green Martian and had suddenly sprouted wings.

"At your store…earlier today…three high school girls? We met right before that," he hurriedly explained.

Remembrance flooded back and she blushed at her forgetfulness. "I'm sorry. I…I'm a little preoccupied."

*She didn't hear from the publisher or from Phillip Beck*, Wayne told himself. "Those girls were really something."

Leslie shifted uncomfortably and glanced up the stairs to the sanctuary of her front door. "Sometimes we get students who really are interested in retailing or sometimes designing. Most of the time we get Fifi and Scooter who go to every store in the mall and then come to us." She shook her head as if to rid it of the thought and started for the stairs leading up to her apartment.

"Say," Wayne called, stopping her. As she reluctantly turned back, he indicated inside his apartment with his head. "I have enough Chinese food in there to choke a horse. I didn't know how generous the chefs are here. I have egg fu yong."

"Appealing as you make it, no, thank you," as she started up the stairs.

"There's plenty."

"Then it looks like you'll be having egg fu breakfast," she

called back without turning. She let out a silent breath of air when she heard his chuckle and the door close. "I don't need this now," she muttered as her own door closed and was quietly locked.

Ten-fifteen a.m. Thursday. Most of the residents of the Brighton Apartments had left for work or had gone out for the day. The gardeners were busy at another section and it was the manager's day off. Wayne Fields had left his apartment at nine-thirty dressed in a dark suit and hat. At ten, he had returned to the complex, parked in the visitor's section in the back, and left the jacket and hat in the car. Under the slacks that he removed was a pair of tennis shorts. The loafers were switched with athletic shoes and a white visor was pulled low over his eyes. Grabbing up a gym bag, he walked unhurriedly past his own door and up the stairs. Using a pick, he entered Leslie's apartment and noiselessly closed the door.

Pausing just inside the door, Wayne set down the gym bag and looked around her living room. He was using different eyes, as it were, than he had used the first time he had broken in. Now he looked for evidence of the two distinct personalities of which he had gotten glimpses. The quiet, almost shy individual was most prominently displayed. Her rooms carried the same Victorian atmosphere as the boutique in which she worked, only not as plush and expensive. The off-white sofa and loveseat had tapestry borders that were highlighted by floral throw pillows. The dark accent tables were cluttered with filigree picture frames, cut-glass vases, porcelain flowers, dried arrangements and crocheted white doilies. The pictures on the walls were inexpensive oils of landscapes and flowers. The largest picture over the sofa was a copy of a pastel garden party done by one of the more-popular Impressionists.

Her one bedroom was more of the same. The queen-sized brass bed was covered with a floral comforter and had lacy pastel pillows at the head. Two old-fashioned prismed chimney lamps hung from the ceiling and were poised over the nightstands. Intricate glass perfume bottles, a gold satin jewelry box, more doilies, stuffed animals, and a Venetian glass cockatoo sculpture were on the top of a triple dresser. The French cradle phone, clock radio, and a small television set seemed out of place in this feminine, old-fashioned setting.

It was in the shadowbox and in the collage picture frames that one began to see another side of Leslie. Here the whimsy was evident, the humor. The shadowbox, at first glance, continued the feminine ambiance. But a more careful scrutiny caused one to see items that didn't seem to belong. A large silver sheriff's badge, a brass sailing ship, a wind-up kangaroo that did flips, and a "Time Police" badge all fit neatly into the wooden spaces but didn't exactly blend in with the miniature white ducks, Tiffany-style lamp, small antique music boxes trimmed in gold, and porcelain thimbles.

On one of the walls he noticed two picture frames that held a total of thirty-five snapshots. They appeared to be of family and friends and vacations. But, mixed in were pictures of a popular singer in concert, the cast members of "The Time Police," and a close-up of Phillip Beck in costume. What made Wayne stop and reconsider was that these were not pictures cut out of magazines. They were not publicity photos signed at conventions—they were taken by a personal camera. Since the quality of the pictures was the same as those of the family pictures, Wayne had to assume that Leslie had taken them herself. But how? It seemed obvious that the parties involved had never met. Had Leslie somehow gotten onto the set to take pictures? How could she sneak through security? Or did she follow Beck somewhere and take his picture without his knowledge?

With a quiet, "Hmm," Wayne turned his attention to Leslie's roll-top desk. Here he found the ivory-colored stationery she seemed to favor—the same paper Sarah Beck had shown him when she interviewed him. In the bottom drawer he found her "Time Police" collection of magazines, newspaper articles, Phillip's letter, an answering machine tape labeled "Phillip Beck—Keep," copies of all the letters she had mailed to him, and a collection of more pictures like the ones in the collage on the wall.

The double-drawer on the left contained her rejection letters from agents, a list of potential agencies, sample letters she had typed, outlines of the two finished novels, sample pages from each book, and the two spiral-bound copies she had printed for herself.

Wayne glanced at her clock. Time was rapidly passing. He wanted to read both books and look over the rewrite that was waiting under the sofa. He just didn't have time right now. He had to send off his first report to Sarah that afternoon.

He heard the clicking of heels on the sidewalk that wound through the complex. The person walking had hesitated at the turn to these particular apartments but then continued towards the manager's office. Hurrying to the living room, he barely moved her lace curtains aside to peek out. It was Leslie heading for the mailboxes. So that was why she hadn't taken a lunch that morning. She must have the afternoon off. Crap!

Wayne's mind started rapidly going over his options. He had approximately two minutes before she returned from the mailbox. Back in the bedroom, he quickly looked around. He hurriedly closed the desk drawers. The closet door.... Had it been open or closed? Open, he decided. Grabbing up his gym bag by her entry door, he quietly opened the door and turned the lock. Now he had to get back to his apartment.

Hearing her heels again as the sound echoed through the quiet complex, he knew he would be seen coming down the stairs and going into his rooms. As her door clicked shut, he pulled out his notebook and a pen and quickly flipped past the notes he had made inside her rooms. Head down, he started writing.

Leslie's mind was on her current chapter in her rewrite and had given the mail an uninterested glance. She stopped abruptly at the base of the stairs. There was a man standing at her door writing something in a small pad. Taking a step back, she looked around. Two empty apartments and the rest were quiet. Wondering if she should just go back to her car, she again looked up at the man who appeared to be dressed to play tennis. "Can I help you?" she called up in a voice that sounded calm.

The man turned as if surprised by the sound of her voice. "Oh, there you are. Hi, again. It's just me," Wayne replied easily as he bounded down the steps. He noticed Leslie had taken another step backwards. She didn't recognize him. "Wayne," he pointed to his door. "Your new neighbor?"

"Oh, right," she answered, looking visibly relieved. "I guess I didn't recognize you. Again," she added with an apologetic grin.

As she didn't say anything else, Wayne indicated his notebook that she had looked at with narrowed eyes. "I was just leaving you a note to see if we could have dinner tonight. Or tomorrow. I didn't think you would be home until later."

Leslie momentarily looked down at her feet and ignored the invitation. "I usually only work half day on Thursdays," she told him and gave a small smile as she headed to the stairs.

"What about dinner, then?"

"Well, I am pretty busy with a project. Maybe some other time."

Halfway up the stairs, he called up to her, "Then, how about Saturday? Hey, you have to eat sometime!" he reasoned with a friendly grin.

"Ask me Saturday," was the noncommittal response.

"Okay, I will. Remember, I know where you live," he said with a laugh and unlocked his own door.

That last remark, meant in a humorous manner, caused a nervous shiver to travel up Leslie's arms. And she didn't know why. Rubbing her arms as if cold, she knew she had made that crack herself to friends who had borrowed something. But, this man wasn't a friend. He was *trying* to be friendly. That much was obvious. He had never been anything but pleasant. *So, why the strange reaction?* she asked herself. Not being able to explain, she set down her purse and the mail and rubbed her arms again.

After kicking off her shoes, she made a sandwich and wandered back to the sofa to eat it. Her wandering glance fell upon her shadowbox and the sandwich froze halfway up to her mouth. Something was different. The box didn't look right.

Leslie knew this wasn't her imagination at work—vivid as it was. No, an old boyfriend had played a game with her each time he would come over. He always, half jokingly, called her a perfectionist. To prove his point that she wouldn't tolerate something out of place, he would rearrange or hide one of her little knick-knacks whenever she momentarily left the room. She would always notice, usually immediately, and find or rearrange the item to its proper place. He had always laughed at her and declared he was right. She gave a small grin as she thought about him. He had ended up unhappily married to a woman who worked full time and never touched a vacuum or dust cloth in her life.

It was the tin sheriff's badge that Leslie had bought years before in Tombstone, Arizona. She had described it as a prop in her Western novel. Now it was leaning over and about to fall off its shelf. As she righted the badge she also noticed one of the music boxes didn't match the dust pattern under it.

Heart pounding, she quickly looked around the living room and then went into the bedroom, her forgotten sandwich still in her left hand. Her desk. The bottom drawer wasn't closed all the way. It was just a fraction off, but…. She pulled it open to look. It was its usual cluttered mess. Slowly closing the drawer, still looking around, she could see nothing else disturbed.

With a look of confusion on her face, she went back to the sofa. Within moments, Leslie upbraided herself for being ridiculous. "Burt was right. One little thing out of place and I fall apart. Hmph. I probably just slammed the door too hard when I left this morning and the badge fell over."

Thus dismissing the matter from her mind, lunch was finished and she changed out of her work dress and into comfortable jeans and a polo shirt. Pulling her lap desk out from under the sofa, she reread what she had written so far and delved back into her own little world of Rex and Jane.


**W**ayne took the earpiece out of his right ear. It had been wirelessly connected to a listening device in inside Leslie's apartment. He heard her go suddenly into her bedroom and then open a desk drawer. He wondered what he had overlooked in his hasty retreat. He relaxed when he heard the sofa creak and figured she was writing again. Turning off the small receiver, he realized she apparently was no longer worried, so neither was he.

After briefly referring to his latest notes, he began his first report to Sarah:

"*Mrs. Beck,*
*As according to our agreement, I have met the third party in*

*question and have had two occasions to briefly examine the residence of said party. A more thorough search cannot be conducted before Monday.*

*Regarding said third party: I have seen two separate personalities indicated. I am attempting to form a more personal contact to get a clearer picture, but this takes time.*

*Regarding the residence: A comfortable, homey, feminine atmosphere. I have found letters to and from your second party. There is also some question in my mind about the origin of some photographs of the second party. It will require further investigation.*

*As the third party is employed locally and busy with another 'project,' there is no cause for concern at this time.*

*I will continue my reports and the surveillance.*

*Have a nice day.*

*W.F."*

# CHAPTER 5

At the airport, Phillip Beck just stood there on the curb next to the black limo. The driver was unloading a mountain of bags and directing the porter. Sarah had just kissed him good-bye setting off a wave of flashbulbs from the media circus that followed her every move. Davey had been distracted from his tearful hug by a whispered promise from Marty to look for a model airplane like the one they would be boarding. Davey tottered off holding "Uncle Marty's" hand and had forgotten to turn and wave one last time to his daddy. The flock of hovering, ready photographers had pushed by Phillip as Sarah regally strode into the terminal. He had been officially forgotten.

He stood by the car until his wife's blond hair was swallowed up by the vast airport. The driver quietly reminded him that they were parked in an unloading zone and would Mr. Beck like him to return after the plane had departed?

"The plane already left," he murmured as he retook his seat in the back. As the door clicked shut, it was eerily quiet without Davey's excited prattle.

Since the limo had been Marty's idea, the driver took Phillip straight home and deposited him on the front walk of his house.

Pausing in the tiled entryway, he listened to the quiet of the house. The tall grandfather clock could be heard ticking down the long hall. There were no other sounds. No maids, no house cleaners, and no gardeners could be heard since they all came on other days.

Phillip looked around the massive house with narrowed, critical eyes. Everything was white. Tile, walls, draperies, furniture, even the bricks of the fireplace were painted white. Touches of color came from a few accent pillows and the oil paintings. Even the chandeliers in the entryway and the formal dining room seemed so stark and sterile to him right then.

He hadn't wanted his house to look like this. He had admired the great manor houses of the English countryside when he had been on location there and had far preferred that kind of look. This house had been selected primarily because of its vaulted ceilings, sweeping staircase, and huge fireplaces. This house had the potential to recreate that warm, inviting, livable atmosphere of those grand mansions.

However, Martin Thomas had introduced Sarah to Didi Goshen at a party one evening shortly after they moved in and Sarah's career was busy skyrocketing. Didi was THE interior decorator. All the celebrities and all the right people had Didi do their houses. The phrase "Land of Goshen" now referred to Didi's work. And Didi said white was in.

The only room where Phillip had his way was his study in the back of the house. This room was home to a large dark walnut desk, burgundy leather sofa, overstuffed tartan chairs, a floor-to-ceiling walnut bookcase, prints of hounds and the English hunt matted in dark green and burgundy, and a large brass hunter's horn arranged with dried wild flowers.

It was in this room that Phillip could retreat, a place where he could really relax. Davey would bring in his plastic horses and play while Phillip read over his mail or a script. It was to this room that Phillip now headed, his footsteps echoing loudly on the white Italian tile floor. But Davey wouldn't be bringing in his toys to play on the thick brown carpet. Davey was gone. For a month. *At least a month*, Sarah had added in the limo on the way to the airport, just before the door flung open to the photographers Marty had arranged to be there. There was a possibility of another major shoot, she had told him. She'd let him know, as she gave him a kiss and the cameras obediently began shooting.

He took out the script for the Zenith picture "Mutiny of Love at Sea." He hated the title. He hated his role as the captain. He hated his perfunctory lines. He hated.... No, he retracted, he hated Martin for his involvement.

Phillip stretched out on his eight-foot sofa to go over his lines once more. He had already memorized them by the second reading, but felt he should review both the words and the action. He was still a professional and would still do the best he could with the material—such as it was.

*"Have you invited the Duchess to dine with me tonight? Good."*

*"Here, here! Stop this fight! You're officers. Now shake hands and remember you're also gentlemen."*

*"You dance well, Madam."*

*"What do you mean we are out of caviar?! That's impossible. Get me...."*

The script dropped onto his chest. Drivel. Silly drivel. Where were the interesting roles? Where was that Western he had read...when? Ten months ago? A year? Oh, yes, now he remembered. A riverboat gambler, a saloon girl, an archrival named...Jack. "The Time Police." That was it. Now, what had happened to that script? It was different than anything they had done yet.

He turned his head toward his desk. Bunny. He hadn't heard from her in months and wondered how her writing was coming along.

He thought back to when his agent Bill had handed him her first letter and a very small script that was only about sixty pages long. This had now been Bunny's third attempt and it, too, centered on his Professor character. Bill had read both the letter and the story before passing them along to Phillip as was the policy for handling celebrity mail. Bill was, at first, a little concerned when he learned Phillip had personally contacted this writer, but, he too liked her short story. He could see the possible potential in a well-written, longer version. Bill had thought, as had Sarah, that a script would be more advantageous to Phillip's career than a book.

Phillip shook his head and sighed. Didn't anyone trust his professional judgment? Bunny wasn't ready to write a script. She needed more experience. Extending her short stories into novel length and working with an agent to get them published was an excellent way for her to gain that experience. Was he the only one who realized this?

Bunny had offered to send him a copy of her first novel to familiarize him with her new character and show how Jane arrived in "The Time Police" squad. It was then he recalled how he had dissuaded her. He told her he was overwhelmed with his *own* books and scripts.

He picked up the script of "Mutiny of Love at Sea" from off his chest and dropped it to the floor. He knew over on the bookcase next to his desk were the scripts for "Senator Steve Goes to War," "The Slasher's Guide to Love," "The Nile—River That Time Forgot," "Moonshine Madness," and the ever-popular serial, "DMV—Part VI—The Senior's Revenge." There were also a few costume dramas, two silly slapsticks that he didn't quite understand, and a science-fiction thriller. A three-hour Revolutionary War epic had been interesting, but Bill had only offered him the role of the officer who takes the first bullet.

At least his sea captain film began rehearsal in a few days and would be over—for him—within two weeks. Then he would play the Professor again. That would take two and a half weeks. Then…nothing. Unless he agreed to take one of the repugnant offerings waiting on his bookcase.

"Sorry, Bunny," he muttered as his eyes closed. "I'm just too overwhelmed."


**T**he phone rang in Sarah Beck's suite at the Tokyo Imperial Hotel.

"Miss Beck's room. This is Mr. Thomas. Can I help you?"

A static-filled voice replied, "This is Phillip. Can I talk to my wife, please?"

"Who is this?" Marty demanded with a smug grin. "I can hardly hear you. Bad connection."

"Phillip here," he shouted. "Let me talk to Sarah."

"Phillip? She can't come to the phone," Martin yelled back, scratching the mouthpiece with his fingernail.

Phillip had to hold the phone away from his ear. He could hear Martin just fine. "Where is she?"

"In the shower," came back the clear response.

"Let me talk to Davey, then," Phillip requested.

Martin scratched the phone again. "No can do. He's not here."

"What? Where is he? You're supposed to be watching him!"

Martin smiled to himself. "Don't throw a shoe, old man. He's with a sitter. We're going out tonight." After a long enough pause, he added, "With her boss. They're throwing a party in her honor at the Fire Dragon."

"Will you tell her I called? Again?" The bitterness in his voice was heard through the fake static supplied by Martin. This was the third attempt to talk to his family and he had always gotten Martin.

"Yeah, sure, old man. I'll go tell her right away. Sayonara," Marty laughed and hung up.

Marty was still laughing as he went to answer the knock on the door to the suite. He bowed his greeting to Mr. and Mrs. Matsui as they arrived to escort Sarah and him to their party. A limo would be waiting outside. He excused himself and quickly went to get Sarah.

She was not in the shower as he had said, but was putting on the finishing touches to her outfit. She was pulling on gold heels to match the golden silk backless dress she was wearing. It was a stunning effect with her blond hair.

Marty put his hands over his heart. "You take my breath away," he declared and then told her their hosts had arrived.

"Did I hear the phone? Where's my wrap, Marty?" she inquired as she hunted for a shimmering stole.

"Wrong number," was the smooth reply as the missing garment was located in her monstrous closet and they left for the gala event.

The photo sessions and the television commercials were going extremely well. The country loved this lovely lady and her well-behaved, respectful child. The advertisements were released sooner than planned because of the popularity of the sample ads. A car company and a cosmetics firm had put in offers for Sarah's representation. The car company even requested Davey for ads aimed at the family.

Sarah was recognized as the trio went sightseeing and were stopped many times for autographs by polite, almost apologetic fans. The people were delighted when she would ask questions or compliment the beauty of their country in their own language. Davey had quickly picked up a lot of the dialect as only the absorbing mind of a youth can do.

Sarah's stay in Japan turned from a one month stay into what now looked like would be two months. Marty arranged a lot of off-time excursions to keep Davey excited and Sarah preoccupied. They cruised the harbor amongst the colorful fishing boats and attended the Kabuki Theater. There were trips to the mountains, the beach, entertainment areas, and beautifully sculpted gardens with intimate tea ceremonies. The shopping was extraordinary. Davey was enthralled by all the new electronic toys that he had never even seen back home. Marty even bought him a small personal computer designed for the young mind.

By now Davey had quit asking when they were going home. The questions about "Daddy" slowed to a trickle and finally stopped. To him it seemed as if his big, tall, strong daddy just wasn't around any longer and what was once concern had now turned into acceptance.

But, Marty was there. And Marty took him to exciting places and bought him neat toys. Martin let him stay up too late so Davey could see his mommy's new commercial. Whenever he was scared, Marty's arms were there to shield and protect him. If he awakened in the middle of the night unsure of where he was, Marty came in at his cry even before his mother did.

The transition was too subtle for a four-year old to grasp. Sarah was happy because Davey accepted Marty better now than at first, and seeing that Marty took such personal interest in her son was very satisfying. The agent, in turn, was satisfied in Sarah's success and her unconscious leaning towards him more and more. Marty slowly developed a real liking for the boy as Davey was well-behaved and looked to him for comfort when needed.

Months later, the final step for Marty and Davey came one morning when Sarah was called to an early shoot. She had to leave before Davey was awake. Marty heard him stirring in his room and went to the door. The boy opened his eyes and saw Marty smiling at him. "Hi, Daddy," was the sleepy greeting that melted Marty's devious heart.

"*M*rs. Beck,

*The third party and friend are talking more and more of vacationing in Los Angeles. The current project is near completion and the author feels she 'needs a break.'*

*I have spent considerable time in this one's company and have become privy to secrets and stories. There is a growing, shall we say, fascination with the world of LA, and much speculation regarding your second party. We have seen what can come of these fascinations. This third project is quite a love story.*

*Shall I continue my current assignment? Our original agreement time has lapsed. I await your decision.*

*Have a nice day.*
*W.F.*"

Marty chuckled over this weekly report. Knowing Wayne, he knew it meant nothing of importance. Knowing Sarah, he knew it would keep her satisfied that her fears and tremendous expense were justified and that this woman was a threat that only she could control.

To Marty, 'considerable time' meant Wayne was probably dating her. And using Sarah's money! That was funny to him.

Marty had called his friend weeks ago to get the real story. Wayne had been vague and had not told him much. Marty told him to spice up his reports or Sarah would likely fire him and fly home to assign someone else.

"What's wrong?" Wayne had been sarcastic. "Aren't your fringe benefits working out?"

"Listen, buddy. You just keep convincing Sarah we're dealing with a fanatic and we'll both profit. Understand?"

"Yeah. I understand. Perfectly. But, do you realize how far off you really are?" he had asked.

"Wayne, I don't care. I've got plans—big plans for my girl here. She needs to feel she is in control of the situation back there—whether it exists or not. You're dealing with an outsider, a nobody. Whatsa matter? You developing a conscience?"

There had been a pause. "Maybe I am."

That had surprised Marty. "Maybe you'd like off the case if you can't do what you were hired to do. There are plenty of other guys I know who can make it stick."

"I didn't say I wanted off, Marty. I just wanted you to know something along the lines of the truth," Wayne quietly told him.

"Since when have I cared about the truth?" Marty declared with a laugh. "You keep everyone happy. All right?"

"Sure, Marty, sure," was the resigned reply as they both hung up.

Wayne had done what he was told. The reports were short, but they convinced Sarah of her need for continued surveillance and that there was a danger to what she considered her own property—whether she really wanted it or not. This last report would probably net Wayne a bonus in case he would have to follow Leslie to Los Angeles and watch her there. Wayne might have faltered briefly for whatever reason, but the all-powerful dollar spoke loud and clear and he would continue to do what he was told.


There was a reception that night for Sarah thrown by the car company responsible for her extended stay. The company was thrilled at acquiring her for their world-release campaign. The party was bigger than any she had been given so far. The food and the champagne were exquisite and plentiful. There were countless toasts to their success and health.

It had been a busy and tiring day for Sarah. Now the reception went into the late hours of the night. She ate too little and drank too much to keep up with the toasts. Her head swam and Marty could see she needed to leave.

He made arrangements with the Matsuis to use their private yacht. He felt the sea air 'would be refreshing to Miss Beck so she could be ready for work.' They were more than happy to oblige and made the necessary call to the dock and even brought around their personal limo.

Sarah bid them all good-night and gave her thanks and was mildly surprised then their car drove past the hotel.

"I have a surprise for you," Marty told her. "I've arranged for you to be given a moonlight tour of the harbor."

That appealed to her groggy mind as the car parked in front of the mooring. The captain, who was accustomed to the eccentricities of the rich, welcomed Marty and Sarah aboard and did his duty.

The couple went to the upper deck to see the lights of Tokyo as they played off the water. Marty excused himself and returned with a bottle of champagne.

"To your new job and to your beauty," he toasted and took a small sip.

Sarah smiled at the compliment and took another swallow. "You've been so good to me, Marty," she sighed as he refilled her glass. "You always compliment me and tell me how nice I look. I'm not used to that, you know," she confided in an overloud voice as the champagne affected her.

"Now, now. People pay you respects all the time," he murmured.

"That's not what I mean. You say it because you mean it. They have to," she said, gesturing with her flute to indicate that 'they' meant everyone in general.

When she shivered in the ocean breeze, he put his arm around her shoulder. She snuggled closer. "You deserve the praise. And more," he asserted quietly as the yacht continued its leisurely course around the bay. "Your beauty is great. And your intelligence matches your looks."

"Hmph. Phillip doesn't think I'm smart. He's...."

"He's not here," Marty interrupted her gently and turned her face to his. "He's never been here for you. I have. And I always will be."

She studied his face as best she could in her condition. When she shivered again, he took her into his arms for an embrace.

"Yes, you have been here for me. You've been a good...," pausing as she struggled for a word. "No, friend isn't enough. You're more. You're...."

Words failed her as she lifted her face to his and her lips parted. He returned the kiss and her arms went around his neck.

The lights of the harbor were forgotten as Marty picked her up in his arms and carried her below.


"**Q**uit giving me excuses, Martin. Let me talk to my wife!" Phillip demanded, growing angrier.

"Who is it, dear?" he heard through the phone as Sarah entered the living room.

"It's for you. It's Phillip. I tried to tell him we're leaving for an assignment," as Marty handed her the phone.

"Phillip? What's wrong?" she asked, looking at her watch.

"Wrong?" he echoed, unbelieving. "I've been calling and calling and this is the first time I've gotten through to you in over three months, and that's all you say?"

"Don't shout. That's rude. All right. How are you? Is that what I am supposed to ask? You caught me by surprise, you know," she retorted.

"Well, dear," acidly using the endearment she had just given Martin, "I just finished "The Time Police" and wanted to fly over to spend some time with you and Davey this weekend. Meet me at the airport and we'll forget this argument."

There was a pause. Sarah had her hand over the mouthpiece telling Martin what Phillip had said. "Phillip, that's not such a good idea this week. We're going to a remote location to shoot. No outsiders are allowed. Only the crew."

"Outsiders?" He couldn't believe the term applied to him. "I am still your husband. Aren't I?" he added bitterly.

"Of course you are. It's just not allowed. I had to make special concessions for Marty to be allowed to come. Davey was no problem as he is in the ad with me."

Phillip sighed. She could make arrangements for Martin, but not for him. "Can I talk to Davey? I really miss him. It's too quiet around here," he confided. *And lonely.*

"He's not here. He's on an outing with the Matsuis and their grandson. He won't be back until it's time for the shoot."

"Will you give him my love, then? Did he like the letters I sent him?"

"What letters?"

Phillip was astounded. "I've written him every week! Eddie even sent a line last time."

Sarah shrugged. "We never received them. It's probably just as well. It would probably confuse him. He's really settled in here. He talks like a native!"

"You sound as if you are staying. Does he ever ask for me?" Phillip sounded dejected.

"Oh, yes. Sure. Uh huh. Of course he does," was her hurried reply.

"Tell him Davey calls me daddy," Phillip heard Martin call out from the background and then he heard Sarah's, "Shh."

All the anger, dejection and hope flooded out of Phillip at hearing that. He felt nothing but empty. "So, when are you coming back to L.A.?" he asked as unconcerned as if he were talking to his butcher.

"I'm not sure," she tentatively told him. "France has been talking to Marty. We're considering some options."

"France? How nice. Well, I won't keep you any longer. Bonjour, Sarah," he said and hung up.

He went to his terrace and sat heavily in one of the wrought iron chairs overlooking the carefully tended flower gardens. But he saw nothing. He only thought. She had said it was just as well his own son didn't hear from him. Davey was called Martin Daddy. Sarah called Martin dear. She didn't want him to come visit. There had been no questions about his latest project or the movie coming up. Nothing familiar. He had been intruding.

He then remembered what he had forgotten to tell her, why he had wanted to come visit. "Happy Anniversary," he told the still water of the pool.

**S**arah looked at the phone in her hand and could hear the dial tone.

"If that doesn't beat all," she muttered.

"What did he say?"

"He hung up on me! He told me bonjour and he hung up!"

"I didn't know he spoke French," Marty commented with a smile.

"A little." Sarah set the phone down. "I wonder if I should have let him come this weekend."

*Oh, great idea, Sarah*, Marty thought. Out loud he said, "I don't know. The company is pretty strict about the shoot. Do you want to call him back?"

"And start another argument? Hardly. I don't know why he is so unreasonable about my career. He always has been. You'd think he'd just be happy for me. It's not my fault he's at a standstill. Is it?" she asked rhetorically.

Marty didn't know whether to answer or not. When she looked at him he just shrugged and told her, "I think you're doing a fabulous job. Soon you'll be known all over the world. You've accomplished all that and raised a son by yourself."

That worked. She walked up to him to put her arms around him. "Oh, no, Marty. It hasn't been alone. I've had you every step of the way. Even with Davey. He adores you."

Marty looked down as if embarrassed. "I feel the same. I'll tell you a secret if you promise not to repeat it."

This always intrigued Sarah. She loved secrets. He wasn't frequent in his displays of personal insight. "What is it, Marty?" she prompted gently.

"Well, I…I," he stammered as he looked at his feet. "Sometimes when I check on Davey in the middle of the night I pretend he's my own son." He looked up and met her eyes. "I can't explain the feeling I had when he called me daddy the first time."

"Oh, Marty. What would we do without you? I can't imagine," she claimed as she embraced him again.

"You'll never have to find out," was his reply as he smugly

smiled behind her back. Even though he had meant most of what he had said, he still considered his master plan and how Phillip didn't figure in it at all.

The housekeeper came to the patio door. "Mr. Beck? The phone, it is for you."

"Who is it, Amy?"

"I don't know, sir. Sorry."

He glanced at the cordless phone on the table next to him. He hadn't even heard it ring. "Hello? Beck here."

"Hey, Phil. It's Eddie. A group of us are going out to Charney's tonight. You're coming with us," Eddie informed him.

"Who's going?"

"My wife's in from the coast. Cindy has a new boyfriend. Tom. Max. Ron. Monica. Maybe Angela."

The last two names meant nothing to Phillip. Probably friends of Tom. "Sure, Edward. Sounds like fun," he replied in a monotone.

"Well, don't sound so thrilled. You might smile and crack your face," he kidded. "What's wrong?"

"Wrong? That's two times today someone has asked me that. First Sarah and now you," was his agitated response.

There was an uncomfortable pause. "Sarah, huh? Any news?" he cautiously asked.

"Not much. Davey calls that scum agent of hers daddy. They're going on to France next and I can't go with them or even visit them for a few days. Other than that, no, nothing big."

Eddie grimaced. It was rare for Phillip to open up like that. Rare? Non-existent was more like it. "Well, a night at Charney's is just what you need. We'll pick you up at six. See ya."

Phillip set down the receiver. He smiled in spite of his mood. This was what he needed. Tom and Eddie would probably make fools out of themselves. Maxwell was always good for an interesting conversation. Eddie's wife, Linda, could fill them in on what's happening on Broadway where she headlined. Plus, it would be interesting to see if that vein in Ron's forehead would finally blow.

He checked his watch. He had two hours. He could review his next role in case anyone asked what "Wall Street Burning" was about. Zenith Pictures was starting production in ten days and Bob Carlson had just contacted Bill. They needed someone tall and older for one of the floor traders. They wanted Phillip.

# CHAPTER 6

Leslie sat on her sofa. For once she wasn't writing as her pen sat idly by a mound of binder paper. Neither was she reading what she had already written. She was actually just staring at a large yellow envelope on her lap. The return address showed it was from her agent Wallace Quimby. Already sitting there for ten minutes, she knew what was in it. This was the reply from Adventure Novels. After five months of waiting for their decision, she found she was afraid to open the tall envelope.

With her stomach in a knot she opened the seal and pulled out a letter. There were more sheets beneath it.

*"Dear Ms. Nelson,*

*Good news finally. Adventure Novels has agreed to print THE LONER FINDS LOVE. There will be a few necessary corrections in the copy as outlined on the enclosed sheets. The changes are relatively minor but will require your agreement and initials.*

*Also enclosed is the standard literary contract. You are given complete say in any changes to the manuscript and Adventure Novels agrees to publish any future novels of yours that meet their requirements and needs at the time. It is a straight-forward contract and of a language I feel you won't have any trouble understanding. You can have your lawyer look it over, if you wish.*

*The editor with whom I spoke was quite enthusiastic about your work and feels they can hopefully have it on the market within four or five months. He also would like to see your next finished work, WESTWARD REX, for appraisal.*

*If you have any questions, please call me at the number above.*

*Look over the contract and return it as soon as possible so the publisher can get to work.*

*Well done, Ms. Nelson. I look forward to hearing from you.*

*Sincerely,*

*Wallace Quimby"*

With shaky hands Leslie pulled out the rest of the papers. She first looked over the changes to the manuscript as that would be the easiest for her to understand.

There were some technical language corrections, location clarifications, and some grammar work. A few sentences were crossed out. As Wallace had said, nothing major. She initialed all the changes where it indicated she should do so.

The contract was short and to the point. Adventure Novels would own the printing rights to her work. They would be given first option on her new writings. They would handle promotion and distribution. The royalties would be sent to her agent and he would send them on to her.

There was a blank space towards the bottom of the contract. Any special requests from the author would be inserted there for consideration.

Leslie had already known what she wanted to request. She typed in that she would provide photographs of the way Jane Barrett would look on the cover of the books. She was as particular about her character's face as she had been about her substance in the novels. Removing four photos from a folder she had set aside months earlier, Leslie attached them to the contract, but she didn't sign it.

Calling Wayne on the phone, she asked him to come up. She said she wanted to show him something.

Within seconds he bounded up the stairs and lightly tapped, letting himself in. He could tell by her wide eyes and blanched face that something big had happened.

"Well?" he asked as she stood on the other side of the room by her phone, her hands behind her back.

She pulled the contract out from behind her back and showed him, a big grin spreading over her face.

"You heard? You got it!?" he demanded as he grabbed the papers and read the letter. "This is great!" he told her, lightly kissing her cheek.

"I'm...I...I can't believe it. After so long they finally said yes! I wanted you to look over the contract, if you would. Since you are in insurance, I thought you'd understand the wording better than I," she explained, looking as if she wanted to break away and run around the complex.

As he sat on the loveseat to read it over, Leslie remembered that she hadn't told anyone else yet. She called her mom first and quieted her voice down. As she started talking, Wayne looked up at her, confused. She winked at him and turned away with a grin.

"Mom? I...I heard from the agent finally.... Do I sound happy?.... Yeah, I know. I tried. I thought I did pretty well, but I guess it wasn't good enough.... What am I going to do with my manuscripts? I don't know. Probably bore my friends with them for the rest of my life.... Or, I could hand them the printed version that will come out in four or five months!.... Really! They will publish my books. I just heard today. Now they want my Western. Is dad home?.... Oh. Does he even remember all this?.... Well, tell him when he gets home.... Yeah, thanks. I'm pleased, too. I have some more calls to make. I'll talk to you later."

Wayne looked up again. "Boy, you're mean! I didn't realize you had such a cruel streak. Let's celebrate," he offered. "Call Janice, whoever. It's on me." *And Sarah*, he silently added with a hidden smile.

"Great! You're on! If I know Janice, she'll be here in ten minutes. Is that all right?" she asked, indicating the contract still in his hands.

"Sure. Call away. Oh, you mean the contract. Yeah, it's fine, from what I can tell. I didn't see anything that could indicate a hidden clause. It seems pretty straight-forward. Sign it, lady!"

"Yes, sir!" after which she got out her personal phone book, forgetting, in her excitement, that she had the needed number memorized. "Boy, I wish I had Phillip's number," she stated, revealing the reason for her preoccupation. "I'd like to tell him personally. But, I'll have to settle on a letter again," she decided as she began dialing Janice's number, the unneeded phone book still in her hands. She failed to see the strange look that passed over Wayne's eyes at the mention of Phillip Beck.

Leslie hadn't mentioned Phillip much in the past few months. Janice regularly referred to "her actor," but Leslie herself had seemed to have dropped the idea. Wayne knew she would now be more grateful than ever for Phillip's first advice so long ago. Hoping she would forget the actor, he would finally be able to report to Sarah that the "threat" no longer existed. His now-unsavory employment would then end. No, his *bondage* would end. Wayne knew he was being used—mostly now by Marty to further his own selfish plans.

Wayne looked at Leslie as she excitedly babbled the news to her friends. Compared to Sarah, Leslie was transparent. She didn't exist. But, that comparison was unfair, he knew. They were two different types of women. Sarah contained all the outer beauty a woman could possess. But, inside, she was a cold business woman. Shrewd, sure of herself almost to the point of arrogance in most matters, but neurotic and troubled when something she felt she owned was threatened.

Leslie.... Well, Leslie had changed his viewpoint of her. As he had gotten to know her, he found her more attractive. She didn't consider herself alluring or charming, but that only added to her appeal. She had compassion and empathy. She didn't reach for the highest goal, but chose one that she felt was sufficient and attainable. Dangerous? He had seen her verbally slaughter someone who had attacked someone she loved, but that was different.

Now she had attained a goal higher than she ever expected. He wondered how it would affect her. Smiling to himself, he already knew the airs Janice would put on in public. But, what about Leslie? Her third book was almost ready to be typed. What then? He knew she wanted to try and turn her books into scripts. He hoped Phillip would ignore this next letter she would send just as he had ignored her last few. Beck would probably recommend the script angle now where he hadn't before, he thought sourly.

Wayne was jealous of Phillip Beck. He just didn't realize it.

*"Hello, again, Phillip,*

*From now on I would appreciate it if you would refer to me a 'Madame Author'.*

*Yes, it finally happened. I heard from the publisher and they will print my book! You know I was always thankful for your encouragement and now it has paid off!*

*By the way, I don't care if you are overwhelmed. I am still going to send you a copy.*

*A group of us celebrated last night. It became pretty silly, I'm afraid.*

*I saw "Mutiny of Love at Sea" last week. You should have gotten higher billing.*

*Keep busy and take care,*
*Leslie Nelson*
*Author"*

**A** few nights later, the light on Leslie's answering machine was flashing on and off. She and Wayne had just come back from dinner and he had followed her inside.

"Hi, Les. This is Pa. We're real proud of ya. Bye," was the message.

"What was that?" Wayne asked with an amused grin.

"Just Dad giving me support and encouragement," Leslie shrugged, a warm smile crinkling her eyes. "That's his way."

"Do you think they'll read your books?"

Leslie gave a light laugh. "No! They hate the television show. But I do know they will want a copy."

Wayne helped himself to a drink from her refrigerator. "Well, I guess I'll have to buy a copy. But," he stressed with an upraised finger, "only if the author will autograph it."

"Hmph. Peasant," she sniffed, her nose in the air. "You'll buy two copies. One for yourself that you will treasure forever. And one to send to Majestic. Of course you will rave about how wonderful an addition to the show Jane Barrett-Newby will be."

"Of course," he bowed his head briefly. "What else could I say or do?"

Leslie looked away and giggled. "It will be interesting at work tomorrow when I tell them about this."

"What are you going to do?" he asked with narrowed eyes.

Leslie looked thoughtful. "I'm not sure, but I do know I'll have a whole different attitude!"

"Uh-oh," he muttered as he took a sip of his drink.

She nodded happily and smiled. Glancing at the clock, she added, "It is getting late, Wayne. I need to get to bed. Mondays are our busiest days."

"Yeah, yeah, I know. You just want to plot what you're going to do." After throwing away the soda can, he came out of the kitchenette and walked up to her. "Are you going to send me out into the cold to go all the way home to my dark, cold, lonely, depressing apartment?" he asked gently, refraining from touching her.

She averted her eyes briefly and then quietly nodded. "Yeah. And if you turn your stereo up too loud again I'll stomp on the floor. Besides," she finished with a small grin, "you snore."

"How the heck would you know?" he scoffed.

"I can hear you through the floor."

"Maybe it's because I'm all alone," he offered, raising his eyebrows.

"Maybe you should sleep on your stomach."

"Maybe that's not the solution I had in mind."

Leslie shook her head.

"How about a good-night kiss, then?" Wayne resignedly asked, knowing when to back off.

She offered her cheek.

"No, thanks. I'll wait for a better offer." As she opened the door for him to leave, he gave a parting, "Night, author."

"Night, peasant."

**W**ayne made a show of stomping downstairs to his apartment and slamming his door.  In return, he heard Leslie stomping into her bedroom with such a force that it made the windows rattle.

He yelled up at the ceiling, "All right, already!  You win!"

The stomping ceased.

Grabbing a beer out of his fridge, Wayne thought back on their evening.  He had interrupted her writing to take her out to dinner again.  She had protested that he was spoiling her and trying to make her fat.  He agreed to the spoiling part as he had taken her arm in his and they walked to his car.

She had still been pretty excited about the book being accepted and talked a lot about the next two novels.  She expected to be done with CHATEAU REX within the week and then she would begin typing it and having copies made.  Then she would wait for word on the Western she was mailing in the morning.  She mentioned starting to do research on scriptwriting and....

Wayne stopped his recital of their evening and tried to picture Leslie in with the Los Angeles crowd that he knew.  All he could picture was a lamb amongst the lions.  She would need someone to advise her on what the double-tongued terminology meant.  She would need someone besides her New York agent.  *A manager?* he thought, throwing the word back and forth.  He thought of Marty and immediately grimaced and shook his head to clear the image.  That would be one of the head lions!  Then he laughed.  Wouldn't Sarah be fit to be tied if Marty represented Leslie?

Thinking about all the contacts he knew, Wayne couldn't come up with anyone suitable for Leslie in his eyes.  He knew quite a few agents and managers and like most of them, but still had an unfocused distrust for them.  She needed someone in Los Angeles whom she could trust since she would probably stay there in Amherst.  He didn't want anyone else around her like that.  He wanted to be there.  He should....

Wayne stopped short.  *He wanted to?*  He sat down heavily on his bed.  *Like he was trustworthy?*  He had been spying on her for months now and making money—good money—at it.  He reported her every move and intention and made her look like a demented loon. Even though he had long since stopped listening in and taping her calls and searching her apartment, he still was misrepresenting her for pay. He was a traitor, a hypocritical traitor. And he had just elevated himself into a position of trust by implying that no one else was worthy of that position.

Four, five months ago he would have thought nothing of spying, reporting and betraying his best friend in the name of his job as a private investigator—as long as the pay was good, that is. That was what he had been doing for twelve years. And he was good at it. Very good.

His eyes narrowed as his self-examination continued. What did he have to show for his expertise in this new decade of 1990? Friends: Marty, Leslie, Janice. Reputation: Cold, hard, no conscience, no scruples, one of the best in his field. Money: Considerable savings built up from his work as a spy. Possessions: New unremarkable car, state-of-the-art surveillance equipment, few pieces of furniture in a rented Los Angeles apartment. Family: Parents disapprove of work, lifestyle and outlook. Older brother a successful realtor who won't speak to him. Relationships: Girlfriend through high school and one in college. No one special in twelve years.

Wayne now knew what had happened to him. In these months in Amherst he had lived on the "other side," as he called it, for the first time since leaving home. He was far away from the flash and glitter and also the corrupt and murky sides of Los Angeles in which he had orbited and snuck around. Leslie and Janice led simple, honest lives. They worked hard for sustenance and covering and now Leslie was working harder for a little extra. If it happened. If not, that would be all right as well. A phone call from someone they considered famous had turned up some excitement in their lives and their friends were envious. That same phone call—had it been made to someone in the business in L.A.—probably wouldn't have been answered.

Wayne had dreaded coming to Amherst. Now de dreaded returning to Los Angeles and his previous existence.

Because of his constant, steady, friendly efforts since he moved in, Leslie now viewed him as a friend and a confidant, but not anything more intimate, much to his chagrin. He was welcomed into her circle of friends and accepted by those within. No one had asked him anything beyond the usual. No one expected anything. That is, except honesty, trust and friendship. This was nothing beyond what they themselves gave.

He could come and go at Le Petite Boutique and was let in on all the private jokes and inside stories that went on there. Her parents liked his firm handshake and the fact that he had steadily met their eyes when they talked. They were glad Leslie had someone near at hand to watch out for her. When he had first heard them say that months ago, he had laughed and laughed to himself. It wasn't funny any longer.

His honest contemplation halted when he heard her walk back into her living room and then heard the creak of the springs in her sofa. He glanced at the clock. It was eleven. He wondered what she was doing. Glancing at the black bag in his closet that now held every piece of surveillance equipment he had brought with him, he knew that wasn't an option any longer.

*High in the foothills bordering the eastern end of the Silicon Valley, in a secluded glen, two people stood together in the darkness on a vine-covered balcony. The gentle breeze rustled the leaves and played with the hair that curled around the woman's contented face. As they gazed at the stars, he would point out this or that constellation. She would follow his finger's direction and, while her face was upturned, he would gently kiss her cheek.*

*"No wonder you are so interested in astronomy," she teased, returning the kiss.*

*Professor Rex Farrell didn't respond to her humor. He was content for Jane just to be near. It had been two months since he had abducted her. Only bits and pieces of her memory had returned. Her husband Jack and the rest of the squad had not come back to her mind. But the Professor didn't care. For Jane was his now. Almost completely. For tonight he would take their relationship to a different level....*

*Rex could now admit to himself that he had been envious of The Loner and the happiness he had found with Jane. Then, after Rex had gotten to know her better eight months ago when he sent them back in time to Dead Horse Gulch, he had been curious. He, who had never needed or wanted anyone close to him, had been drawn to the feisty woman the squad has rescued from her own past. He had wanted to observe the woman to see what she would be like in his secret chateau. The accident and memory loss had given him just the chance he had awaited. Only he hadn't expected this. He had fallen in love with Jane.*

*He realized it when he took her back to Scotland and helped her discover her royal heritage. He had known she wasn't a peasant. She could never be lowly. He had decided then that his life had been incomplete and lonely.*

*She had been delighted in learning all about his elaborate hideout deep in the wooded hills. The laboratory was her classroom. The chateau was her playground. And Rex was her teacher, guide, and constant companion. She delighted in teasing and exasperating his patience. And, without even realizing it, she came to love him in return.*

*Each morning he was impatient for her to come out of her suite of rooms so they could be together again for the day. Now she had unconsciously gone into his arms under the canopy of stars that shone in the clear mountain air. She had allowed the light kisses and even timidly returned them. She was leaning against his body as they both gazed heavenward.*

*Jane turned suddenly. "Do you know what we need, Rex?"*

*He looked down into her brown, liquid eyes. "I can't imagine what else I could possibly need besides you."*

*Jane broke away and went into the living room. "We need music."*

*He shrugged and smiled. Whatever she wanted. He programmed the computer for something soft, quiet, romantic.*

*She nodded appreciatively as the sounds came into the*

*room and flowed around them. "Perfect," she declared.*

*"Will you dance with me?" Rex asked, surprising himself.*

*They moved together and swayed in unison as they circled the room in a sweeping waltz. Eyes were closed and hearts beat as one.*

*One of the Professor's assistants came to the door with a message. He was stopped by the scene before him. Never had he seen his master as happy and content. The woman had made a wonderful difference in the Professor's life. The message could wait. Smiling and humming to himself, the assistant tiptoed away.*

*Did hours fly by or was it only mere minutes? Neither could have told. Time didn't exist. They were in their own portal that had no dimensions. Only each other and the soft music existed.*

*The creak of a shutter in the breeze disrupted their music-filled silence. Their eyes opened and looked at the offending window. When their gaze returned to each other, their eyes held and his hand came to raise her face to his. Their lips met in a moment of tingle and a nervous tremble. Jane's arms encircled his neck and his arms surrounded her waist.*

*The music was smooth, mellow. Rex and Jane could no longer hear it.*


The postal clerk Fred looked at the familiar face in front of him. She had tiredly set down a large padded envelope on the counter and asked for correct postage to New York.

"Won't you be needing postage for the return envelope like usual?" he asked.

Leslie glanced at his face. Fred. Her old postal buddy Fred. She always got Fred. When she sent her first novel off to Mr. Quimby, Fred couldn't comprehend the need for a return envelope of the same size with the same postage. "Why are you mailing it if it is just coming right back?" he had asked in a rather snippy voice.

Her reply had been pert. "If things go well, I *won't* get it back. I'll never see it again in this form. If not...."

When she first mailed her short stories to Majestic Studio, he glanced at the address and rolled his eyes. When the addresses had been to different literary agents in New York, he had snorted.

Leslie would like to rub his face in the letter from Wallace Quimby, but she mildly told Fred, "This one won't be coming back. Either," she added as she took out her wallet.


"**W**ell, look what the cat drug in," Mona chided. "Stay out too late with Wayne?"

"Wayne?" Leslie's tired mind didn't register the connection between her current condition and Wayne Fields. They weren't related.

"You remember? About five-feet-eleven-inches tall? Brown hair? Brown eyes? Hangs around you a lot?" Mona grinned, amused. Leslie never looked like this in the mornings.

Now Leslie looked irritated. "I know who Wayne is," she snapped. "Boy, first the postal clerk gives me a hard time...."

"Fred? Was it Fred again?" Janice interrupted, coming into the back room to see what was going on. When Leslie nodded, she laughed out loud. "Wouldn't you love to tell him off now?"

Mona was quicker on the uptake than Leslie who, at that moment, was yawning. "Why now? Something happen?" asked their curious boss.

Leslie threw a sour glance at Janice. "Thanks, Mouth."

Janice's feelings were hurt. "I didn't say anything. You're sure a grouch when you don't get enough sleep," she declared with a pout as she went out front.

Leslie sighed and muttered a "Sorry" after her. "I had a sudden inspiration and wanted to get it written down. Took longer than I thought."

Mona set a cup of strong tea in front of Leslie. "You're working awfully hard on that story. Shouldn't you wait until you hear on the first one?"

Leslie looked up from the cup with just her eyes and suddenly smiled, but remained silent.

"You heard? Why didn't you say so?"

"Yeah. Saturday. It will be out in four or five months and they want to see the Western now," Leslie yawned.

"I guess you were more excited Saturday," her boss decided at Leslie's unenthusiastic response.

"I was awake Saturday," was the flat reply.

"Well, this will perk you up. Mrs. Penney asked for you. There's a dinner/dance Thursday at The Ballroom. The van is ready to go."

"Naw. Send Janice. I don't need this," was the only remnant of her plan for her new attitude that she could recall.

Mona smiled indulgently and tossed the keys onto the table. "Oh, but you get along so well with dear Mrs. Penney. She asks for you every time."

"Mine's the only name she can remember. It's the same as her cat," grumbled Leslie as she headed for the back door where the van was parked.

"Don't forget. Happy. Perky. Friendly. Smile!"

Leslie called back, "Grumpy and Sleepy were the only two who made it," as the door to the van slammed shut.

Leslie looked over the information sheet on Mrs. Penney. Dress size twelve. Shoe size eight wide. Favorite color was yellow. Looks best in blue. Address. Previous purchases. Names of family members. Pet's names.

In the van were ten different dresses, twelve pairs of shoes, twelve pairs of earrings, twelve necklaces, six bracelets, four wraps, six purses, and four shades of hosiery. Leslie groaned. She would be there for three hours. At least. But, she reminded herself, there's always that five dollar tip and all the sugar cookies she can eat. Wahoo.


Around lunchtime Wayne wandered into the boutique. He waved a greeting to Mona and snuck up behind Janice who hadn't heard him come in.

He said in a deep, gravely voice, "Hey, Red, you got anything in a size fourteen husky, preferably backless?"

She was startled both by the voice and the request.

"Wha...Oh,          Wayne,          knock          it          off! she blushed.  "And don't call me Red!  I hate that," she added testily.

"Sorry, Beautiful.  Where's Madame Author?"

Janice's feelings were still hurt.  "You mean, Madame Grouch?  She's out on a call."

"What's wrong, Jan?  She write you out of her will?" he teased.

"Madame stayed up too late writing and now she's a grump," was the brief explanation.

*Ah, so that was what she was doing*, he thought.  "Well, when do you expect her?" he asked as he helped himself to a cup of coffee and a cookie.

Mona looked up from the invoices.  "You never know with Mrs. Penney."

"Mrs. Penney?" Wayne laughed and spilled some coffee on the antique table.  "Oh, that will help her mood!" He had been told numerous stories about the different patrons and felt as if he knew them personally.

He looked at one of the mannequins and got an idea.  He stood next to it and put his arm on its shoulder.

Janice looked back to see what he was doing since he had suddenly become quiet.  "Oh, for crying out loud, Fields.  We're not that kind of a store!" she exclaimed.

"No.  No.  I have an idea.  Do you have a blond wig for the little lady here?"


**A**round one o'clock, Leslie trudged in.  There was a five dollar bill sticking out of her jacket's breast pocket like a hanky.  "I get there," she started in as if she was in the midst of a conversation already, "and she's eating a sandwich.  Looks over the ten dresses and claims she's been on a strict diet and is now a size eight.  Don't we have anything else?  Do we have a backless yellow chiffon?  Are they still wearing black in Paris?"

Leslie continued her monologue as she unloaded the van with Paula's help.  Mona looked over the invoice.  One dress, two pairs of shoes, all the hosiery, one purse, and one necklace.  Not bad.

"We've been busy, too," Mona told her. "It was difficult keeping track of where everyone was. While we restock this, would you check over the dressing rooms, Leslie?"

Someone always forgot something. Glasses. Sweaters. You never knew.

Leslie quickly checked behind the velvet curtains. In dressing room number three she gasped to find a man and a woman in the middle of a passionate embrace. The man was irritated at the interruption and looked up angrily.

"Wayne!" Leslie cried. "I...what...You...Oh!" she stammered.

He turned his partner around. "Meet Sarah. She's a little stiff, but I think she likes me!"

"Oh!" The curtain was thrown down. "That's not funny."

All the others disagreed with Leslie's assessment as they joined Wayne in laughing at his joke. Leslie was red and flustered and embarrassed by her own reaction.

Wayne helped Mona return "Sarah" to her proper place in the shop.

Leslie, still red, tried to change the subject. "Say, Mona, the van seemed to be smoking out the exhaust," she told her boss and ignored Wayne who was eating another cookie and looking awfully pleased with himself.

"I know," Mona replied. "Our mechanic at the dealership ordered some part or other. I think he called it a Cadillac converter."

Wayne looked at her incredulously. "A what?" he demanded with a laugh.

Mona waved him off. "I don't know cars. Something for the exhaust."

Janice piped up. "Well, order a Cadillac converter for my car, too. Mine must be broken. I've had it for five years and it still hasn't converted into a Cadillac!"

Wayne started laughing and had to sit down. "Women! Oh, this is great! It's a...it's a catalytic converter! Cadillac converter! Oh, ow, my side!"

The four women present failed to see what was so funny while Wayne tried to regain his composure. His face was all red as he wiped his eyes.   He found himself ignored when they went about their duties.

"Well, you've got to admit…" he started to explain, but then, wisely, decided to drop it.  "Hey, Les, when are you going to be off for lunch?"

"Don't know.  When are you going to get some manners?"

"Okay, fine," he said good-naturedly, raising his hands in defeat.  "I'll just eat alone.  All by myself."

"Take Sarah," four voices offered.

"Touché!" he declared and waved his good-bye.

Leslie watched him walk out of the shop.  She sniffed.  "Does that mean I don't get lunch?"

# CHAPTER 7

"*Dear Leslie,*

*Congratulations on your book. That's great news. I look forward to receiving a copy. I'm glad you got your good work out there.*

*I just finished another "Time Police" episode. Be sure to watch for it.*

*Thanks for writing,*

*Phillip Beck"*

Phillip put down his pen and looked over his brief letter. He really was glad that Leslie's book had sold. While he would have liked to have given her some of the tips she had broadly hinted about regarding scripts, he hesitated getting too involved. He knew most celebrities wouldn't have replied at all, and he knew he was taking a chance.

Still, she wrote a nice letter and at least she asked about his career and seemed interested. Even though she had his home address, he didn't feel she was taking advantage of the situation.

Sitting back in his chair, he wondered about this Bunny person. For some reason, her actual name "Leslie" didn't stick in his memory once his short letters to her were written and in the mail. To him she was "Bunny." He had learned bits and pieces about her through her letters, such as the fact that she worked in some kind of a boutique with another clerk with whom she had done some traveling. She had mentioned a trip to New York once and the Caribbean twice, and her friend had been to Europe. He also picked up that she was divorced. She had an interesting way of expressing herself. His agent Bill had thought she was funny. As Phillip looked over her latest letter once more, he wondered if she was serious about being called Madame Author. *That would be a little presumptuous*, he thought with a frown.

"Handsss up, you dessspicable fiend, or I'll blassst you with my ray gun!" demanded an angry, lisping voice from the door of his study.

Startled by the unexpected voice, Phillip jerked around in his chair, dropping Leslie's letter to the floor. He frowned at Eddie Chase who, in turn, gave him a big, charming grin.

"Amy let me in," Eddie causally explained as he scooped up the fallen paper and plopped down on the sofa. "What's this? A smoldering love letter?" he asked as he began reading. Quickly answering himself with a grunt, he uninterestedly mumbled, "Nope. So, who's this Madame Author Leslie? Anyone I know?" He held the page out to the still-frowning Phillip who snatched it back and set it on his desk.

"No, you don't know her," Phillip began with a short, clipped voice. Then, remembering his manners, he calmed himself and continued in a more friendly tone, "Actually, I've never met her, either. She wrote me on the set about a year ago and sent me a script. You were there, if you recall. You called it a dog letter," he reminded Eddie who was watching him with an amused twinkle in his eyes.

Trying to think back, Eddie was shaking his head. "Which episode? Last season? Oh, wait, I remember you were late to the set a lot, and you were very defensive about someone you called Kitty. Puppy. No, that's not right. It was Bunny, wasn't it? Was that her?"

Phillip nodded as he leaned back in his leather desk chair. "That's her. She took the advice I gave her back then and made that script into a novel. This letter is the latest I have heard."

His friend started to look a little concerned. "The latest you've heard?" he repeated, leaning forward. "Are you two regular correspondents? That isn't something we're encouraged to do, you know."

"No, no, no. It's not like that," Phillip hurriedly said with a dismissive wave of the hand. "She does all the writing. I've only contacted her twice. Well, three times when I send this," he explained, indicating the obviously brief note still on the desk in front of him.

"Well, more power to her if she's gotten published. Just as long as she doesn't get all spooky on you all of a sudden." Eddie silently wondered if Sarah knew anything about this Bunny. He could sell tickets to that event!

Phillip had irritably waved off that possibility, and, pushing his chair back, put his feet up on the desk. "What's up, Edward, or did you just come over to go through my mail?"

Eddie stretched out on the comfortable sofa, put his hands behind his head and gave an amused smile. That was the closest Phillip ever came to telling a joke. "I just wanted to tell you about the party Friday night," he told his friend, his eyes closed.

"Friday? What party?"

"The one you are throwing here for all your good friends and co-workers."

Phillip cast a heavy sigh. This was probably another silly prank. Tom was probably hiding around the corner, waiting for him to get irritated—which was probably going to happen pretty quickly the way the conversation was going. "What are you talking about?"

"Tom, Cindy and I figured you've kept yourself shut up in here too long, so we're giving you a party." He paused and then added, "Actually *you* are giving you a party. You need to see people more often, buddy," Eddie told him half serious, half worried. "So, we made all the arrangements. All you have to do is provide the music, food, and drinks. We've done everything else."

Phillip's feet abruptly came down from the desk as he jerked forward with a glazed expression on his face. "What?! You've got to be kidding! That's only two days away! I don't know how to plan all that!"

Eddie could tell he was really getting upset and was about to lose it. He kept forgetting Phillip had no sense of humor.... "Hold on, old man! Don't lose it!" he quickly said, holding up his hands. "We've taken care of all that. Really! All you have to do is clean the bathrooms and remember to be at home." The message delivered, he stood to go and added, "And try to wear something pretty. You never know who you might meet."

Having risen to see Eddie to the door, Phillip frowned at his last words and grabbed his arm. "Hey, I'll go along with your little party, Edward, but I'm not looking to meet someone. Understand? I don't know what you know or what you *think* you know, but I am still a married man. All right?"

Eddie glanced at the letter on the desk. "Yeah, Phil, I know. I didn't mean anything. I just think you need to have a little fun. I'm concerned about you. We all are. Okay? So sue me."

Phillip dropped his hand, embarrassed by his outburst. Running a hand through his hair, he looked down. "Sorry, Edward. I know you mean well. It's just...." He hesitated, hating to make his troubles public again. "It's just that things around here are still off." He looked at the far wall and took a deep breath. "I already told you Davey calls Martin Daddy. Well, Sarah now refers to that scum as Dear. I don't know when, or if, they are ever coming home."

Eddie let out a low whistle as Phillip sat heavily on the sofa. "Sorry, old man, I had no idea things hadn't worked out yet. I heard through the trades how well she's going over in Japan, but now the France deal is definite? Why don't you go spend some time with them?" he offered for thought.

The reply was a sick, despairing laugh. "I tried that, remember? I had it all worked out. Only they didn't have the time for me. They were too busy," he said with a bitter edge. "Every time I call I get Martin. I've only talked to Sarah twice in three months. Davey has always been out on some outing. Or, so I've been told. I'm getting sick and tired of this, but I don't know what to do."

Eddie didn't know what to say to his friend. This further confiding from Phillip hadn't been expected. He usually never knew what was going on with this private man. But he now knew everything and was surprised by the depth of anger and hurt he was seeing. Phillip usually betrayed no emotion.

Eddie hesitated. "Well, maybe this party isn't such a good idea. We could make some calls...."

"No," Phillip surprisingly interrupted. "Go ahead. You're right. It might do me some good."

"That's the spirit," Eddie grinned. "Some good food and some good friends always help."

Phillip glanced at the papers on his desk. "Yeah. You can always count on some people to be there when you need them," he muttered in a quiet voice that sounded far away.

Following Phillip's glance to the letter on his desk, a worried expression wrinkled Eddie's brow once again as he looked back at Phillip. Phillip didn't notice the look on Eddie's face. He saw only the ivory-colored stationery.

As Phillip strolled through his house chatting with the different guests, he noticed the soft classical jazz albums he had playing on the stereo system had been changed. Now hard rock blared over the hidden speakers throughout the house and terrace. The only notice the guests gave of the switch was that they were not talking a little louder and dancing a little faster out by the pool.

He could tell the usual assortment of partiers were present: Fellow actors, directors, writers, agents, realtors, young hopefuls, lawyers, speculators, backers, patrons, and a few people whom no one knew but always showed up. The mood was relaxed and friendly. Deals would be discussed; movies would be argued over; past roles would be ribbed; lunches would be set; starlets would be introduced; real estate prices and locations would be considered; gossip would be exchanged.

Phillip was mildly surprised to discover he was actually enjoying himself. Tom and Eddie were minding themselves, which was a relief all in itself. He had just had a fascinating discussion on the latest art exhibit downtown. He bypassed the lovely young hopefuls that threw wide-eyed, smiling glances at his handsome face. He had partaken in the debate about the quality of the plays coming out of New York as compared to their own here in Los Angeles.

He found he was at ease in his role as host. Sarah had always planned and invited everyone with most of his friends never included. He was always easily bored by her models, photographers, agents, decorators and prospective employers. Almost nothing that her particular bunch discussed interested him. His world was equally unappealing to them. Phillip felt he *should* miss his wife's presence either at his side or mingling around the room. But, he didn't. The only twinge he felt was that Davey wasn't constantly sneaking halfway down the stairs to peek out at the colorful guests or wave at his Uncle Eddie. Phillip would always go up the stairs with some little dessert off one of the trays and carry him back up to his room. This memory was the only shadow on Phillip's evening.

The host resisted his impulse to go look once again at Davey's room. Instead, he went out onto the terrace where ten or so couples were dancing. A few of the more adventuresome were frolicking in the heated pool, the rising steam in the cool air making it look like a misty sauna. He sat with Tom Young and a realtor introduced as Mike Upson. They were talking about some available beachfront property along the coast. Tom was interested in getting out of the hills and onto the ocean. Mike happened to know of one or two prime locations. When Mike's wife interrupted and took him away to dance, Phillip could see Tom was still contemplating the offers.

"Say, Phil," said Tom, suddenly looking over. "I need to make a call while this is still fresh in my mind. Can I use your phone?"

"Sure. If you want some privacy in this madhouse, use my office in the back. Just close the door. No one should disturb you."

Tom began searching through some papers in his wallet and apparently couldn't find what he wanted. "Shoot. Do you have a phonebook in there?"

"In my desk. Help yourself," Phillip offered, glancing over at the pool where a sudden shriek was heard over the deafening music. He smiled briefly at Tom who rolled his eyes. It was an old trick. One of the young hopefuls had a friend "accidentally" throw her into the pool. Some of those on the terrace quit dancing and talking and came to the aid of the pretty girl whose dress was ruined but clung provocatively to her shapely body. Phillip couldn't recall many parties with a pool where that didn't happen.

Too bad the girls didn't realize that trick didn't work any more. It would save a lot on dry cleaning bills, he mused as he went inside to get something to eat and see what Maxwell Marlowe was doing.


Tom Young, at age thirty-four, had been amused to find himself an over-night star after being an actor for more than ten years. His role of The Loner had made him instantly popular with the women. Although having acted on a television series before, he had never been one of the leads. What most people did not realize was that, in real life, Tom was a lot like his "Time Police" character—intelligent, quiet, and alone.

Tom was the youngest of five children. All of his brothers and sisters had gone into the family business that his mother and father had started, Youngtown Clothes in New York, forty-five years ago in a third-floor walk-up with two sewing machines and a head full of designs. Now, Youngtown Clothes was the fourth largest line in the United States. All the family was still active in design and sales and promotion. All, that is, except for Tom.

He had gone to college to major in business as was expected of him, but found he had little interest in the whole idea. Realizing, even at the time, that he was becoming a cliché, he followed a certain charming lady into a drama class as a chance to be near her. She dropped out, but he had been acting ever since.

Tom's current popularity with the female fans didn't faze him much. He was well aware of his plain appearance by movie standards. He didn't have the square-jawed, manly ruggedness or the dimpled, boyish handsomeness found on most popular stars. He was just under six-feet tall, amber brown eyes, straight brown hair that always looked windblown, and a serious countenance that belied his quiet sense of humor.

Like his character, he had never married and spent most of his free time traveling. Tom had not set out to be single, but had never met that certain, special Someone. And it wasn't the fault of his co-workers and friends as they were forever setting him up to meet this or that perfect companion. Even Tom couldn't fully explain what was wrong, what he was seeking. Absolute beauty didn't appeal to him, even when it was combined with an intelligent mind or a good sense of humor. Most of the actresses and models who looked his way lacked something indefinable.

One of his sisters was now vice-president of the family business, second only to their father. Her tough business sense was helping push the company towards the number three spot. While Tom admired her expertise, he knew he wasn't looking for someone of her particular type either.

It was Tom's humor that surprised people the most when he allowed someone to get close enough to discover it. While Eddie was the chief instigator in most of their capers, Tom was always the right-hand man when it came to execution. When left to his own devices, Tom would silently do private deeds. He would keep adding sugar to someone's coffee when their head was turned. Or tighten knobs of props on the set so the action would have to be halted. Or lock the door to the time portal that resulted in a four-person pile-up. Or invite fifty people over the Eddie's house for a party when Eddie was off visiting his wife in New York. During the festivities, they would make it a point to empty both the refrigerator and the liquor cabinet. When they were all ready to leave, everything would be completely cleaned up and put in order, and all attending would sign a huge thank you card that would be left on Eddie's dining room table.

Tom was now seated behind Phillip's desk, the forgotten phonebook pushed off to the side. For in his search for a blank piece of paper for some notes he had to make, he had come across a pile of letters and two scripts. When he picked up the edge of one to see what it was, a picture had fallen out of the upper pages of the letters and landed face down on the carpet. On the back of it were the words: "This is my word processor. Don't need none o' them fancy gadgets." He had turned the snapshot over and laughed. On an off-white sofa sat a smiling woman holding a pen ready in one hand and had some kind of lap desk on which she was writing. The sofa was literally covered with papers and reference books. The woman's sock-covered feet rested easily on her coffee table and a large yellow and white cat overlooked her work.

As Tom returned the photo, his eyes caught a few words of

the letters and he read "Time Police," and "my novel." Curiosity aroused, he found himself reading all of the letters from this Leslie Nelson, not really meaning to be nosey or pry into Phillip's business. He would have quit reading immediately at the first indication of a love letter or some business he should not be privy to. But, instead, he found well-written, funny letters of thanks, friendliness and observations. He chuckled over some of the passages and wondered about others—ones that mentioned his Loner character and a Jane Barrett. He thought her descriptions of "The Time Police" conventions were hysterical as he was a regular guest at such events and knew what they were like.

Like Eddie, once he thought about it, he had remembered Phillip's preoccupation on the set and figured the larger dog-eared script had been the reason. After checking his watch, Tom knew he wouldn't have time to read the whole manuscript. And he could think of no way to ask Phillip for it without revealing how he came across it. So he allowed himself a few more minutes to thumb through the pages. He was surprised to find in the first chapter that his character was now married. The letters had told him what he was now reading was a second novel. The first was the one being published. Now he was interested, for the first time, in novels written about his television show. He wanted to see how this Leslie managed to do what their writers wouldn't.

After carefully collecting all the papers and replacing them in the drawer, Tom sat a moment thinking. Leslie had told Phillip she sent a copy of her first manuscript to Tom over a year ago. By now it would have been read, charted, and destroyed with all the other unsolicited manuscripts and mail that poured into the studio for him. He felt he would have liked to have seen that one. *Oh, well*, he thought, *I'll just have to wait for the book*.

Glancing at his watch again, it was now too late to make his call. Looking around the quiet, well-arranged office, he smiled as he preferred this room to any other in the bleak, white mansion. He would have liked to stay in there shut away from the noise and the hilarity of the party, but a giggly young woman boldly threw the door open and declared that she had been looking for him just everywhere. When she shut the door behind her and gave him an inviting smile, Tom hurriedly excused himself and made his escape around her. The woman looked around the quiet office, wrinkled her pert nose, and turned off the light as she left.

**E**arly the next morning, Phillip was doing his usual laps in the pool. The party had gone on into the late hours, and he actually had no idea who was still asleep inside the many guestrooms. Eddie had arranged with his own housekeepers to come by later that morning to help with the clean-up.

As Phillip continued his workout he was unaware of the ringing phone. In one of the downstairs bedrooms, a moan was heard as a hand reached out for the horribly loud noise.

"Hmmm?" came out instead of hello.

There was a moment of silence at the other end and then a static-filled voice asked, "Hello? Who is this, please?"

"Mindy," she replied, not yet awake.

"Cindy?" Sarah demanded, straining to hear. "Is that you? What are you doing answering the phone?"

A yawn. "It wouldn't stop ringing any other way."

The static increased. "Where's Phil? I want to talk to him. Now."

Mindy turned to her sleeping husband and nudged him. "Bill, it's for you. Bill?"

There was no reply.

"He's asleep. Good party," Mindy mumbled and hung up the phone.

"**P**hillip? This is Bill. Did you ever get your house straightened out after that party?"

Phillip smiled and shifted the phone to his other ear. He leaned back in his office chair and put his feet up on the desk. He figured this call from his agent might take a while. "Oh, yes. Between my cleaners and Edward's, it only took one whole day. We found four pairs of shoes in the backyard in case you hear of anyone missing any," he smiled.

The agent laughed. "Only shoes? After my last bash we

found…. Oh, well, never mind. I wanted to know if you were all set to begin filming next week. Any problems?"

Phillip looked at the script entitled "The Drums of the Red-coats" sitting on the desk. "Well, I'd rather have played the Major, but I guess I can take the first bullet. Rehearsals went well. The director still calls me Fred."

"Well, he's an idiot. Always has been. But, he does know his historical drama," Bill pointed out. "One other thing. Did Tom or Eddie mention the convention coming up in two months?"

There was a long pause and a groan from Phillip. "Don't start on me about that again, Bill. I don't like those things and you know it!"

Bill was quick to cut in. "Hold on, now. This one will be different. It's really big. The major "Time Police" fan club in the Silicon Valley is sponsoring it in honor of our fiftieth show."

"Aren't they a little late? That episode was earlier in the season. And I wasn't in it," he added as a passing shot.

"So they are a little slow. So what? Everyone else is going. Even Maxwell and Ron and two of the writers," Bill reasoned. "They really want you to come. As your agent I feel the public exposure will do you some good. It will be after your part in the picture is done. Saturday and Sunday, the twelfth and the thirteenth. They're even talking about a parade."

Phillip rolled his eyes. "I hate parades," he mumbled in a flat tone, thumping the script with a pen.

Bill knew Phillip well enough to know he was just stalling. "All you'll have to do is just sit there and wave. The pay's good. They've already booked you a room."

"Well, I'm not staying with Tom again. The last time I did he stapled all my underwear shut."

Bill chuckled. That had been a riot. "No, no. You'll have your own suite. It's at the Fairington Oaks Hotel."

Phillip perked up a little. "Really? Those are nice." He gave an elaborate sigh. "Since it seems I again have no say in my own affairs, fine. I'll do it this time."

"Good. I mailed you all the details yesterday. You should get it today or tomorrow. Oh, the wife wants you to come for dinner Thursday around seven. It's been a while since you've been over."

Phillip opened his top drawer and pulled out a calendar. "Sounds good. I'm free."

"Fine. We'll boil another hot dog for you. See you Thursday," Bill told him and hung up.

As Phillip put down the phone, he wrote the date onto his calendar. Pen still in the air, he frowned. "I hate hot dogs," he muttered.


In two days Bill's brochures of the convention arrived in the mail along with a small box from Amherst.

"Come on, Bunny," Phillip sighed. "Don't start sending me gifts. You know better than that."

He opened Bill's envelope first and took out the standard convention brochure covered with pictures of all the cast and come-ons for all the "exciting events" that will take place over the "two fun-filled days." "Meet your favorite stars and chat with the writers" claimed the colorful paper. There would be the usual question and answer periods, "never before seen" slides from behind-the-scenes, autograph sessions both days, a trivia contest, costume judging, an auction for memorabilia, and a photo session. An attached note from Bill said the convention was expecting in the low thousands in attendance.

Phillip had to find a knife to cut through the packing tape on Leslie's little box. He had never felt comfortable when fans sent him things. He always felt obligated in return. Now Bunny was stepping beyond that silent boundary that he thought she understood.

What he found inside surprised and pleased him. There was her standard ivory-colored letter and two paperback books. He grinned as he pulled out the books and looked at the cover.

Adventure Novels Presents:
The Time Police
THE LONER FINDS LOVE
by Leslie Nelson

The picture on the cover showed a smiling Tom Young as The Loner and a frowning Eddie Chase as Andrew Fox facing each other.   The face on the woman standing between them looked vaguely familiar to Phillip.  Brown hair, blue eyes, shy smile.  He had seen the model for the drawing somewhere, but where had it been?

As he stared at the book cover, a recollection came to him. He opened his lower desk drawer to take out Bunny's letters and a picture fell to the floor.  Picking it up, Phillips started laughing. It was Bunny's face on the cover of her own book.

"Well done, Bunny," he laughed.  "I don't know how you pulled that off, but good show!"

He turned to the back cover and read the outline of the plot. He nodded.  Yes, that was what she had said it was about.  He then turned his attention to her letter.

*"Hello, Phillip,*

*How are you?  I am slightly ecstatic!  Can you believe my book?  I can't!  It's not real just yet.*

*I'm surprised they moved up the printing date.  My agent said it was because there were no major rewrites. (Of which I am most thankful!)*

*I well remember you told me you were too overwhelmed with your own work to read mine, but I don't care!  I was sent five copies right off the press and I wanted you to have one of them. I'm sure you have a bookcase and I'm sure you can arrange to have a beacon of light illuminate my book.*

*The second copy, if I may impose on you, is for Tom Young. I didn't know how to send it to him so he would actually receive it.  I was hoping you could help me out there.  Please!*

*The book ought to be in the stores in a week or so.  I hope someone else, besides my friends and me, likes it.  Time will tell.*

*I hope you are well and working.  I'll look for you at the movies!*

*Thanks again,*

*Leslie*

*P.S. How do you like the picture of Jane?"*

Phillip put down her letter and immediately pulled out a blank piece of paper. As he hesitated, thinking about what to say, his eyes fell on the convention brochure. He wondered if she knew about it. The dates had been advertised on the weekly show a couple of times already and would be repeated. But he didn't know if her town of Amherst was anywhere near the Silicon Valley.

His curiosity had been aroused over this fan of his. Now that she ranked as an author, she was elevated above the fan level. Perhaps it would be all right to say hello to her in the midst of several thousand convention-goers.

*"Dear Leslie,"* he wrote,

*"I was pleased to receive your book. I'm glad it has worked out for you. I will try to look through it when my schedule allows.*

*I will also attempt to get the other copy to Tom, but I can make no promises.*

*Enclosed is a brochure for an upcoming convention. I wasn't sure if you knew about it or not.*

*Again, congratulations.*

*Sincerely,*

*Phillip Beck"*

# CHAPTER 8

*T*he days flew quickly for Jane. There had been so much to learn from Rex during her months at the hidden chateau. Being very happy and very much in love, now knowing him so well, she knew immediately when something was wrong. Rex would come away from the computer console looking tense and uneasy. She knew something was going to happen. Soon.

Whenever she asked Rex to confide what he was thinking, he would momentarily look sad and draw her close to him in a warm embrace. But he wouldn't tell her the reason. Rex would follow her movements around the kitchen with his eyes, or he would stand on the terrace for an hour just holding her without speaking. Studying her face or running a soft hand over her cheek, he was trying to emblazon her features into his memory, becoming more tender and more loving than ever.

One warm evening they stood together on the balcony overlooking the swaying trees. Rex broke the silence as he stood a step back from her so he could see her face. He held her hands in his. "Jane," he started in a soft voice. "I want to tell you something. I have come to love you more than I have ever felt possible…. No, let me talk," he interrupted her attempted response. "I have been alone for many years. You have been the light to my darkness. Even when *you have to go I will still have your light within me."*

Jane looked confused by his words. *"Go? Why should I go? I'm happy here with you. Is this why you have been troubled lately?"* her quick mind picked up. *"Rex, tell me what you know,"* she implored.

His hand caressed her upturned face and he gently kissed her lips. *"I can't tell you just yet what will happen, but it will come soon and you will be gone."*

Tears came to Jane's eyes at his words. *"Are you sending me away?"* She had been sent away before, a long time ago in Scotland. The pain in her heart still burned.

The first tear the Professor ever shed now fell slowly down his cheek. *"I would never willingly do that. You have to believe me. But, in the next few days—I fear its close—you will choose to go. And it will break both our hearts."*

*"But, darling…."*

He put a soft hand against her lips. *"Please, Jane, let me finish. I want to tell you now that my chateau will always be waiting for you. And so will I. I will find some way to watch over you when you are gone from here. Some day, somehow, I will reclaim you. The portal is at my disposal. When your other life is complete, the portal will make you mine again."*

*"Other life? I don't understand."* Her tears were falling again, her face showing her confusion by his words.

*"I'm afraid you will understand. Just don't despise me, for I do love you,"* he finished and his arms reclaimed her.

Jane couldn't comprehend the reason behind his words, but yielded to her love and trust of her dear Rex.

The next day Rex shocked Jane by giving her a small handgun. *"I know you hate these, but keep it in your pocket, hidden,"* was all he told her.

Returning to his computer, he frowned over the readings. It was almost over. His hideout had been located and they were closing in. He programmed the portal and went over to the worried Jane. He took her in his arms one last time and kissed her.

A loud noise startled them. A horrific crash had toppled

*their front door, and now the sound of running feet could be heard searching the house.*

*Two men burst into the lab and aimed their weapons. They were shocked when Jane pulled her gun and stood protectively in front of the Professor.*

*"Andrew! Jack!" she shouted. "Put down those...." Her words trailed off as confusion hit. She knew these intruders. Her memory flooded back in that instant. "I know you! You're my.... Oh, dear! My husband, Jack."*

*Behind her, unseen, Rex closed his eyes as if in pain. It was just as he had feared. Her memory returned at the sight of those most familiar to her. It was all over. For now. He could see Andrew was watching him like a fox, but Jack could only see his beloved wife. In these few moments, no one had lowered their weapons. Jane still shielded Rex.*

*Jane's face was a mixture of happiness at her memory and confusion about the past three months. "Maggie? I killed Maggie. I caused the explosion and Maggie fell. I ran away because I was scared. I remember hitting something and pain and then I was here. I...."*

*Andrew quickly explained, "Maggie isn't dead, Jane. She was hurt by the explosion, but she is fine. She... We all have been worried about you."*

*Jane stared at Andrew. "But you...you said you were going to have me arrested for murder."*

*Andrew looked ashamed. "I was upset and angry. I...I shouldn't have said that."*

*Jane had turned pale. Her mind couldn't keep up with all these conflicting images. "But Rex, he's always been there. We...I...love...Oh, Jack!" she cried as she fainted and sunk to the ground.*

*Rex took advantage of the diverted attention and leaped into the portal. He had no fears for Jane. She would be all right and was back with her husband. They had been tracking her ever since he had abducted her and knew this was the way it had to be. He would wait. She would be his once again some day.*

*Jack and Andrew let Rex go. They gently lifted Jane*

*and Jack kissed his wife. As her eyes opened, she looked into his concerned face and her arms encircled his neck....*

Ring. Ring Ring. Leslie looked up suddenly from her sofa. The phone. Drat, she was almost done....

"Hello?" she demanded shortly.

"Hi, honey. It's Mom. What are you doing?" Bonnie asked, choosing to ignore the sharp tone of her daughter.

"Umm," her mind was still with Jack and Jane. "I'm finishing my last chapter."

"Oh, you're always writing. I'd like you to go to the mall with me. There's a dress I would like your opinion on," her mom requested.

Leslie looked back at the sofa. "I'm almost finished, Mom. I think it's pretty good."

"Of course it is. But we don't get out to the mall much any more. I'd like you to go with me."

"Mom, all the cash registers light up and spell out 'Hi, Leslie and Bonnie' when we walk in the door."

Her mother didn't think that was funny. "Well, if you're too busy...."

*Guilt. Lovely,* Leslie thought to herself and gave a resigned sigh. "No, I'll go. There are only a few more pages to write. I could use the exercise," she relented. "My rear end is getting flat from the sofa."

She knew Bonnie was smiling into the phone. "Great. I'll pick you up in fifteen minutes."

Leslie looked down at her rumpled clothes. "Okay," she said slowly. "Meet you out front."

Ten minutes later Bonnie looked her daughter over as Leslie slid into passenger seat. "Is that what you're wearing?"

Leslie buttoned her coat to cover her old flannel shirt. "Hey, I only had ten minutes. I brushed my teeth and put on shoes. I hadn't planned on going out, you know."

Her mom became serious and got to what was really bothering her. "Les, between your job at the boutique and your writing, you don't have much free time. Dad and I are worried about you working so hard. If it weren't for Wayne, you probably wouldn't go out at all."

Leslie shook her head and tried to explain. "But I don't feel like my writing is work. I enjoy it too much. And pretty soon it will start paying off…I hope," she muttered under her breath. "When I'm not writing, I feel like I'm in a void. I have all these ideas in my head and nothing to do with them. It keeps my brain active."

"You know we're proud of you no matter what becomes of your little books," Bonnie smiled condescendingly, but added dryly, "Even though we don't understand how you can be so interested in that silly television show! We tried watching it once. Horrible thing! Why can't you write something more wholesome?"

The familiar buildings passing by were unseen as Leslie stared out the window of the car. "Mine are different. They'd make terrific episodes for the show. Mine are more human drama than science and technology."

"What does Wayne think of all this?"

Leslie shrugged. "He seems to like the stories. And, in answer to your next question, I haven't seen him lately. He suddenly had to go to Los Angeles on business, I don't know, weeks ago. He didn't know when he'll be back."

"He's such a nice boy," Bonnie smiled. "He's so polite to us. Renee was asking about the two of you," she told Leslie, glancing over at her. "She says she never sees you any more."

"I still have the same phone number and address," Leslie remarked dryly. "Mom, she's married now. They all are. I just don't fit in. If it weren't for Janice and Wayne, I wouldn't go anywhere," she stated, inadvertently admitting the same thing her mother had pointed out.

As the car pulled into a parking space near their favorite department store, Bonnie turned to Leslie. "We really like Wayne, Leslie. He seems to like you. Has, umm, anything been said?"

The warning bell in Leslie's head went off too late. She should have noticed how many times Wayne's name had come up in the conversation already and been able to deflect what she should have known was coming. "There's nothing to declare, Mom. He's a good friend. That's all right now. Now that my book has sold, I don't know what's going to happen in the near future.

I want to be open in case I have to go to New York or Los Angeles."

Knowing when to drop it, Bonnie gathered her purse and keys. "I just don't want you to shut the door on a possibility."

Leslie wasn't thinking of Wayne. She was picturing the cast of "The Time Police" and putting herself in-between Tom and Phillip. "Don't worry, Mom. I'm considering all the possibilities."


"Dizzy blond model," Wayne muttered angrily for the hundredth time as he sat in his surveillance van across from Sarah and Phillip Beck's house. He had been ordered by Sarah to temporarily stop his watch on Leslie and find out what was going on at her house. All Wayne could piece together from her frantic, angry phone call was that some actress—she was sure it was Cindy Sanders from the show—slept over and Sarah wanted to know what was going on.

Wayne hadn't wanted to return to Los Angeles. He was becoming more comfortable with his life in Amherst and more familiar with Leslie. He spent a lot of time with her and would quietly sit and watch her when she worked on her novels. Immersed as she would get, she didn't even remember he was sitting there. He considered it a victory when he could get her away for the evening to go to dinner and a movie.

What he couldn't comprehend was his lack of progress on a personal nature. She still offered her cheek for a requested goodnight kiss and an offer to stay the night resulted in a silent, red-faced shake of her head. He could tell she cared for him and enjoyed his company. But there was some barrier between them that prevented any intimacy.

Wayne found himself reviewing all their times together as he continued his boring watch of Phillip. He could not come up with anything that was said nor done that would explain her refusal to carry things to the next, normal level. He knew she had a passionate side because of her scenes between Jane and Jack or, lately, between Jane and Rex. Leslie had even asked him to try out a certain position to see if a scene would work before she wrote it down. Wayne had enjoyed holding her briefly like that and had received a mild admonition when he failed to let go soon enough upon request.

His occupation as a private investigator still bothered him. While hating to lie to both Leslie and Janice, he couldn't picture their reaction to hearing the truth. Finding he respected them, explanations would have to wait. Perhaps he could find work of another kind in Amherst. *Too bad*, he thought, *that I'm not good at anything else that's legal.*

Contacts of his had provided Wayne with all the details of Phillip's party and the guest list. He had known within the first three days what had happened and who had had to spend the night. He knew what they had to eat and drink and what music had played. He even found out which house Tom Young was going to buy on the beach.

Now he was just wasting time until Sarah was appeased. Phillip led one of the quietest lives of anyone he had ever watched—well, perhaps except for Leslie. At Marty's request he had provided the names of the women guests at the party and of the three who had been in no shape to drive home. The other names hadn't been wanted. Wayne knew Marty's angle and figured it would work on Sarah's jealous nature. Phillip didn't stand a chance with Marty around.

When Phillip finally drove off to the studio, Wayne gave a sigh of relief as he started the van and headed to his apartment. He hoped there would be a message from Sarah sending him back to Amherst.


"**B**eep...Wayne? This is Janice. Hi, how are you? We haven't heard from you in so long. I thought one of us ought to do something. I thought Leslie would, but she is so preoccupied.

"Her agent sent her five copies of her first book. We're all excited about it. It'll go on sale any day now. I'm sure she just forgot to tell you. She sent two copies to her actor, Phillip Beck. One was for the actor who plays Jack. She kept a copy, her folks got one, and she gave me the last one.

"Well, anyway, that's the latest around here. They keep asking about you at work. Hope you're all right. Give us a call or something.  Bye."

Wayne clicked off his answering machine.  Hoping that Leslie would have called by now, it was Janice who had to tell him the good news.  He could imagine how excited Leslie must be to finally have her book in her hands, but became hurt that she didn't save a copy for him.  Instead she sent two to "her actor."  *Like Beck really cared.  He probably won't even read it*, Wayne snorted.  *He was probably still too overwhelmed with his own career.  Ha!  If Leslie only knew the truth about "her actor" she might be very surprised.  He was just a too-bit....*

Wayne stopped his pacing and stood still.  It just occurred to him that he was jealous of Phillip Beck.  The actor had gotten two novels, probably another letter, and he had gotten nothing.  He'd have bet anything that Beck sent Leslie another of his short, say-nothing letters that meant so much to her.

Wayne strode into his bedroom and angrily packed his suit-cases again.  He had had enough of Los Angeles and Sarah.  He was going home to Amherst.  Sarah could take a flying leap.  And she could take Martin with her.


The Amherst Times
    Book Reviews
THE LONER FINDS LOVE
by Leslie Nelson
"Local author Leslie Nelson's first literary attempt has been enthusiastically received by fans of the popular "The Time Po-lice" television series.

Her writing style is simple and direct and has managed to combine the futuristic storyline with old-fashioned romance.

Early predictions indicate the novel is headed for the best-seller list."


Leslie was handed the page out of the newspaper when she entered the boutique.  Her boss Mona smiled at her.  "Congratu-lations, Les.  Your book seems to be a hit.  I'm surprised you came to work today," she kidded.

Leslie glanced at the review that had already been read.  Her parents had already called about it. Pretending to yawn, she joked back, "Oh, that. What a bore. What else could the little people say? Bring me a grape. And peel it." Leslie dramatically flung herself into a chair and closed her eyes.

Janice rolled hers. "Brother! Don't tell me we're going to have to put up with this from now on!"

Leslie looked up at her. "Where's my grape?"

"Where's your brain?"

"I don't need one. I'm famous," Leslie sighed.

All the women laughed and threw their coats on top of her before they went out front to get to work.

Leslie dug out from under the pile and fixed her hair in the mirror. "How rude!" she sniffed and strolled over to the pressing machine.

"Seriously, Les, what do you hear from your agent?" Mona wanted to know. "Anything on the second book?"

Leslie started steam pressing some dresses that had just arrived. "Well, he said he liked it and already sent it on to the publisher. He didn't seem to think there would be any problem getting it into print. He does want me to come to New York this spring to meet him and the editors."

"That's great!" Mona beamed.

"Tell her about Phillip," Janice prompted.

Leslie shrugged. "It's nothing really. You know I sent him a copy of my book," to which Mona nodded and waited for her to continue. "Well, he wrote back thanking me for it, and he also sent me a brochure to an up-coming convention. He didn't say so, but he is supposed to be there. I don't know," Leslie said casually, keeping head down so they couldn't see the excitement in her eyes. "Maybe he wants to say hello or something."

Janice looked at her unbelievingly. "What do you mean maybe? Why do you think he sent you the invitation?"

Leslie shook her head as she continued working on the dresses. "It wasn't an invitation, Jan. Just a brochure. All he said was that he didn't know if I had heard about the convention or not. That's all," she stressed, managing to kill her own mood.

Janice wasn't convinced. "He's going to be there and he wanted to make sure you would be, too," she stubbornly insisted, hands on her hips. *Sometimes Leslie could be so dense!*

"Well," Leslie said to end the conversation, "if he is there, and if we do meet, I hope he can tell me how to approach Majestic Studio with the idea for a script."


It took Leslie and Janice two hours to get to the convention site in the Silicon Valley. It was a cold, clear day in February, and there was a long line of cars waiting to get into the Fairington Oaks Hotel's parking garage.

Janice had driven as Leslie was jittery and nervous and quiet. Janice knew Leslie had brought her copy of her novel for the cast to sign. She also knew how many different outfits Leslie had tried on before choosing her blue rayon dress that highlighted the blue of her eyes.

What they both didn't know was that Wayne had followed them in his own car dressed in a disguise of a wig and a fake beard and mustache. He had been hurt that Leslie hadn't invited him to go along. She had told him he would get bored since he didn't like the television show as much as they did. Janice was also disappointed in Leslie's decision as she had wanted him to drive, but Leslie had been firm. Put off, now Wayne wouldn't have missed the meeting of Leslie and Phillip for anything in the world.

When the women finally parked, Leslie again checked her reflection in the car's vanity mirror.

"Your clothes look fine, Les. Don't know why you didn't wear contacts, though. But lighten up. You look like you're going to cry," Janice bluntly told her.

Leslie took a deep breath. "I'm so nervous," she admitted. "I don't know what to say so I don't come off sounding like some tongue-tied teenybopper."

"Just throw yourself into his arms and kiss him!" was Janice's suggestion as she started walking to the elevator.

"Very funny," Leslie scoffed as she looked around. "With all these people I probably won't have time to say much of anything anyway. Just as well. I do better through letters."

"You'll do fine. Wow, this place is great!"

Leslie glanced up at the ornate chandeliers, the glass and brass elevators, and the fern-enclosed grotto. "Close your mouth, Jan. We don't want to look like two geeks from the country who have never seen a grand hotel before."

"We *are* two geeks from the...."

"We are not! Shh!" Leslie insisted as she led them to the back of a long line.

After they stood in line for about ten minutes and had advanced a few yards, Janice started in with her favorite game: "Did you bring Phillip Beck's letter with you?" and "Do you think there is enough room in the front of your novel for all the cast to sign?" and "What did your agent say about your personal appearances?" and "Do you think your book will be on sale here?"

After a few people had turned to look at the red-faced Leslie and the smiling Janice, Leslie hissed under her breath, "Knock it off! This isn't for me."

Janice wasn't bothered in the least. "It will be. Some day."

In an hour they reached the desk and paid their admittance. They received a hand stamp in indelible red ink that read "Enter" and would last longer than the two-day convention. They each grabbed up an information sheet, scanning for the guest star's appearances. The whole cast would field questions at eleven o'-clock and sign autographs from noon until half past two. That gave the two women an hour to browse.

The room into which they were admitted was huge. It was lined with display booths filled with badges, fan magazines, uniforms, dolls of the cast, lapel pins, posters, postcards, copies of scripts, coffee mugs, blooper tapes, tapes of each episode, and anything and everything that could possibly carry "The Time Police" insignia. Leslie found her novel mixed in with all the other books for sale. There were other adventure shows produced by Majestic Studio that were also represented in the booths.

All this time, as the pair wandered around, they never noticed the bearded man who followed their every move.

At ten-thirty, they found seats towards the front of the auditorium to watch a slide show that featured behind-the-scenes looks at the cast and stills from various episodes. Leslie found herself looking over at the long white-draped table that had eight empty chairs behind it. She didn't even notice the elaborate floral spray that extended the length of the table.

The announcer, Frank, finished the narration on the slides and again welcomed the conventioneers. He was greeted with loud applause and verbal affirmation.

"Well, I see all of you are in high spirits," he beamed. "That's great. We're glad each and every one of you is here. Are you having fun yet?"

Feet were stomped and whistles were heard.

"That's great!" Frank replied. "So are we. And now, we won't keep you waiting any longer, Silicon Valley. Here they are! The stars of your favorite show—Maxwell Marlowe, Eddie Chase, Cindy Sanders, and Tom Young!"

Leslie's mouth dropped open and she looked at Janice. "Where's Phillip?" she yelled over the thunderous ovation the stars were given. Janice could only shrug.

The announcer then introduced the director, Ron Nickles, and two writers for the show. The crowd was still on their feet. Only Leslie and Janice remained seated. Wayne looked over from one row away and could see the obvious disappointment on Leslie's face. He smiled smugly to himself.

The crowd finally quieted down and retook their seats. The stars smiled warmly and waved at some children who ran to the edge of the stage. Flashes from dozens of cameras were still going off.

"Well," Frank cooed into his microphone, "I can tell you know who these people are!"

The crowd went wild with applause again.

Then Frank told them, "I know you all notice the empty chair. That was for Phillip Beck who, as you know, portrays Professor Rex Farrell on the show. Well, he was planning on being here to meet all you wonderful fans, but he was called back to the set of a movie he is filming and had to cancel."

There was a small groan that came from a few of the fans. Leslie looked over at Janice and muttered, "Oh, well, we tried."

The announcer opened the floor for questions and was greeted with a field of waving hands.

"Tom, are you married? Wanna be?"

"Eddie? Will your Andrew and Maggie ever really get together?"

"Cindy, want to go out for a drink later?"

"Has the show been renewed?"

"Can we take pictures?"

"How much money do you make an episode?"

"What is your favorite episode?"

"How long does it take to shoot a show?"

"Who makes the most mistakes?"

"Will The Loner ever get to keep the girl or will you keep killing them off?"

"Mr. Nickles, my cousin directs at a local theater. Need an assistant?"

"Would you accept a script from a local writer?"

"How old are each of you?"

"Which current problems in the world will you be fixing next season?"

"Will you ever do a theater-released movie?"

And so it went for the entire hour. The stars were generous and laughing with their answers or deferments. The writers told about some episodes coming up next season and how ideas are transferred into scripts.

Frank interrupted them all to say there would be another question and answer session later from four o'clock until five, but, for now, the stars would take a fifteen minute break. Then all were invited to the autograph session to be held in the fern grotto. Another ovation was given as the seven panelists exited waving and smiling. There was a rush of noise and movement as the fans streamed out of the auditorium. Some headed back to the merchandise room. Some went to lunch. Some stood around and exchanged fan club gossip. Quite a few—including Leslie, Janice and Wayne—headed for the fern grotto and patiently got into another line.

Janice started in again. "Did you see they have your book for sale?" and "Are you going to send a message back to Phillip Beck?" and "Did you hear what they said about looking for scripts? You're all ready for them."

"Janice!" Leslie pleaded, "Stop! I already told you Phillip

probably didn't intend on meeting me. He probably knew about this all along. They'll send him a cut of the take, no doubt. Two extra losers came to the convention."

Janice just smiled. "Oh, sure. Now you're being silly. He was called back to the studio. You heard that. He told you he was really busy."

"He always says that," Leslie pouted, noticing a few people looking back to catch their conversation. "Drop it for now, okay?"

"Do you think he gave your book to Tom?" Janice persisted.

"Doubt it. It didn't sound like he was going to. Maybe I can find out when we go through the line. With all these people I'll only have a few seconds."

"Well, you'd better get that look off your face," Janice told her. "You look like a thundercloud."

Janice finally fell silent, to Leslie's relief and she looked around the crowded hotel. A few fans were strolling around in homemade versions of the show's uniform. Some were browsing through magazines. Janice suddenly nudged Leslie who jumped as though startled. "Hey, look, Les. They're reading your book!"

A couple of conventioneers were indeed relaxing in chairs reading the opening pages of THE LONER FINDS LOVE. Leslie found her mood lightening as she watched them for a while.

"Well," she remarked to Janice, "that makes seven books in public hands."

"Eight. There goes another one," Janice pointed.


**A**s the line moved forward Leslie took her copy of her novel out of her purse. She felt her stomach tighten as she got closer to the table where the four stars of the show were greeting people. First Maxwell, then Cindy, Eddie and lastly, Tom. There were large eight-by-ten studio pictures to be bought and signed at the head of the table. There were no pictures of Phillip. Most of the fans bought one of each star, Leslie noticed, but she passed them by.

She shyly offered the front blank page of her book to Maxwell, and then to Cindy and thanked them. When it was his turn, Eddie looked up at her and smiled as he took the book. He said hello, and as he asked for her name he glanced at the front of the book at the picture on the cover.

"I don't look very happy, do I?" he remarked as he looked back at Leslie. His smile altered as he again looked at the front cover. It was obvious he was comparing the faces.

Leslie blushed. "I guess it is because Andrew isn't too happy with the newcomer Jane."

"What did you say your name was again?" Eddie asked in a friendly way, his pen poised.

"Just Leslie. That's fine," she mumbled.

"Nice to meet you, Leslie," he said as he handed the book back. He then tapped Tom as Leslie moved down a step and said, "Bunny," in a low voice.

Leslie heard what he had said and saw Tom do a double-take at her. She got all red and flustered again. Janice, who was having the time of her life, prodded her to go to Tom's station.

"I wonder if you could sign this for me," Leslie managed to choke out.

"Did anyone ever tell you that you look like the girl on the cover?" Tom smiled as he looked at the novel's front. "I'll sign yours, Leslie Nelson, if you'll sign mine. Phil told me you might come to the convention when he brought over my copy. I really enjoyed reading it," as he pulled the book out from under his chair.

Leslie looked from Eddie to Tom. She grinned broadly to match theirs. Before she could reply, there was a loud, "You're holding up the line" yelled from the back.

Leslie blushed again. "Oh, dear. I...sure, I'll sign yours."

Tom took her book with the cast signatures and put it under the table. "Tell you what, Leslie," he said quietly, coming to an instant decision without thinking it through—or discussing it with Eddie. "Have dinner with Eddie and me after all this is over. We'd both like to talk about your book. Okay?" he smiled warmly.

"I'm not alone. Janice, my friend, is with me," she stammered, motioning with her hand in the wrong direction from where Janice was standing.

"Great! The more the merrier," Tom grinned, ignoring

Eddie's kick under the table. "I'll make the necessary arrange-ments. See you later," he said as he motioned over an assistant. He pointed out Leslie and Janice, and the aide came over to them, leading them away from the nosey crowd.

"If you two ladies will come to the El Dorado Suite at six this evening, Mr. Young and Mr. Chase will be waiting for you. I do advise you not to mention the suite name to anyone else. Now, if you will give me your names, I will meet you at the door at six."

Leslie and Janice complied. Leslie then remembered, "Oh, I have Tom's book and he has the one signed by everyone else."

The aide told her, "You can exchange them at dinner tonight. It would be best not to say anything here. See you later, ladies."

The two women looked at each other as he walked off. "We're having dinner with Tom Young and Eddie Chase," Leslie murmured, wide-eyed.

"If you scream, I swear I'll slap you!" Janice warned. "I re-member your reaction when Phillip called you that time."

"No, no, I'm fine." Leslie was actually stunned. "What did he mean by 'bunny' after he looked at me? Do my teeth look funny?"

"I don't know. We'll ask him at dinner," Janice told her, peer-ing at her friend's white face. "Are you really all right? You're awfully pale."

Leslie put Tom's copy of her book in her purse. "I'm fine. I just can't believe this. Let's have lunch," she said suddenly and started walking towards the hotel's main restaurant.

The bearded man had seen Tom switch the books and then motion for the assistant. He could tell Leslie was shocked and Janice was excited. He just didn't know why. Following them into the restaurant, he figured Janice would soon announce what was going on.


**B**oth women found themselves getting nervous as six o'-clock approached. Janice became more talkative, and Leslie be-came more silent. They had attended the rest of the convention events scheduled for that day and finally entered one of the brass elevators. As they weren't alone in the elevator, they discontin-ued their on-going speculation on what the evening would be like.

Leslie took off her glasses to clean them just for something to do with her hands. Janice looked mildly disgusted. "You should have worn your contacts," she stated again.

"How was I to know? We would have been home by now."

"Well, we could leave," Janice kidded.

"Yeah, right!" Leslie laughed. Both of them knew nothing on earth could turn them away now.

After numerous stops, the elevator eventually reached the top floor. There were only Leslie, Janice and the disguised Wayne left when the doors slid apart. The view down to the main floor lobby was lovely with all the white lights in the trees and the six-story tall waterfall.

The same assistant met them at the door marked El Dorado Suite, ushering them into a large living area with an L-shaped white sectional sofa, glass and brass accent tables, a desk and chair done in antique white, and a honey oak entertainment center. Their gaze fell on a dining table set for four near the picture window overlooking the lights of the city. Three large fresh flower arrangements, oil paintings, and an Oriental silk screen that half-hid an oak bar did not escape their notice, nor that the room was beautifully tasteful.

From behind one of the three closed doors was the muted sound of male voices conversing. The far right door opened, and Tom Young came out with a grey-haired man who looked like he was in a tremendous hurry.

Tom smiled his greeting to the two women and brought the man over for introductions.

"Ron Nickles, this is Leslie Nelson, a new author for "The Time Police." And this is...uh..." he faltered at Janet's name which had eluded him. "I'm so sorry."

Leslie extended her hand which was cold. "Hello, Mr. Nickles. This is Janice Woods."

Ron shook hands with each of them and abruptly turned back to Tom. "I need to call the studio. Tell Eddie I'll see him tomorrow. Ladies? A pleasure." He nodded and rushed out of the suite.

Tom explained, "He's the director of the show. But, you probably knew that. Why don't you two go ahead and take a seat.

Eddie is talking to his wife in New York. He'll be out in a minute. Can I offer you a drink?"

"White wine would be fine," Leslie answered as she took Tom's book out of her purse. "This suite is lovely," she commented as she took her glass of wine.

Tom looked around as if that was a new thought. He shrugged. "I guess so. In our line of work we travel so much that we get a little jaded. I never really notice."

Leslie took a tentative sip. The wine proved to be excellent. "So, you don't like to travel? I love it. I only wish I could do more."

Tom seemed to be thinking back. "Oh, yes. New York once and the Caribbean twice. And Janice, you have been to Europe."

The women looked confused and a little wary. "How do you know that?" Janice asked him. She looked over at Leslie who likewise didn't understand how he could know that personal information.

Tom smiled a little sheepishly and looked down. "I *could* say that Phillip told me, but that wouldn't be completely true. I actually found out through your letters, Leslie."

"My letters? To Phillip?" She blushed again. "I didn't think they were anything special to be passed around," she confessed.

Tom grinned again. "Well, he didn't exactly pass them around. Phillip threw a party recently and I needed to use the phone. While looking for something to write on, I came across your letters and a picture of you fell out on the floor. A few lines caught my eye and I ended up reading all of them. I thought they were quite funny," he told her as he looked steadily at her over his own wineglass.

"I'm surprised he kept them," Leslie murmured. "But I am glad he gave you my book. The first manuscript I sent you apparently never reached you."

He shook his head. "No, we don't see much mail," Tom replied, looking disgusted. "We get so much. Then there are the legalities if we read something the general public wrote and it ended up in a show without going through the proper channels. But Phillip..." he broke off for a second. "Well, Phillip doesn't get that much, plus there are different rules for guest stars."

The middle door now opened and Eddie Chase came out.

He smiled at the two women with his trademark dazzling smile. He looked as if he was in a very good mood.

Walking up to Leslie first, he shook hands. "It's nice to meet one of our authors," he told her. "I hope Tom isn't boring you too much."

"No, not at all," Janice grinned. "He was just telling us how he came to know about Leslie."

Eddie picked up Tom's glass and took a healthy sip. "Ah, yes. The snoop! I actually first heard mention of you over a year ago. When Phillip received your first letter. He was quite impressed by the story."

That pleased Leslie. "How come you said the word bunny when you saw Leslie?" Janice asked.

The men exchanged a grin. "That's what Phillip calls you," Eddie told Leslie. "He can't seem to remember your name. Was there some picture or something you sent?"

Leslie looked as if she was trying to decide if she should be hurt or not. Janice immediately knew what they meant and began laughing. "It was that picture! Remember, Les? The one I took when we were at that amusement park together. You were being hugged by a six-foot tall rabbit."

"He calls me Bunny," Leslie muttered. "I guess it could be worse."

There was a knock on the door and Tom arose from one end of the sofa to answer it. "I hope you don't mind. I've already ordered dinner. That's probably room service."

He was correct. Eddie, ever the gentleman when he wanted to be, led them to the dining table and held out the chairs for Leslie and Janice. He took his own seat as Tom brought over the wine to refill their glasses.

Leslie removed her glasses and rubbed the bridge of her nose. When she set them on the side of the table, Tom peered at her face. She noticed his close scrutiny and turned red again.

"You look better without your glasses," he remarked with a kind smile.

Leslie glanced at his face and made a show of squinting. "You look better without my glasses, too," she kidded dryly.

Eddie started laughing and Janice giggled. Tom lifted his

glass to Leslie. "Well said," he saluted with a satisfied grin.

As they continued eating their filet mignon, the talk loosened up as the women relaxed more. Tom and Eddie seemed very interested in Leslie's novels.

"How did you happen to develop Jane into a wife for Jack?" Tom asked. "Our writers won't do that."

Leslie looked down at her plate, carefully cutting a stalk of asparagus as she answered. "I really like The Loner character. And...I don't like to see anyone alone like that. I like happy endings. So I wrote one," she ended simply as if the whole process had been that easy.

"I do, too," Tom replied good-naturedly. "I've tried to get the writers to give Jack someone, but they haven't."

Janice gave them a wide grin. "Well, there's always next season. We happen to know of an excellent storyline."

"How many have you written? This isn't the Western, is it?" Eddie asked.

"I've done three so far. The second, the Western, is at the publishers now to see if they will accept it."

"They will," Janice, ever the optimist, stated.

Eddie nodded. "That's good. What's the third about?"

Leslie looked pleased with herself. Her eyes shone as she talked about her work. "It's called CHATEAU REX and Jane is hurt in an explosion she inadvertently caused and gets amnesia. The Professor has been watching her since the time and setting of the second story and abducts Jane. He takes her to his hidden laboratory in the hills around the Silicon Valley...." She broke off at the looks on the men's faces. "Oh, that's right. You know where that is. Ha, sorry! Anyway, the two of them go back in time to Scotland to discover Jane's past—which she knew nothing about. All this time the squad has been searching for her. Even antagonistic Andrew is worried. Jack is distraught. During the three months she is there, Rex and Jane fall in love...."

"Interesting triangle," Tom commented, intrigued.

"Her memory returns when Jack and Andrew arrive to rescue her, guns in hand," Leslie finished, out of breath and a little embarrassed that she talked so long.

"So, you gave the Professor a love scene? That's a first!"

Eddie laughed.

"Actually, he gets three or four and a touching farewell," Leslie explained, turning red again for some reason.

"Does Jack get his wife back?" Tom wanted to know.

"Oh, yes. Jane, of course, is very confused as her memory returns, but she would never leave Jack."

"Of course she wouldn't," Tom declared, lifting his chin. "That Jack is one terrific guy."

Leslie steeled herself to meet his direct look and gave a small smile. "Yes, he is," she responded quietly.

When they were done eating the foursome returned to the sofa and chairs. Tom sat next to Leslie on one end of the sofa as Eddie sat across from them in one of the chairs. Janice sat at the opposite side of the sofa so she could watch everyone easier. She didn't want to miss a thing.

"So," Tom started when they were finally settled. "Tell us about your adventures traveling. I enjoy going to exotic places myself when I'm not filming."

Leslie shook her head slightly and looked at Janice. "I wouldn't call it adventuresome, but it was enjoyable. I've been to seven islands in the Caribbean, and I spent five days shopping in Manhattan, but I prefer shopping in the Caribbean."

"My wife's appearing on Broadway," Eddie told them. You wouldn't go back to New York? She seems to like the pace of the city when she's there."

"Oh, I really liked New York," Leslie was quick to insist. "My agent wants me to come in the spring to meet the publishers. But, I do prefer St. Thomas and Martinique."

Tom looked interested. "When are you going?"

"To New York? I don't know for sure," Leslie frowned slightly and looked back at Janice. "Maybe in April. I'm kind of leery about just Janice and myself going. I was in a group before."

"Take someone else with you," Tom suggested.

Janice piped up here to make a point in Leslie's behalf. "There isn't anyone else, really. All our friends are either married or broke. Or both," she added with a laugh. "We'll just have to stick together."

Eddie glanced at Tom's face and changed the subject.

"What are you planning on doing next with your stories, Leslie?"

Leslie looked away from Tom's face. "Next? I'd like to turn them into scripts and submit them, but I'm not sure how."

Tom looked surprised. "Haven't you ever seen a script?"

"Not a real one," Leslie replied and then grinned. "I'm planning on having all my friends send copies of my novel to Majestic with letters extolling the wonderful storyline! I'm hoping there'll be interest in it before I start another rewrite to try and turn it into a script."

Eddie nodded at this strategy, not knowing for certain if she was completely serious. "Public opinion carries some weight. You'll want to contact Richard Avery. He's the head of the studio. If your work is good and enough fans show interest, something could happen."

"It's good," Tom said quietly, studying Leslie's face as she listened intently to Eddie's words. Janice continued to observe Tom and smiled contentedly to herself at his scrutiny of Leslie.

"Thanks," Leslie said brightly. "That's good to hear from a professional." She glanced at her watch. It was almost ten o'clock. "Oh, my, it's getting late, Jan. We shouldn't have taken up so much of your time," she apologized as she stood from the sofa and looked around for her purse.

"No, don't go yet," Tom hurriedly said, standing as if to block her. "We don't often get a chance to talk to people like this."

"We have a two hour drive home," was the reluctant argument from Leslie. She glanced at Janice for back-up. Janice was still seated, her arms across the back of the sofa, settling in for the duration. "Jan?"

"I'm fine. So we get home a little late," she shrugged, knowing this was a once-in-a-lifetime chance for her friend. "No one is waiting for either of us. We both live alone," she added with a smile.

Leslie threw her a "What-are-you-doing?" look and turned back suddenly when Tom picked up one of her hands. "Please stay for a while. If nothing else, we can arrange for you to have a room here. If it gets too late, that is," he told them as he pulled Leslie back onto the seat on the sofa.

It was Eddie who stood next. "Well, after that meal and sitting for so long, I need some exercise. If that crowd is gone, I'm going down to the main lobby."

Janice perked up at this. "I'll go with you," she suddenly interjected, seeing a perfect opportunity to leave Tom and Leslie alone for a few minutes.

Hesitating for a fraction of a second, not seeing any other polite option, Eddie offered his arm. "That would be charming. We'll be back in a few minutes."

Leslie's eyes grew alarmed as Janice strolled out the door with Eddie Chase. "You two are full of surprises. I wish I had a camera. No one will ever believe this," she muttered as she turned back to Tom. He had kicked off his shoes and had his feet up on the coffee table.

He shrugged. "Eddie's the energetic one. He likes to work out and jog and keep active. Plus, he has a son to run after."

"And what about you?"

"Me? No, I don't run around after his son," he teased and was rewarded with a wide smile. "I don't know. I try to keep in shape, but I'm not a fanatic about it. Tell me about yourself, Leslie Nelson. Where are you from? What do you do in your boutique?"

So they talked on and on about their lives and found similarities in likes and dislikes. They told of pranks and jokes at both of their workplaces. Talking about their private lives, there were past loves mentioned and what they were both looking for in a partner. The television show came up and the possibility for Leslie's character in the next season. They went back to traveling and the destinations they would most like to reach. Never once was Phillip mentioned.

Eddie and Janice had returned after an hour only to be quickly, surreptitiously waved away by Tom. Leslie hadn't even noticed the door opening, being so caught up in their discussion and the moment. Somewhat concerned but not wanting to argue with his friend in front of the ladies, Eddie had no choice but to take Janice to his suite as the hour was so late. Always the trooper, she turned on the television and promptly fell asleep on the sofa. Eddie brought in a bedspread to cover her. Returning to his bedroom, he went to sleep himself, wondering what in the world Tom was doing.

Leslie awoke suddenly. There was a man's arm around her shoulder, and she was leaning against someone's chest. Her own arm was encircling a waist. Her shoes were off with her feet tucked up under her wrinkled dress.

She looked up at Tom Young who was still asleep, his head back against the cushion of the sofa. Alarmed, she tried to get out of his arms as quietly as she could without awakening him. However his eyes opened and were momentarily shocked to see someone in his arms. He was quick to recover and quietly murmured, "Morning," with a grin as she sat away from him looking extremely embarrassed.

"I…I can't believe we fell asleep like that," she muttered as she smoothed down her messy dress and pushed absently at her hair.

Tom stretched his cramped arms. "Where's your friend? It's five a.m."

Leslie stood awkwardly and looked around. Her nerves were making her shaky. "I don't know. Maybe in the bedroom?" She checked all three shut doors before she found the right room. "No. Is she with Eddie still?" she gasped at the thought.

"Maybe," Tom shrugged as if he didn't care one way or the other. "She'll be all right. Eddie's a happily married man. Everything's fine. What's wrong?" he asked as her face was far from calm.

"I can't believe this happened! What about your reputation if someone found out? This is terrible," she exclaimed getting herself even more upset.

Tom reached out to her and put his hands on her arms to calm her. "No, it's not terrible…unless you had a really terrible time," he added with a small grin. "We fell asleep on the sofa after a most enjoyable evening. That's all." He put a finger under her chin and raised her face so he could see her eyes. He gave her a sincere smile. "I can't remember the last time I enjoyed an evening so much. You're different from most women I meet. And you're certainly not like most of the fans. You're funny and serious and shy and bold all mixed together."

Leslie didn't know what to say. She was staring into his amber eyes. Her embarrassment had fled at his kind words. He bent down and lightly kissed her cheek. Her hand went up and touched the spot where his lips had been.

"I guess I enjoyed it, too," she almost whispered. "I must look a fright," she claimed wiping at her eyes and looking down.

Tom grinned showing his even white teeth. "Well, you do look like a raccoon."

"Oh!" That was the last thing she wanted to hear and tried to cover her eyes with her hands.

He laughed and pulled her hands down. "I like raccoons," he told her and lifted her face again. This time he gently kissed her lips.

"No, don't," she whispered, turning her head and trying to push away as all the years of brow-beating took over her actions. "I'm nobody. You deserve...."

"Shh," he cut her off, not relinquishing his hold. "You're not a nobody. I think you're special and I'd like to see you again sometime."

"I live in Amherst. You live down in Los Angeles. That's over three hundred miles away. You're just being nice," she argued weakly, her heart pounding at his words.

"Just leave your address and phone number. You'll see. I don't spend the night with just anyone," he added lightly. He was surprised to see her eyes widen.

"We...we didn't spend the night together! Don't say it that way!"

Tom was touched by her protestations. That was all the other women usually wanted from him. He now knew for sure that this one was different. "Okay, I won't. Sorry. Are you going to stay for the convention today? You're already here. We could have lunch together," he offered, hoping.

"No, I have to get home. If my parents knew I wasn't home they would worry." She saw the dubious look on his face. "I know I'm not fifteen," she smiled, knowing how it sounded. "But they still worry. Plus, I've taken up too much of your time."

"All right," he sighed, relenting. "Do you believe what I told you?" he asked, suddenly getting serious again.

Leslie turned away from his look. "Well, you are a good actor. I think you're trying to make me feel better."

Tom shook his head as he reached for her hands. "My, you're stubborn, too!" he claimed and grinned at the frown she gave him.

"Am not," she sniffed.

"Then kiss me," he murmured, bending down to her lips. He brought her close in an embrace as one hand touched her back and the other dropped below her waist and pushed her even closer.

The ringing of the phone disrupted his convincing Leslie. It was Eddie inquiring what the heck was going on. Tom explained what had happened and asked about Janice. Eddie had already called Cindy to bring over some make-up for the visitors. When Leslie overheard that, she asked for the same help.

When Janice arrived with the needed cosmetics, the two women retreated into one of the bathrooms to make their repairs. Eddie then assaulted Tom.

"Whatintheheck are you doing, Tom!? Are you nuts," he demanded in a low voice.

"It wasn't like that, Eddie," Tom shot back angrily. "We talked all night and fell asleep on the sofa. That's it. Her face is still dented from the buttons on my shirt if you care to check."

"I don't care to check. It was bad enough that you invited them to dinner, but this is terrible. What if the papers pick this up? I'm married, you know!"

"Oh, is that what you're worried about? Yourself?" Tom charged. "Well, this has nothing to do with you. I...I like Leslie. A lot. Her reaction was the same as yours, by the way," he added, trying to end the argument before the women walked into the middle of it. "It wasn't planned. We just fell asleep. Don't worry about Linda. I'll tell her everything if you think it's necessary."

Eddie attempted to smooth his own ruffled feathers. "She already thinks you're a terrible liar. I doubt that would help. I just don't want anyone hurt by gossip. You know how bad it can be."

Tom nodded quietly as he looked at the closed bathroom door. "I know. We've all been burned.... This one is different,

Eddie. And she's going home just as fast as she can."

Eddie gazed at Tom but said nothing. He could tell Tom meant what he had said. Tom did seem affected by this woman. Maybe he had been too harsh with his criticism. "Do you know how to reach her again if you wanted to?"

"Not yet," he sighed. "But, I will. Even if I have to ask Phillip."

The bathroom door opened and the two women emerged looking somewhat repaired and refreshed.

"We really need to go," Janice spoke first.

Leslie walked shyly up to Tom. She didn't seem to know what she should do or say to him. "Thank you for the dinner and the…the interesting evening." She extended her hand.

Tom, torn between being amused and hurt, took the offered hand and kissed it. Then he surprised all of them by using that hand to pull Leslie towards him and kissed her on the lips. "No, thank you," he told her. "I meant what I said. I will see you again."

Leslie said nothing as she took up her purse and her signed book. Janice brightly said good-bye to the actors, mentally high-fiving herself. They left the suite without looking back.

# CHAPTER 9

**P**hillip Beck looked up from the current trade sheet. The article had been about the most successful model in Europe—Sarah Beck. France was even more enthusiastic than Japan had been. Davey's face, the paper reported, was becoming as well known as his mother's. But now there was a new angle for the model; a new opportunity had opened. For, the paper reported, she was pregnant. Three months along. Europeans had a more relaxed attitude towards expecting women and realized the body was natural and beautiful. Pregnancy was natural and beautiful. Her career would continue and flourish throughout her term and her development would be followed by all. By the time the baby came into the world, he or she would be welcomed and loved by all of Europe—for Sarah belonged to them now and the baby would belong to them, also.

Phillip felt old and tired for the first time in his life. He had just turned forty-one alone. He still worked steadily and Majestic was talking about making some big changes next season in "The Time Police." But that didn't interest him right now.

Upset and lonely, he wanted his family back. Fighting down his anger and repulsion, he dialed the number Martin had given him weeks ago. He had to try again.

Sarah answered the phone. "Bonsoir."

"Sarah? It's Phillip," he started reluctantly, suddenly unsure of what he was going to say or how he would be received.

"Yes?" she asked, reserved and cool. "What can I do for you?"

He silently shook his head. He should have known. "I wanted to see how you and Davey are. How's my son?" he asked, stressing the last two words.

"He's really grown, Phillip. He's learning French faster than he picked up Japanese. This has been so educational for him."

"Can I talk to Davey? I'd like to say hello," Phillip told her hopefully.

"Marty took him to the Louvre. I didn't feel up to going," was her evasive reply.

Phillip's jaw tightened. "Oh? Why not? Are you ill?" he pointedly asked.

He could sense her hesitation. "Well, not sick, exactly. You see, I'm...well...I'm expecting."

He wouldn't let her off easily. "Expecting what? A pizza? A phone call from your husband?"

Sarah exploded. "Oh, for Pete's sake, Phillip! I'm expecting a baby! What did you think?"

"So, who is the fortunate father?"

Sarah swallowed. "I'm pretty far along. Who do you think the father is, silly?"

"That's funny. The papers say you are only three months along. I think I would remember coming to Japan, if you will pardon the pun," he asserted hotly.

"All right! It's not yours. You knew all along. It's Marty's baby and...and we're both thrilled about it. Davey calls it his baby already," she added just to hurt him.

It worked. Phillip closed his eyes. "What about us, Sarah? When are you coming home?"

Sarah tried to appeal to his business sense. "I wouldn't have any career in this condition back there. I'd have to shut myself up in a dark room!"

"Is that all you care about? Your career? What about our family life? What about me? What about Davey?" he asked quietly, his emotions spent.

"Don't whine, Phillip. It isn't manly," she sighed. "All I can say is that my career is here. Sweden has contacted Marty and we are considering it."

Phillip was quiet. "So, you aren't coming back to Los Angeles. I want to see my son, Sarah! I have rights."

"I spoke to a lawyer already, too. She has spent a lot of time with us as a family. She has questioned Davey. He barely remembers another man in his life other than Marty. He's happy here, Phillip," she told him, less unkindly than he expected. "He accepts Marty. If you get back into the picture, that means he will have to fly back and forth from Europe to America for a few days of visitation. I think its best he stays here. When he gets older and has questions, then you can come back in the picture."

"No way! There's no way you are going to take my son away from me. I want him back here in the U.S. right now! There's no way I'm going to give him up, Sarah. That's cruel, even for you," he told her, his heart clenching.

"It's honest, Phillip. If you want to test me out, then come here and see for yourself. He won't know you. Listen, I can give you the number of my lawyer. Maybe that will help."

"What would *help* is for you to come back home and bring me my son. But, you're not coming back to Los Angeles, are you?"

"At least not for the next seven or eight months. I'd be foolish to leave now. Marty wouldn't advise it."

"Yeah, I'll bet he wouldn't," he asserted angrily. "Our friends have been asking, and I don't know what to tell them any more because I've been confused about what's been going on."

"*My* friends already know what's going on. I don't know about your friends," she coolly informed him.

"The studio is talking about some major changes next season. The Professor role could be broadened."

"That's nice. Say, listen, Phillip, I really need to go. I'm supposed to be resting."

Phillip bit his lip. "Well, I certainly don't want to take up any more of your valuable time. Au revoir."

"Good-bye, Phillip."

The dial tone sounded in his ear and he slowly hung up the phone. What else was there to say? His wife and his son were out of the country and, now, it appeared, out of his life—probably forever. She was carrying another man's child. His son probably didn't know him any longer and now turned to someone else for love and comfort. Phillip had nothing now but his career.

Eyes narrowed in anger, he picked up the phone again and called his travel agent. He wasn't going down without a fight. He was going to go get his son.

The secretary came to the door of the largest office on the Majestic lot. "Mr. Avery? The mail was just delivered. There's five more of that same book."

Richard Avery swung his huge leather chair around, turning away from the wide windows, a knowing half-smile on his face. "Are all of these from Amherst as well, Margaret?"

"No, sir," she said, checking the return addresses. "These are from different states. There's also another letter from an agent, a Mr. Quimby, from New York. He says he represents the author," Margaret informed her boss as she referred to a sheet of paper in her hands.

Richard rubbed a hand over his face. This pile of books made thirty-five copies of the novel that had been sent to him. Even one of his own actors had recommended the book. "All right, Margaret," he sighed briefly, "she wins. Leave me a copy of that darned book, the letter from the agent, and contact Tom Young. Tell him I want to see him here tomorrow at three. And tell him to leave his whoopee cushions, joy buzzers, exploding cigars, pepper gum and dripping cups in his dressing room."

Margaret grinned as she made some notes on the pad she carried. Tom was always pulling some stunt when he was called into this office. "Yes, sir. I'll leave them here on your desk. Mr. Avery? I started reading the novel during lunch a few days ago...." She broke off at the look on his face. "Well, there are over thirty copies lying around here.... I think the author has a good grasp on the characters."

"Uh-huh." He tilted his head as he look up from the letter from the agent. "I've always valued your viewpoint, Margaret. After I read it tonight, we'll see."

He gave the letter from the agent another perfunctory

glance. It was the usual letter extolling the wonders of the new discovery. Looking at the cover of the book, he was slightly surprised at the picture of the heroine. The women on novel covers were usually beautiful and voluptuous. Comparatively, this woman was rather plain with large blue eyes. He opened to the first page and started reading, hoping to find a quick clue about the cover girl.

Two hours later Margaret found her boss deeply engrossed in the novel, feet up on his desk, and neglected work pushed aside. He chuckled now and then as he read and nodded his head.

Margaret smiled as she returned to her desk. She knew she would be calling New York soon.

"Tom? What do you know about this Leslie Nelson?" Richard asked as he leaned back in his chair. "I heard you met her at the last convention."

Tom never ceased to be amazed at how fast news and gossip traveled over the lot. "Yes, I met her. Eddie and I had dinner with her that evening. I found her interesting, intelligent, funny, and a little enthusiastic about her work."

"Uh-huh. I suppose you've read her book," Richard commented, tapping the novel with his pen.

Tom nodded, wondering where this was going and how much Richard *really* knew. "Months ago. Phillip Beck brought me a copy that Leslie had sent through him. I enjoyed it. It would make a terrific opening for the new season," he added with a wide grin.

"Uh-huh. Considering how much it affects your character, I'm not surprised at your recommendation," Richard retorted and waved off Tom's attempt to sanction his claim. "Yes, yes, I know. It affects the whole show. I read the book as well. I intended to do in last night, but once I started, I couldn't put it down," he confessed, frowning as he looked off into the distance, pondering the possibilities. "I think you're right about next season. Do you think Miss Nelson would be willing to work with us? A few of her ideas aren't feasible for the show."

Tom nodded as he tried to remember the different parts of the novel. He couldn't think of any idea that wouldn't translate well onto the screen. But he didn't voice his disagreement. "She seemed pretty level-headed. She already is thinking ahead to scripts."

"Uh-huh. How do you think she would react to meeting here with all of us? Is she capable of handling herself, or should we deal just with her agent in New York?" was his next concern.

There was a smile from Tom as he recalled how nervous Leslie had been with him when they first met. "She might be a little shy at first, but I think she'd do fine. It would help if Eddie or I were here at the same time. She's already used to us...sort of. I'd volunteer to be present if you think that would help," he offhandedly offered.

Richard looked at him steadily. "Uh-huh. I'm sure you would. I also heard about your...uh...evening," he added and again waved the actor off. "That's your business, Tom, and I don't care what did or didn't happen. It usually helps to have someone familiar at the first conferences, however. I'll contact her agent and arrange the date. You and Eddie will both be present. And Nickles, of course. Margaret will let you know when."

Thus the meeting was adjourned. Tom arose without another word and left to go back to the rehearsal from which he had been called. He grinned to himself on how thrilled Leslie would be to get such an opportunity. He hummed a little tune as he thought how much he would enjoy seeing her again.


*Los Angeles Daily*
*"Majestic Signs New Writer*
*Majestic Studio today announced the appropriation of the newest "The Time Police" novel entitled THE LONER FINDS LOVE to begin the highly-rated show's fourth season. Yesterday, the author, Leslie Nelson, met with the studio heads and agreed to work closely with the show's creators in getting her work onto the air.*

*Ms. Nelson's novel, her first published work, has been one of the most widely-accepted books based on the popular show.*

*The next effort, WESTWARD REX, will be released within the month. Both parties are quite enthusiastic about the upcoming season."*

Phillip reread the article and looked again at the picture in the paper. Tom Young had his arm around Bunny's waist as she smilingly held up a contract. Richard Avery stood on her other side holding the pen. Eddie Chase and an unidentified man stood in the background. The photo was shot in Avery's office.

Phillip set the paper down with a sigh. *Why was it he always had to find out what's going on from the papers*, he wondered? He hadn't heard from Bunny in months and didn't know Majestic knew about her. Now she had signed a deal with Avery and she didn't even tell him about it.

He suddenly realized, once he stopped to think about it, that Bunny also hadn't written him about that convention he hadn't been able to attend or about the latest on her books. She hadn't told him she would be in town or for how long. He found, surprising himself, that he missed her letters.

Glancing again at the photo in the newspaper, Phillip's eyes stopped on Tom's arm around her waist. *That didn't seem a very appropriate pose for a publicity shot*. His mind clicked to a new thought: Maybe Tom could fill him about that conference with Avery.

After dialing Tom's home number, the phone was answered by Tom's housekeeper. No, Mr. Young was out to dinner with some author at Charney's. No, she didn't know who. They were celebrating some deal. No, they would probably be back late. Could she take a message?

Phillip didn't leave a message. He decided to go to the posh restaurant in Beverly Hills and join them for dinner. His curiosity had piqued over Bunny, and he felt this would be an excellent opportunity to meet his fan.

Running a hand over his jaw, he decided a quick shave and a change of clothes would be a good idea. Charney's was one of the better restaurants the actors frequented.

Phillip was pleased with his decision to take the initiative to finally meet Leslie. Pulling into the parking lot to leave his car with the valet, he figured out what he would say to congratulate her. There would also be an offer of his help with the scripts—something she had asked for and he had failed to do thus far in their correspondence.

The maitre d' warmly welcomed Mr. Beck and asked if he was meeting anyone or would he like a table for one? Phillip asked for Tom Young's party.

"Oh, but Mr. Young and his guest left over thirty minutes ago. I am so sorry," Roberto told him. "We still have some excellent seats, Mr. Beck."

Phillip thanked him and went back out front. He handed the card to the valet who rolled his eyes in disgust. He had just gotten back from parking that car. Phillip didn't notice the reaction as he handed over a generous tip. He was trying to decide whether to go to Tom's new beach house or to go back home. After glancing at the clock, he headed home and figured he'd call Tom in the morning.

"Thomas? Beck here."

"Hey, Phil. Long time," Tom answered in a friendly tone. "How's that television movie going over at North Star Studio?"

"It's all right. My part will be finished in a week and a half. I wanted to ask you about the deal Majestic signed with Bunn...I mean, Leslie. I saw the picture in the paper. How did it go with Avery? Did he try any of his tricks?" Phillip asked with a knowing grin.

Tom laughed. "Did he! Boy, I tell you, he tried them all. But that Leslie was sharp. She came prepared. She knew what she wanted with her books and stuck to her guns. Her agent mostly just sat there and helped with the contract. She handled all the fine print."

"Like what?" Phillip wanted to know as he leaned back in his chair.

"Oh, like how Jane Barrett will look on the show and how much of her book will be used in the script. Things like that," Tom replied.

"Did Avery try to buy the book outright?"

Tom gave a disgusted snort. "Yeah. For a ridiculous price. But," he emphasized, clearly enjoying the telling of the tale, "that was not acceptable to Miss Nelson. She wasn't about to hand over her precious book with no say attached."

"Where did Bunny learn those techniques of dealing with Avery? She didn't seem like that determined of a person to me," Phillip commented with a puzzled frown.

"Well," Tom confided, "she surprised all of us. Even herself, I found out later. She was pretty nervous about the whole meeting concept and having to deal with the head honcho and all. She was even shy and nervous when I met her at the airport. I hadn't contacted her since the convention and I guess she didn't believe I had been sincere."

Phillip frowned to himself. He didn't know what Tom was talking about, but didn't want to ask. It sounded personal. Apparently they had spent more time together than he knew about.

Unaware of Phillip's level of concern, Tom continued. "She was surprised I met her or even knew she was coming. Then she was relieved to learn Eddie and I would be there at the conference. I told her what to expect from Avery." Tom paused and laughed. "You wouldn't believe how mad she got in the back of the limo when she heard Avery wanted all the rights to her books! She wasn't about to do that! I thought she was going to turn the limo around and go back to Amherst right then and there."

"What did you tell her?" Phillip prodded as Tom again fell silent and was laughing.

"Oh, just the usual advice about dealing with studio heads. I told her that Avery really wanted her work and what a good position she was in. I took her to the hotel and we both met her agent. Nice chap, by the way. We decided on a battle plan and I filled Eddie in on it before the meeting the next day. She was still nervous. I could feel her shaking as we went in. But, as soon as Avery came in, the show started."

"Show? What show?" Caught up in the narrative, Phillip was confused.

"Leslie's show. She'd make a terrific actress, Phil. The scared look left her eyes and her mouth set in a most determined fashion. She lifted her chin, and then shook his hand as if he were the one being presented to her. Her voice didn't even quiver."

Phillip smiled. Mr. Avery liked people to be afraid of him. "How did Richard react?"

Tom laughed out loud again and switched the phone to his other ear. "You should have seen the look he gave Nickles! Even Ron was amazed. They expected to walk all over her. As it ended, Les will do the rewrites herself—with some assistance from the main writers, if needed—and will have final say in which actress we hire, plus any changes."

There was a low whistle. "Good job, Bunny," was Phillip's comment. Those conditions were unheard of. "So she's moving down here?"

Tom paused as he thought back. "No, she never mentioned that. Avery is installing a fax machine at her place in Amherst— that was part of the deal. I offered my help with the scripts and all."

"That's great," Phillip muttered. "I'm glad for her. Is she still in town? I'd like to say hello."

"No. I took her to the airport earlier today. Her agent left the day the contract was signed and took her third book with him. I asked Leslie to stay a few days."

There was silence from both men. Tom expected Phillip to ask something else. Phillip was surprised by this revelation from Tom. "Oh. Did you show her the sights around here?"

"Naw, that wasn't necessary. Les is already pretty familiar with the area. We spent a lot of time here at the house. You know, talking about scripts and walking on the beach and all. Too bad I didn't know you wanted to meet her, Phil. I would have had you over or something."

"Maybe next time. When is she coming back down to Los Angeles?"

Tom had to think on that. "Hmm. I don't know. She wanted some time to start on the scripts before I see them. I'll probably go north and surprise her. I'd like to see where she lives. She's a terrific person, Phil."

"Yeah. Sounds like it," was the quiet response. "Thanks for the update, Thomas. I'm glad everything went well. I'll see you soon."

Phillip pondered his strange reaction to the news about Bunny. He felt like he was an outsider on something he himself had helped initiate. He felt Bunny was his special fan and he was jealous of Tom's association with her. Yes, it was jealousy, he admitted. Even though he hadn't been interested in her personally, he now resented Tom's apparent interest—whatever the reason behind it. If only he had sent her the script pages she had requested. If he had written more to her than just a few measly lines. If only he had been able to go to that blasted convention. If he just hadn't given Tom the book she had sent for him. He should have been at the meeting with Avery. After all, it was because of his original phone call that Bunny was even in the position she now held. It was he who should have taken her to celebrate at Charney's, he thought. It was he who should have strolled with her on the beach and then lit a fire to ward off the chill of the evening....

As soon as Phillip noticed he was pacing, it abruptly stopped as he stared at a photograph on his desk. It was a beautiful blond woman, a darling tow-headed four-year-old, and himself. Sarah and Davey. His wife and son. He looked down at the wedding band on his left hand as his pulse seemed to throb under the gold and diamond ring.

All the negative feelings about his good friend Tom flooded away. All the what-ifs concerning Bunny left his mind as he sat heavily on his sofa. He had no right, no claim on Bunny. He was a married man. Even though his abrupt trip to France proved all the awful things Sarah had told him were true—that he no longer had a family—he was still married. He had made vows and promises.

Exhaustion encompassed Phillip as he put his head back on the sofa and closed his eyes. "Sorry, Bunny."

# CHAPTER 10

"**S**he doesn't know what she's doing, Jan! She's in over her head!" Wayne fumed angrily as he stormed around Janice's apartment.

Surprised by his sudden outburst, Janice remained silent. He had shown up unexpectedly at her door and hadn't even waited for an invitation to enter. Ever since the convention Wayne had been getting more and more angry at Leslie. Now that she was back from Los Angeles, he was livid.

He continued his tirade without waiting for or apparently wanting any reply from Janice. "She doesn't know what kind of people she's dealing with. They're going to devour her. Sure, they *pretend* they like you, but they'll knife you in the back! Especially those actors!" he spat out, gesturing madly.

"Wayne!" Janice pleaded from the far side of the room, as far away from his mad pacing as she could get, deciding to head off his tantrum. "Please! I'm sure you're exaggerating. The two men we met at the convention were as nice as they could be. How would you know what they're like? You weren't there. And you aren't in show business!" she pointed out.

His head snapped around to look at her. He seemed about to say something and then thought better of it, clamping his mouth shut. He ran a shaky hand through his straight hair and finally sat down on her sofa. "I...I know what I'm talking about, Jan," he insisted in a quieter, more reasonable voice. "I am from that area. I've had…dealings…with that type of people. I just don't want to see Leslie get hurt," he said to his feet as his head had drooped.

Janice smiled knowingly when he settled down and she felt it was safe enough to come over to put a hand on his shoulder. "You care a lot, don't you?"

Wayne glanced at the far wall and frowned. "Yeah, I guess I do," he replied eventually. He then added bitterly, "But I know she doesn't return the feeling."

"Now, Wayne, you know she's fond of you. I…we all are. You have to realize there are a lot of new things going on in her life. Les is very excited right now—especially after the success of the meeting at the studio."

The private investigator turned to look at Janice. She could see anger and something else flash across his eyes. "I don't want her to be 'fond' of me. By now it should have been something a little more significant. Now all she can talk about is that blasted script she is trying to work on and that Tom Young. And whatever happened to that wonderful humanitarian Phillip Beck? She used to go on and on about him," he snapped acidly.

Janice shrugged as she tried to explain. "Phillip was never real to her. They never even met. Tom is flesh and blood now. It sounded like they spent a lot of time together when she went to L.A.—without me," she added sourly to herself. "Leslie's been pretty quiet about what happened. Even to me." She was disappointed about that, too.

Wayne scoffed at that. "No kidding. She hadn't told me anything. She used to tell me everything when we went out to dinner or I spent the evening with her. Now she doesn't have the time for us less-important ones. Sure it's exciting, but we're still her friends! If it weren't for you, I wouldn't have anywhere to go," he claimed.

"Well," Janice told him, putting a soft hand over his, "I'm always here if you want to talk or spend some time or something…."

At her words and the shifting tone of her voice, he looked at her again, but this time with different eyes. Her beautiful green eyes stared steadily at him as he appraised her. "You always have been the supportive one no matter what was going on. Ask me some day to tell you a little story about my business in Los Angeles. You might be surprised." He stood to go and briefly put a finger under her chin.

"I'm a good listener," she told him. "Any time."

He stood with his hand on the doorknob. "Yeah, you are. See ya."

Janice remained seated on the sofa long after he had gone. She had known for a long time how much Wayne cared for Leslie, but she had been taken aback by the force of his anger. Right now she thought about the look in his eyes...how they had turned soft just then when he had looked, really looked, at her as possibly something other than Leslie's best friend. Would that cause a problem with Leslie? Janice frowned as she stared at the flower arrangement on his table. Would there be any fallout with the person who had been her best friend since grade school? Yes, Leslie was fond of Wayne, but she had never seen that spark that showed something more—that same tangible *something* that she saw when Leslie was around Tom Young. *Interesting,* she concluded as she got up to make herself some lunch. Something else had intrigued her about this little visit from Wayne. She was immensely curious about his life in L.A. He had never mentioned much about it before. Perhaps now was the time for disclosures and confessions.

She smiled to herself. She had an interesting revelation of her own for Wayne.

The shrill siren on a fire truck blasting past the boutique caused Mona Green to look up from the jewelry display that she was rearranging. Only then did she notice the white limousine that had pulled up in front of the shop. It must have just arrived as no one had gotten out yet. She called one of her clerks. "Hey, Jan. Come here and look at this."

Janice peered around the corner from the back where she was working. A large shipment had just arrived and the three other women were busy checking the invoices. "Look at what?"

Mona cocked her head towards the front door. As the two

women peered at the car, they saw the driver walk around and open the back door. Janice's eyes became wide as she recognized Tom Young right before he lowered his head and quickly ducked into the boutique, hoping not to be recognized out on the street.

Intentions momentarily forgotten, Tom stopped suddenly just inside the door, amazed at the interior of the boutique. Not expected anything as posh and lovely as what he was viewing, he might have just stepped into a shop on Rodeo Drive back home in Beverly Hills. Finally spotting Janice, who was still frozen in place, he smiled and put a finger to his lips to convey the surprise he wanted to give Leslie. She mutely nodded as she walked over to say hello. Leslie and Paula continued working on the shipment unaware of the new arrival out front.

Janice shook his offered hand and introduced him to the star-struck Mona. She whispered, "Tom, it's nice to see you! I suppose this means Leslie doesn't know you're here?"

He grinned. "Righto. I wanted to surprise her. Is she here?"

Janice motioned towards the rear of the shop. "She and Paula are working on a new shipment. Do you want me to call her?"

Tom thought a minute and whispered back, "No. Send her to one of the changing rooms. I'll let her know I'm here myself!"

As he went behind one of the velvet curtains, Mona, always quick on the take, handed Janice a dress and picked up another one, calling, "Leslie? Could I have your help, please?" When Leslie came out, Mona continued with the charade, "Janice, take that dress to the back. Leslie, take this one to dressing room two. I'll go get the shoes to match."

Leslie gave a small sigh as she shook her head. She had been making headway in the back and couldn't see why she was being disturbed. There appeared to be only one customer which rarely required three clerks. *Unless it was Mrs. Penney*, she suddenly thought with a groan. It would be just like Mona to make her wait on the difficult customer.

She tapped lightly on the wall next to the dressing room. "Ma'am? Here's the blue dress," as she put her hand on the drape.

There was a small shriek when her hand was grabbed and she was forcibly pulled into the mirrored room. Before she could further react, Tom had her in his arms and was soundly kissing her hello. When recognition fell on Leslie, she quit struggling and happily returned his gesture.

Suddenly the drape was pulled back and the rest of the women in the store applauded the scene. Leslie blushed as she pulled away from Tom, embarrassed.

"Now *that's* the way to say hello!" Paula commented, nodding approvingly.

Leslie, once she became composed, handled the rest of the introductions. "What brings you here, Tom? I haven't gotten much done of the script yet," she told him.

He shrugged good-naturedly. "I was done filming for the season and didn't have any other plans. Just thought I would drop in and say hi."

"Drop by?" Mona echoed. "Three hundred miles is not a drop by! Boy, I wish my kids were home. They'd love to meet you!"

Tom glanced at Leslie's blank face. "I plan on being in town for a few days. I'll be sure to see them. I brought a few "Time Police" badges with me."

"Oh, that would be great!" Mona exclaimed. "They love your show. They've been pestering Leslie for months about you and Eddie Chase."

"I'm afraid you'll find our city a little boring after what you're used to," Leslie remarked, her mind still revolving around work on the script.

He gave her a half-grin that wasn't lost of the other women watching. "Oh, I'll find something to keep me occupied."

"Good. I sure could use your ideas on the script. I'm having trouble cutting it down," the oblivious Leslie commented.

Tom winked at Janice. "Yeah. That, too. When do you get off work?"

Leslie checked her watch. It was two in the afternoon. "In about three…."

"Minutes," Mona cut in with a grin. Sometimes Leslie could be so dense. "She was just given the afternoon off, Tom."

"Great!" he declared. "My carriage awaits," as he made a sweeping gesture towards the waiting limo.

"Oh," Leslie hesitated, not on the same page as the others yet. "Uh, my car is out back. Can I meet you at your hotel?"

Tom shook his head, clearly enjoying himself. "Don't have one. I came straight from the airport. I wanted to make a grand entrance. How about if I dismiss the driver and we'll use your car?" was the next suggestion.

As Tom went out to retrieve his bag, Leslie groaned. "What in the world am I going to do with him here for a few days? This town is boring!"

All the women looked at her as if she had lost her mind. "You've got to be joking," Mona told her. "One of the most popular actors on your favorite show travels three hundred miles to see you and you wonder what to do with him!!?"

"Boy, Les, you need to get out more often," was Paula's parting comment as she went back to work.

Janice had been happily intrigued, just silently watching back and forth as if she was at a tennis match, taking in every word and nuance.


"Okay," Tom was saying, "you have the right idea here for the dialogue, but leave out the action. That goes over here. Stage directions go there. Leave off these reactions. That's for the director to do."

Leslie let out a frustrated breath of air. "My. There's more involved than I thought. I'm glad you're here to help. Mr. Avery would have buried me if I had turned in that mess."

Tom shrugged. "That's why I came to see how you were doing. Well, one reason," he added with a sly grin.

Leslie missed the meaning of his last remark in her preoccupation with the script. She was sitting on her sofa with her feet tucked under her bottom, lap desk in place. Tom sat next to her at an angle to see what she was writing.

"Do you think I should start over?" she asked with a sigh. The paper looked like a mess to her.

"That would be a good idea unless you can remember all

the changes when you start typing. Why don't you just type it from the beginning? Why bother with writing it by hand? Wouldn't that save duplicate work?" was the same query everyone asked her.

She nodded. "It would save work," she agreed, "but I have a better feel for my work by doing it this way. Plus, if my papers fall into enemy hands, no one else could possibly read it!" she admitted with a laugh, holding out the script page as a prime example.

"Boy, that's the truth. Your letters to Phillip Beck were written a lot neater." He made the observation just so he could watch her reaction to the other actor's name.

"Letters are different," she explained and then paused, her hands falling into her lap. "Phillip. My, I haven't written him in a long time. Not since before the convention. Hmph," she thought out loud, not seemingly over-concerned about the lapse. "Oh, well, he's probably thankful for the reprieve."

Mollified now, Tom sniffed. "You never wrote me. You can't say you didn't know my address."

"I...well...I didn't want to bother you," Leslie mumbled as she nervously began to shuffle some papers.

"You still don't believe me, do you?" Tom inquired unbelievingly as he put a blocking hand over her work.

Leslie looked at his hand just to avoid his intense eyes. "I think you are being very nice," she replied in a low voice.

"We went through this before, Leslie," he said earnestly. "Why can't you believe I like you?"

"Because things like this don't happen to me," she was blunt. "I usually get hurt. I guess I'm just trying to protect myself."

Tom shook his head at her protestations. "Leslie, we are going to be working closely together on these projects until the second or third episode of yours airs. Then we feel you won't need the extra help. I'm not here because I had to be. I'm here because I want to be here. We could have used the fax machine and the phone, you know," he pointed out. "And, I want to go with you and Janice to New York to meet the publishers."

This surprised Leslie. "It would be nice to have you along," was her quiet, unexpected acceptance of his offer.

He took the lap desk from her and set it on the coffee table. "Let's go out to dinner. Just forget all this for now. Where do you recommend?"

"After Charney's all the restaurants here look like hamburger stands."

"Forget L.A. We're here and I think your city is nice. Now, let's go!"

"*Popular actor dines with local author*" read the caption of the picture that made the front page of Amherst's only newspaper. An overwhelmed Leslie and a smiling Tom were being mobbed in a local restaurant. The next day, the picture hit the wire service with a story about the joint effort on the script. And sales of Leslie's books jumped.

Her Western was becoming more popular than her first book had been. At book signings, Leslie was now being asked questions like: When will the shows would on the air, and when will her next book would be out? She was gaining recognition around town, especially so after Tom's visit.

When the trio arrived at the LaGuardia Airport in New York they were immediately mobbed by fans. The picture that made all the papers this time showed Tom's arm protectively around a wide-eyed Leslie and a smiling, waving Janice right behind them. The caption read "*Jack and Jane flee for their lives.*"

The two-day stay in New York was hectic. The publishers treated them on the first night to a wonder luncheon at the famous Tavern on the Green restaurant in Central Park. Tom then took the two women on a carriage ride through Central Park and on to Broadway to see a play. Eddie's wife Linda was thrilled to see Tom unexpectedly and to meet the two friends. Her new play had just opened, so she wouldn't be home for a while. Hungry for all the news and gossip from home, she arranged for the trio to come backstage after the play.

The next day was spent shopping on Fifth Avenue where Leslie and Janice were able to stop in briefly to say hello to one of their boutique's main suppliers. They had just three hours in a museum, and then off to another hectic scene at the airport.

Leslie didn't even realize that she was digging her nails into poor Tom's arm as they made their way to their gate.

With a collective sigh, they sunk into the wide leather seats in first class—another surprise from Tom. "Is it like that everywhere you go?" Janice asked Tom as she accepted a glass of champagne from the flight attendant.

"Like what? Oh, that. No, not always. But, thanks to the newspaper coverage, Leslie is now getting better known. I guess the combination with me in the mix will make a difference now," as he rubbed his sore arm.

"Do you ever get used to it?" Leslie wondered out loud.

"You do look a little dazed," he commented as he took her hand. "It helps to get used to the attention. But, for now, all you have to do is relax. We have five hours until we get back to California."

"And go through it all over again," Leslie murmured as they titled their seats back and got comfortable.

When the plane had leveled off and Janice had fallen asleep—as she did on every flight they had ever taken—Tom moved the armrest between his and Leslie's seat up out of the way. Gently tugging on her, he had her lean against him so they could talk quietly as they munched on the meat and cheese platter they were served.

"Do you think you'll be ready next month to face Avery and Nickles with your script?"

"If you're there, I will be. I hope they like what we've done," she sighed.

"What *you* have done," he corrected. "It's all your work, all the way. Don't forget that. And don't let them change anything you feel strongly about, either," he counseled. "It's a good storyline the way it is."

"Thanks."

"They'll also have you give your choice on the actress to portray Jane. I know they have already done the first interviews and will have you there for the selection."

Leslie groaned at this.

"What's wrong?" he asked. "That was one of your stipulations, unusual as it was," Tom reminded her with a private smile.

He could never figure out how she got Avery to agree to that.

"I know. It's just...I don't know," she broke off, looking away.

He couldn't read the expression on her face. "What? Talk to me, Les," he encouraged.

He could see her trying to figure a way not to tell him what was really bothering her. Finally, though, she took a deep breath and forged ahead. "I just can't imagine someone else playing Jane opposite you. I'm...I mean, she's my.... Oh, forget it. I'm being silly," Leslie muttered, turning red.

"Oh, I get it!" he brightened up. "You don't want somebody else doing the love scenes with me! Is that it?"

Leslie pulled away to her own seat. "No! Well, I mean.... Oh, stop."

Tom chuckled at her flustered denial. "Well, I'm happy to see I am making some progress with your after all. You're jealous!" he stated, obviously happy at the revelation.

Leslie's embarrassment faded as she got a little mad. "Oh, I shouldn't have said anything to you! You'll probably blab to Eddie and I'll never live this down!"

"No, I won't tell Eddie," he assured her as he pulled her back to his shoulder. "Besides, you know how detached we are when we're at work. There are lines to remember, marks to hit, cameras to worry about, Nickles yelling at us to put more passion into it. We don't consider what we're actually doing. Unless, of course, she is really pretty and then we flub the shot on purpose so we can retake the love scenes!"

He felt her tense up and put an arm around her to keep her from pulling away again. "I'm kidding! You know I'll be thinking of you when I'm kissing someone else."

"Hmph. That really helps," she muttered. "Remember, I can always change the script," she warned. "The Loner could become a dirty, smelly hermit living by himself in a cave."

Tom laughed at that. "Touché! Sheesh, you writers are such an over-sensitive bunch, I'll tell you. Maybe this will help your bruised feelings." He reached inside his coat's inner pocket and pulled out a light blue box with a very familiar logo on it.

Leslie's eyes got wide as she looked up at him, her heart suddenly pounding. "When did you get that?" she stalled.

"Well, you weren't with me the whole time, you remember. I have my ways. Open it," he prompted, eager to see her reaction.

Leslie's hand slightly shook as she sat up to open the elegant box. Inside was a necklace. The brilliant diamonds were alternating baguettes and marquis in a full heart design. A delicate gold chain dropped behind the back of the display.

"Oh, Tom," she whispered, stunned. "It's beautiful! But...I can't...."

"Yes, you can," he interrupted, his eyes shining, and looking very happy. "Now, maybe, you'll quit your silly protests. Put it on."

Leslie's fingers wouldn't cooperate, so Tom had to fasten the clasp. "I don't know what to say," she admitted, her eyes filling.

"How about thanks?" he kidded as he first kissed her cold hands and then moved to her warm lips.

Leslie took another week off from the boutique and frantically typed the last of her script. Monday she was supposed to fly to Los Angeles and meet with the studio again.

A persistent knock on her door brought a disgusted groan. She flung the door open to find Wayne and Janice standing on her stoop. "Want to go to dinner with us?" Janice offered, overlooking the less-than-welcoming expression on her friend's face.

"Dinner?" Leslie repeated incredulously. "It's only...." She looked back at her cuckoo clock. "Oh. How did it get to be six o'clock? I thought it was only around three."

Janice nodded. "That's what we figured. You're getting a little thin, Les. We thought you'd like some food."

"Sure, Mom," she retorted with a grin as she noticed Janice's arm was through Wayne's. "I've never had a deadline before. I guess I will be all right," as she threw a longing look at her dinette table that held her typewriter. "Let me get my coat."

"Les, you don't need a coat," Wayne told her. "It's May."

Leslie looked out her window at the flowering trees. "So it is. What happened to March?"

"You know, you've been a real barrel of fun, Leslie!" Wayne kidded as his arm moved to Janice's shoulder.

"I guess I've missed more than just the seasonal changes," Leslie observed dryly as she followed them down the stairs.

For the first time Leslie sat in the back seat of Wayne's car and it felt strange for her. She had been so wrapped up with her work that she had neglected her friends and now it appears she had lost an admirer. While she was happy for Janice, she still felt sorry for herself. Even as she fingered the diamond heart hanging from her neck, she still didn't consider Tom as a suitor or her boyfriend. She thought of him often, though, and they talked on the phone weekly, but he was so far away. Wayne had always been just one floor down. But now, as she thought back, she hadn't seen him much in three or four months. Apparently Janice had.

"You're sure quiet," Janice called back to her as they drove downtown.

"Hmm? Oh, I was just thinking."

"About Tom or Phillip?" was Wayne's comment, still tinged with a slightly bitter edge.

"Oh, among others," she relied vaguely.

As they pulled into a parking lot, Leslie looked confused. "What's this place?"

They both turned to face her, amazed. "You're kidding, right? It's been open for six months. It's the hottest spot in town. We come here all the time."

Leslie shrugged and smiled. "Oh. Maybe I should have changed clothes."

"Naw. It doesn't matter here. Come on. We have reservations. If we're late we lose them."


As Wayne and Janice said good night to Leslie at the bottom of the stairs, she walked up alone. All she could hear inside Wayne's apartment was the muffled sounds coming from his stereo. They had told her they figured she would want to get some more work done tonight and hadn't invited her in. At the sound of their laughter, she wondered what was so funny. Leslie always figured she would be included in whatever was going on and most of the gatherings used to be at her place. Now her parents called a week in advance to ask her over for dinner. She hadn't been shopping with her mom in ages. Someone had mentioned that Renee had had a baby. Was it a boy or a girl? She couldn't even remember. Mona was talking about hiring someone else part time to help out as Janice had been given some of Leslie's responsibilities. Mrs. Penney had been asking for Janice now. The high school students were also given to Janice. *Okay, those last two weren't so bad*, she grimly smiled to herself. All the students ever asked her about now was Tom Young and her books. The teachers had felt it was better for the students if someone else handled the interviews....

Leslie noticed the laughter had stopped downstairs. All she could hear now was soft muted music.

She looked at her cuckoo clock to see it was only nine-thirty. Picking up the phone, she dialed a familiar number.

"Hello, Mom? Hi, it's.... No, nothing's wrong. I just wanted to say hello. What's new?.... Yeah, I know. It's been a while. How's Dad?.... He was? When? Was it serious? Why didn't you tell me?.... I'm not that busy.... How long will his foot be in a cast? Do you need anything?.... Well, that's good.... No, Wayne won't be going to Los Angeles with me. He and Janice seem to be dating.... No, I don't know when that happened.... Well, maybe I was too busy. They seem to be happy together. We went out to dinner tonight.... I don't know. Some new place.... Yeah, that's the one.... Yes, Tom will probably meet me at the airport. He did last time. If not, I'll get a cab.... No, I'll be all right. It sounds like I'll have to get used to it for a few months or so.... Yes, it is exciting. The first episode airs in four or five months.... Well, you'd better watch it!.... I'd better let you go. I just wanted to see how you were.... Okay, you, too. Bye."

Leslie hung up the phone. Now all she could hear was the ticking of her clock. With an inaudible sigh, she sat down at her kitchen table and turned on her electric typewriter.

# CHAPTER 11

Tom Young met Leslie at the airport early Monday morning. She was dressed a soft pink suit that nicely complimented her complexion. The diamond necklace dangled in front of the embroidered white silk blouse she had chosen. In her white-knuckled grip was a new leather briefcase that Tom knew held her script. As she returned his embrace he realized she was shaking.

He stepped back surprised. "I didn't think you'd be so nervous. I thought this would be old hat to you by now. Tell me," he kidded, halfway serious, "is it because of me or Avery?"

Taking off like a racehorse at the starting gate, Leslie headed for the baggage claim area. "Of course it's Mr. Avery. This is it, Tom," she exclaimed with nervous energy when he caught up, trying to gesture with the arm he had slipped through his. "I feel like its do or die. What if they don't like my script? What if I have to rewrite it again, or they decide I can't do it and give it to their usual writers? I...I don't think I can do another rewrite," she groaned.

Tom glanced at her with a worried look on his face. "I've never seen you this upset before. Did you sleep at all last night?"

Leslie just gave him a noncommittal shrug.

"Hmph, I thought so," he muttered. "You should have taken me up on my offer. You could have come yesterday and stayed with me. You would have been more relaxed by now."

"Well, it's too late now. I really thought I was fine," she admitted, "but I just kept thinking about this meeting and getting myself more and more worked up. By the time I finally fell asleep, I had to get right back up and catch this stupid commuter flight." To try and calm herself down, she changed the subject slightly. "What did you think of the pages I faxed to you? Were they all right?"

Tom nodded. "They were excellent. That's why I don't understand your nerves now. You did a great job, Les. I'm proud of you," he told her softly.

She looked up at the change in his tone and smiled for the first time that morning. "You're such an ego-booster, Tom. Thank you," she said sincerely, and belatedly added, "And thanks for coming to get me. I do appreciate it."

He patted her arm as the luggage started crashing down the chute. "Which is yours?"

Leslie pointed out one large paisley suitcase. "You sure have a lousy memory. That's what I took to New York."

"That was months ago," he muttered as he excused himself to the other people waiting and grabbed for the bag.

"And that garment bag and the little one there," she pointed as he gave her a frown. "What? You told me to plan on a week, maybe two," she smiled as she picked up the garment bag.

"Weeks, not months," muttered Tom as he hoisted the heavy bags, wondering why he hadn't thought to hire one of those luggage carts.

"And you wanted me to move down here," she kidded as she watched him balance the load.

"That's different," he snorted. "You said no, if I remember correctly. But," he added, "the offer still stands."

**A**fter cramming all her luggage into the trunk of his classic 1969 Mercedes 280SL, Tom drove directly to the studio as their meeting began mid-morning. Leslie had become completely quiet by the time they reached the offices. As Tom escorted her through the maze of corridors to the private elevator, she had a death grip on his arm. It tightened in the quick ride to the top floor. But, inexplicably, as soon as the doors opened, she removed her arm from his, lifted her chin, and strode out of the elevator first.

Mr. Avery and Mr. Nickles were talking together by the door to Ron's offices and they smiled pleasantly as she stepped out.

"Ah, Miss Nelson. Good to see you again. I was told you were on the way up," Mr. Avery said as he offered his hand.

"Please, call me Leslie," she replied mildly as she accepted his hand and then greeted the director. "Mr. Nickles. Hello."

Tom looked on, silently amazed. She was cool, almost aloof, as if she had been doing this all her life. He chuckled to himself. He was there to give her moral support. That was funny!

"I hope you had a good flight," Richard Avery chatted as he led them all into his office.

"Oh, yes. It was a fine. A little early, but uneventful," was the steady comment as she opened her briefcase and removed the script. "I believe this is what you've been awaiting. I trust you saw my sample pages and they were satisfactory."

Richard gave her a quick look-over as he took the proffered papers. Shooting a glance at Tom, the actor was busy with something under his nails, seemingly unconcerned. The studio head was secretly impressed by her composure. She betrayed no fears, no nerves or doubts. She met his look with a slight tilt of her head as if to reinforce whatever stand she was going to take and dare him to question it.

"Uh-huh. They were well done. If the rest of your script is the same, there won't be any delays in our normal schedule."

"You see, Miss…er, Leslie," Ron explained, "usually, with their first scripts, new writers tend to put too much unnecessary, oh, dialogue, action, everything, into their work. We find we must go through and trim a lot to make it fit the one or two hour time slot."

Leslie had listened politely. "Yes, Mr. Nickles, I was aware of that problem. That's why I was careful to time the dialogue and action as I felt it should be done. Allowing for the commercials and the credits, I believe I'm within a minute or two. I also wasn't sure how the new actress's name or mine would appear and couldn't judge it correctly. So, there's a little leeway," she explained as she settled back in her chair and calmly folded her hands in her lap.

Tom rubbed a hand across his face to hide a grin that he couldn't repress. Richard and Ron were obviously taken aback. They were used to groveling and total agreement from writers who weren't on the air yet. Leslie was looking around the room as if she was deciding on how to rearrange the pictures.

Mr. Avery called for his secretary and had her run two copies of the script. While Margaret was gone, Leslie was handed twelve photos.

"Let's not waste time, Leslie," Richard said as an explanation. "These are some of the actresses who impressed us at the auditions. They read directly from your book, if you are interested. We have our own favorites, of course, whom we would choose. But we respect your desire to have your say—unorthodox as that may be," he couldn't help but add as an aside.

Leslie didn't respond as she looked at the pictures, mentally willing her hands not to shake. After the first four photos she shook her head, displeased. "They're too beautiful. That's not Jane. The book cover should have given some clue as to her less-than-glamorous appearance."

Mr. Avery folded his arms and frowned. She had already passed over his first choice. Ron was not silent. His choice was likewise passed. "Leslie, we do realize the face on the cover of your book is your own. We doubt, however, that you will find an exact clone of yourself. Unless you intend to play the part yourself, I suggest you be less critical," was his pointed remark. Tom well knew that tone of voice and was about to step in and say something to warn Leslie.

But she didn't give him that chance. She looked up slowly from the next headshot and met Ron's eyes. Her face slightly pink, she waited for a few seconds to tick by before she responded in a measured voice, "The thought did cross my mind, Mr. Nickles. But," she mildly emphasized the word, "regrettably I haven't the training. You must likewise respect the reason behind my request to help choose the right actress. I made Jane plain on purpose. The airways and your show are filled with beautiful faces of both men and women. Cindy Sanders is one of the leading beauties. There aren't enough plain ones in lead- ing roles for those of us in the world who do realize we aren't beautiful or ever will be. We can relate better when we see one of our own. Let the heroine be less than perfect. The vast ma- jority of the world is just that way—less than perfect. I believe you will find tremendous support from your viewers. I know I've heard from both men and women who have read the book who were so glad Jane was just like them," she finished, almost, but not quite, glaring at the two powerful men before her.

The men were silent after her speech. Tom grinned smugly to himself. At a look and nod from Richard, Ron silently took the photos from Leslie's hands and gave her another batch from in- side the folder at his elbow. A satisfied look came across her face as she went through them. "This is more like it," she mut- tered to herself, pleased.

She picked out the three who she thought most closely re- sembled herself and the ideal she wanted to convey and handed those to Mr. Avery.

He spread them out before him and, with Ron looking over his shoulder, referred to their audition notations. Richard pointed to the face on the left and Ron nodded. When Margaret came back in with the copies of the script, the picture was handed to her. That meeting would be at eight o'clock tomorrow morning.

Richard then gave Leslie back her script as Ron took one of the new copies. She handed hers to Tom, who had been ignored throughout the meeting so far, and took another out of her case. At the men's look, she explained, "This is the original. I always keep it myself."

Richard cleared his throat. "Uh-huh. Fine. What we'll do now is read the script and also time it ourselves. We usually make notations in red as we go and discuss it when we're through. Any problem with that, Leslie?" he queried, expecting some kind of argument from her.

She smiled placidly. "Whatever you say, Mr. Avery."

Leslie was getting sleepy by the end of the two and a half hours it took for the three men to read, time, and mark up her script.

Mr. Avery began the discussion. "All right. It is pretty good."

He glanced at Leslie, but she was mildly watching him, no outward show of pleasure at his praise. "If you will turn to page fifty, we will begin there. I'm not comfortable with Andrew's reaction to Jane. It's not in line with his character."

Leslie spoke up. "Don't you feel it was sufficiently explained by the closing act?"

"Well, yes, but the viewers won't understand at this point why...."

"They aren't supposed to," Leslie interrupted. "That's one of the wait-and-see elements I added on purpose. It's supposed to make them stick around to the end and see the hows and the whys."

"Let's skip this for now," Ron injected. "I don't like Jane's lines on page one hundred twenty. I don't feel they're true."

"How are you reading them?" Leslie asked as she looked over the scene.

Ron glared at her. "How am I reading them" he echoed sharply.

Leslie looked up as if he didn't understand what she had meant. "I mean, what are you emphasizing? What...."

"I know what the term means, Miss Nelson!" he broke in, turning red as he tried to control his temper. Mr. Avery gave him a little shake of his head. "I believe I interpreted them correctly," he said finally. "But Jane shouldn't be angry here."

"She isn't angry," Leslie explained out. "She's confused, perplexed."

"You should have indicated that," Ron pointed out.

Leslie glanced momentarily at Tom. "I was told not to."

Tom gave a self-conscious grin, spread his hands apart, and shrugged.

So it went for four hours. Avery's and Nickle's protestations were met with firm explanations and demonstrations using Tom and herself in the roles. The changes were minor and were made on all four of the scripts.

There was one last point Richard brought out. "Leslie, we had a little problem with some of the costumes you gave Jane. You were quite detailed in your books and included them in the script. Fans will want to see the same clothes exactly as the books described them."

"Would you like to see three of the outfits?" Her question surprised them all. "I brought them with me."

Tom left and came back with the garment bag. Leslie brought out the dresses she had detailed for a picnic of the beach, a formal dance, and the wedding of Jack and Jane. "They're mine," she explained, trying not to think of the wedding dress and its previous use. "You may copy them, but I keep these."

Mr. Avery smiled. "Our costume department will certainly thank you. It will save a lot of time not having to draw up those designs," and then he added in an undertone to Ron, "and not have to run them past her for continual corrections...."

A tired Leslie looked from Avery to Nickles as if to ask what was next.

Mr. Avery, likewise relieved, stood to indicate the meeting was over. "Tomorrow, Leslie, we will meet with all the actors and have our first run-through with the script and get ideas and their feedback. As a courtesy, you will be there as an invited observer, not a participant," he pointed out. "We will begin at nine and will see you then. Tom, could I see you for a minute before you leave?" It was not a request. "And close the door."

Leslie waited patiently by the elevator with her briefcase and empty garment bag in hand. It was twenty minutes before Tom came out of the office and drove her to his house on the beach.

Tom was still chuckling to himself by the time they reached his beach house. Leslie had become quiet the moment they sat in the car. Her nerves were played out, the act was over, and she was exhausted.

"Boy, you sure buffaloed Avery!" Tom exclaimed as he pulled into his garage. "Are you sure you're not an actress? Ha!.... No, let me get that. You're tired, I can see that. He told me to talk to you, by the way," as he pulled her remaining bags out of the trunk. "He said it was his show, not yours. And that Ron was the direc- tor, not you. He said for you to get your own studio if you're not going to let him run his." Tom continued laughing, looking back when he got no response. Leslie had sunk down onto the first piece of furniture she had come across. "Are you all right, Les?" he asked, putting the bags down as he went over to her. Sitting next to her on the sofa, he put an arm around her.

She was slightly shaking as if a chill had hit. She leaned her head onto his shoulder and confessed, "That has got to be the hardest thing I have ever done. It was worse than when I first came to sign the contract."

Tom chuckled in spite of her condition. "Ol' Avery still hasn't gotten over that meeting either! I'll tell you this—blustering aside, he really respects you. He'd rather have you cower like everyone else," Tom admitted, "but he still admires your spunk as he called it."

Leslie sighed as she looked out of the huge picture window towards the lapping waves of the ocean. "It was all show. You know that. Just as long as he keeps things the way I write them. That's all I'm trying to do. I figured a strong front would accomplish that goal. Maybe I overdid it."

"Nonsense," he declared. "Don't change a thing. I love seeing Avery and Nickles on the defense. They aren't in that position nearly enough. Wow, Eddie would have loved being there today. I'll be sure to fill him in tomorrow before the reading."

"What a beautiful view," Leslie murmured, nestling closer to Tom's warmth. As she gazed out the window, there were a few colorful sails far out on the water. No clouds could be seen anywhere on the horizon. A jogger and her large dog ran past the property. "How you must love it here."

Tom's jovial mood changed as he glanced at the scene she was seeing. He encircled Leslie with his other arm and rested his chin on the top of her head. They sat that way in silence for a few minutes before he spoke again. "Yes, I do love it. It's almost perfect."

"Almost?" she repeated incredulously, looking around his large, comfortable Cape Cod-style home. "What on earth is missing?"

Tom was looking just at her now. Not at the view. Not at his belongings. Just Leslie. "Just one thing. You," he told her quietly.

Not expecting that, she pulled away a little to look up at his face. She could see that he meant it. She had hoped he would have forgotten what he had said in the past, that there might be somebody else by now. Somebody who she felt was "worthy" of him.

As his face neared hers she dropped her head. "You can't mean that, Tom," she told him as her heart pounded and her throat constricted, her years of low self-esteem pushing her backwards, away from this incredible man. "You need someone...someone wonderful and beautiful and talented. Like Cindy," she offered in a choked voice. "Not me."

Disgusted, Tom dropped his arms. Leslie always replied the same way. He hadn't been able to convince her he was sincere. "Look at me," he demanded, "and tell me truthfully—do you care for me at all?"

Leslie had slowly raised her face to look into his flashing eyes. He thought she would deny it and say she really didn't care. But, instead, she answered in a level voice, "I care very, very much."

"Then why do you refuse me? Don't you feel you could come to love me?"

Leslie hadn't averted her face like she usually did. "I already do."

Tom shook his head, his own heart rapidly beating. "Then, why? Why won't you move down here and be with me?"

"I'm not the same type of person you're used to. I'm an outsider. How could I ever fit in your world?" she asked as her eyes filled with tears—tears that dissipated as fast as they formed. *I couldn't even fit into the world of someone I went through school with....*

"What? That's the most absurd thing I have ever heard. There is no such thing as an outsider! There are no types! You already fit in my world. You fit in Avery's world, too. My word, Leslie, you just set him on his ear and controlled a studio head! You're now a professional writer and in two months your name will appear on the credits of a television show. What do you think it takes to 'fit in', as you insist?"

She got up from the couch and nervously went to the win-

dow. "What I did today was all show and you know it! That was-
n't me. I was doing what I felt I had to do. I'm not like that."

"Leslie, I became interested in you long before you ever met
Avery." Tom came up behind her and put his hands on her shoulders. "You impressed me at the convention, and even more as
we enjoyed dinner together afterwards, and you *still* impress me."
His arms went around her waist and she leaned back into him.
He gave a sigh and a disparaging laugh. "I never thought I'd
have to argue with someone to convince her how much I love
her. Listen, Leslie. You'll be here at least a week. Think about
what I said. I'm not going to give up yet," he told her, moving
away and taking her bags into the extra bedroom.

Still silent, still looking out of the window, a lone tear fell down
Leslie's cheek. Tom would never know how her self-imposed
exile was breaking her heart.


The second day was another full and exciting day for Leslie.
All of the people involved with the show, including Tina Rowan
who would play Jane, met for a round-table discussion and reading of the new script. Tina did a wonderful Scottish brogue and
seemed to fit right in with the regulars.

Tina was two inches taller than Leslie and had slightly more
prominent cheekbones than Leslie's fuller face. She, too, had
short brown hair and blue eyes and a cheerful smile that revealed
her warm personality.

The script reading took nearly four hours as there was much
discussion, laughter and clowning around, plus a few more
changes from the regular stars. Leslie was quiet through most of
this session other than answering questions about the characters or demonstrating what she meant to convey. She enjoyed
this time and could tell her script was getting everyone's approval.

After the changes received the final approval, the script was
read again and timed. Leslie was surprised at the complete difference in attitude. The actors became the professionals they
were and there was no joking.

At one point, Leslie leaned back, closed her eyes and
smiled. It was coming true for her. The familiar voices of the ac-

tors reading her lines! She could picture them in costume and on the set just as she had done when she first wrote the words she was hearing. It was a special moment for her. The only dark spot was hearing Tina's voice. Leslie had always injected her own voice in Jane's role and it was a little bit of a let-down for her. Somehow, some way, she had always wanted to do the part herself. Now realizing she must let go of that unreasonable fantasy, it was a poignant moment for her.

Right then and there, her eyes still closed as she listened, Leslie came to a decision. After the first dress rehearsal she would go home to Amherst. She wasn't needed here. She was only being mollified because of the special concessions in her contract. They were following her script and her wishes. The show would be done as she intended. There was no reason to stay longer.

If she did capitulate and stay longer, she felt she would give in to Tom. As much as she had come to love him, she still felt, deep down, that he would be better off without her. It had been mentally beaten into her. She couldn't convince herself that someone as special and wonderful as Tom could be happy with her. Perhaps with time and distance away from her he would realize that, too.

Looking across the table as the reading continued, Leslie received a pang in her heart as she looked at Tom who was busy with his lines. In just a few days she would never see him face to face again. She would see him on the television and she would see his face as she continued her writing. But she would never feel his arms around her or the touch of his lips on hers. She fought down the lump in her throat and concentrated on the reading.

Friday night a stunned Tom Young answered his doorbell. Phillip Beck stood on the porch holding a bouquet of flowers and a bottle of wine. Phillip was silently gestured to enter and the door clicked shut behind him.

Phillip glanced around as he followed the silent Tom into the living room. He seemed to be alone.

Taking the offered chair, Phillip set the neglected wine and flowers on the floor next to him. He was puzzled by Tom's face. He didn't quite know how to read it. He cleared his throat to begin speaking as Tom was now gazing out of the window at the darkness outside. "I...uh...heard the filming had started for the new season," he ventured. "Which storyline are you using?"

Tom turned at the query and looked confused. "I thought you knew. We are using Leslie's first novel. We had the first dress rehearsal today."

Phillip smiled broadly at the news. "Good! So Richard saw the value of the idea, did he? Great! I was hoping he would. Did Bunny get what she wanted?" Phillip's smile faded as Tom stared at him. He didn't know if he would get answered or not.

"Oh, the integrity of her books was what Leslie insisted on all the way. That seemed to be all she cared about," was the bitter reply.

Phillip became uncomfortable. "Well, I am sure that pleased her. Is she still in town? Where is she staying? I wanted to congratulate Bun...Leslie on her success. I look forward to working with her on WESTWARD REX."

Tom gave a dry laugh. "Well, old man, I'm afraid you will be disappointed. Bunny won't be back to work on her episodes. She made that announcement today."

"Really?" Phillip was quite surprised. "That was one of her unusual stipulations, as I understood from the papers."

"Really." Tom continued in a mocking tone, "She said she felt satisfied in the way her work was handled and there was no need for her to hang around and be in everyone's way. Nickles, of course, was delighted to hear her little announcement. Whenever there was a question in dialogue, Leslie was asked, not Ron."

Phillip smiled at that. He could picture the look on Ron's face when that happened. But he knew there was more involved here. Tom seemed too upset to fit the mentioned circumstances. Phillip had already swallowed his own disappointment at missing Bunny again, and now his curiosity was aroused.

He didn't have to ask as Tom suddenly sprang from his chair and started pacing the floor. "I don't understand it, Phil," he started.  "What did I do wrong?  What did she expect from me?"

Having no idea what he was talking about, Phillip prodded, "What happened, Thomas?"

"What happened?  Nothing!  I pour out my heart and offer all I have and nothing happened!  I finally meet someone with th e very thing I was searching for.  I can't even describe what it is, but Les has it.  And I know she felt the same.  I know she did," he exclaimed, flinging his arms as he continued pacing.  "After the night we spent together in the Silicon Valley and the trip to New York and the time here together—Zip!  Nada.  She walked out on me."

Phillip felt himself bothered by these personal references of Tom's, but put that feeling aside for now.  This was too interesting.  "She must have given you some explanation, Thomas.  From what I know she wouldn't be the type to leave without a word."

"Oh, she talked.  Plenty.  Some crap about her not being good enough and some time apart would do us both good.  She said I would realize she was right.  I'm not to contact her.  Can you believe that?" Tom raved, shaking his head at the memory.  "I can't call or write or go see her.  Dang it, Phil.  I asked her to marry me, not gun down the eastern seaboard!"  Spent, Tom threw himself onto the sofa and glared at his friend and co-worker who had simply come to visit.

Phillip was at a loss.  He was going through conflicting emotions of his own.  He still considered Bunny *his* special fan, and this revelation from Tom was now bothering him a little.  Secretly he was pleased at Bunny's response, but he was still sorry for Tom.  He, too, well knew the pang of lost love.  He also failed to see what he could say to help.  These things usually took time.  He tried, "Well, maybe things will work out.  She probably had a lot on her mind this week and couldn't deal with it all.  Give yourself some time, Thomas.  I've found that helps."  He looked away sadly before he continued.  "After a while you get used to the hole in your heart and it doesn't bother you so much any more.  It might not go away, but it's not so sharp," he finished with a quiet voice.

Tom looked over at Phillip again, his anger dissipating.  He had forgotten in his own problems that Phillip had many of his own. He too had read about Sarah's pregnancy and now remembered that she—and his son—would be gone for a long time to come, if not forever. "Hey, Phillip," he sighed, "I'm sorry. I go on and on and forget to play host. Can I get you a drink or something?" he offered with an apologetic smile.

Phillip reached down for the wine and showed him the bottle. "Not really. I'm not in a celebrating mood either. You can save this for another time."

As Phillip stood to leave, Tom arose from the couch and grinned. "Nothing like coming over here for a relaxing evening, huh, Phil?" he kidded. He then remembered some news for the other actor, not remembering that Phillip had just mentioned it himself. "Oh, we will be doing your Western in about another month or so. Les will be doing that script next. Did you see the book?" he asked with a flash of pride overshadowing the hurt in his eyes.

Phillip nodded. "I went out and bought it when she didn't send one. I compared it with that small manuscript she sent before. It's very good. It'll make a good episode."

"Wait'll you see this one. I don't think Leslie ever realized what she had done. She certainly didn't believe me," Tom quietly remarked.

"I'll probably see you next on the set, then. I'm finishing up a movie next week. Take care, Thomas."

"Thanks for coming," as the door closed and Phillip was once again on the doorstep thwarted in his efforts to meet Bunny.


"*D*ear Leslie,

*I wanted to congratulate you on your success both with your novels and with the television series. Not many authors have made a name for themselves so quickly. I have been told by a few others how fine a job you did with your first script. I look forward to seeing the finished show and also appearing in the Western next month.*

*I bought a copy of the second book and have already read it. You did a good job expanding the short version I had seen before. I liked the extra interactions between Rex and Jane. It* gives another dimension to the character of the Professor that will be an asset to the show.

I realize you must be overwhelmed at this time with your next script. I just finished another movie myself. It was a wonderful costume drama set during the Revolutionary War. But I still wanted to take a couple of minutes to say hello and congratulations. Have you submitted CHAETAU REX for publication yet? I am eager to read that episode as well.

I wish you continued success and if you need any help, just let me know.

Sincerely,
Phillip Beck"


"Hello, Phillip,

It was nice to hear from you again. I'm glad you are well.

The script is coming along fine and the third novel will be out in about four months.

Thanks for writing,
Leslie Nelson"

# CHAPTER 12

At seven-thirty Friday night, guests began arriving at Le Petite Boutique. The shop was actually closed, but the ornate lights still burned. Janice and Wayne, Mona and her family, Leslie, Leslie's parents Lou and Bonnie, and a photographer from the local newspaper were gathered inside to see THE LONER FINDS LOVE on this week's two-hour season opener of "The Time Police."

A big screen television had been rented for the occasion and champagne was passed around in crystal flutes for the guests. All were in a festive mood for this was exciting. One of their own would get her name on the opening credits of the popular show!

Everyone was excited and talking all at once. All except for one person present—the one person who should have been most excited and proud of the moment—Leslie. Oh, she looked happy and smiling as they all fluttered around her and watched the clock for the magical hour of eight. But, inside, Leslie was aching. She would rather have been alone in her small apartment where she could watch Tom Young in privacy. She was already emotional about seeing him. She also knew how she would feel seeing him with Tina doing the lines she had always, somehow, meant for herself. Her own video cassette recorder was programmed and she would have another day to cry in private.

And mourn she would. Tom had kept his reluctantly given promise to keep away and it was really hurting her—even though she had set it all in motion. Her own feelings for Tom hadn't diminished in all the months that had passed. How could they? She saw him in every word she typed and pictured him in every action she wrote. The face that she put on Jane in her imagination was still hers. Tonight she must again accept the inevitable—that Tina Rowan would become Jane. And she was supposed to be happy and excited about it.

The photographer snapped a few group pictures and then one of Leslie holding up the script he had asked her to bring. He hurried out so he could get home to watch the show himself. Leslie wished she could do the same.

She smiled as she looked at her parents, though. They still didn't enjoy the television series, but they had supportively read every word of her novels and were so proud of her they could burst. Leslie knew they had supplied all of their relatives with copies of her books, as well. Her parents now eagerly awaited eight o'clock with the rest of the group. Their personal feelings about the show were pushed aside. This was Leslie's night.

Leslie had never told them about Tom. Oh, they knew she had met him and that he had helped Janice and her get safely to New York and back alive. But they didn't know about the deep attachment their daughter had developed for the actor and they certainly didn't know about his proposal. No one did, not even her best friend Janice. Leslie clutched the diamond necklace hanging around her neck until the sparkling heart left a deep impression on the palm of her hand.

At the end of October and then again at the end of December, the scene at the boutique was repeated. Leslie's two other episodes aired. CHATEAU REX aired a month before the book was released to an enthusiastic public. She again submitted herself to the pain of watching, but it didn't seem quite so deep this last time.

She had to begrudgingly admit that the shows were just as she would have done them, even though she would rather have been there herself. Phillip Beck came across just as she had pictured him playing her Professor and she wrote him a brief note telling him so.

Now immersed in her fourth novel, she again had time for something new. All the scripts were done, and she was free to start being creative again. She titled this one ANDREW'S RE-VENGE and would end the animosity between Andrew and Jane that bothered the vocal majority of the fans of her previous books.

There were letters coming in now from readers of the books. Most were complimentary. Some were critical. She had attempted, at first with Janice's help, to answer all she could. Now that the shows aired on television, there was so much mail that she hadn't the time and hoped her new book would satisfy a lot of the questions she received.

By the end of February Leslie was ready to begin typing. A letter from her agent in New York caught her eye in the stack of mail on her desk. She figured he was going to tell her to get busy as she was a month behind schedule. She wasn't prepared for what she read.

*"Dear Leslie,*

*I won't beat around the bush. You have been selected as a candidate for the 'New Writer of the Year' category by the Public Opinion Award Committee. The ceremony and awards presentation of which you will be a part will be held on April twelfth in Los Angeles. I'm sure you are aware of the show. On the thirteenth the actors, shows, directors and producers receive their televised awards. I'm at liberty to tell you that your first episode and both Tom Young as leading actor and Phillip Beck as guest actor are up for awards.*

*Well done, Leslie! You will, of course, attend the presentations on the twelfth. Highlights from the night will be announced during the next night's broadcast.*

*May you receive the award you deserve!*
*Sincerely,*
*Wallace Quimby"*

Leslie spent the next two hours on the phone, much like she did so long ago after she had received Phillip Beck's phone message. Anne was thrilled. Janice was more pragmatic. "What are you going to wear?" was the question Janice most wanted to know.

"I don't know. I sure don't have anything appropriate. Maybe Mona will help me pick something."

"What about that black evening dress you put into your first book," Janice suddenly remembered.

Leslie closed her eyes and was glad she was just talking on the phone. "I can't. Tina wore it on that episode."

"But you've never wore it!" Janice argued. "I remember when we found it at the mall and you were just waiting for an opportunity to wear it."

"I know," was the quiet response, "and I never will wear it."

Janice was too excited to notice the change in Leslie's tone of voice. "Well, Mona will help, I'm sure. I want to be there when you try the dresses on. Who are you taking? No one goes to those things alone."

That stopped Leslie. Her mouth fell open into an O. "I...I don't know. There isn't anyone to take," she thought out loud, her heart sinking as she realized how true was the statement.

"Maybe Tom will take you."

Leslie flinched. "I don't think that's going to happen," she said slowly. "The papers say he is dating Tina."

"Oh, you can't believe everything you read," Janice replied brightly. "They also said you made a deal with the devil to get on the air," she laughed.

"Not those papers!" Leslie exclaimed, laughing in spite of herself. "Real papers. And...I believe it's true. They've been working together for months now. I'll think of someone. It's more than a month away."

Janice giggled. "I'd offer Wayne, but he refuses to wear a tux. We've been going round and round about that with the wedding plans!"

Leslie hadn't even known they were engaged. "I'm sure he'll come around," was her quiet comment. "I have to go, Jan. I have a few more calls to make and some typing to get done."

"Okay. Let me know. Bye."

Leslie slowly set down the phone. She hadn't even thought about having to be escorted. She then realized how busy she had made herself and how little she got out any more. As pleased as she was with the nomination, she wished she didn't have to go to Los Angeles for the ceremony. At least she wouldn't be there for the actors' awards. That was a small compensation for her.

An insistent knocking on her door interrupted Leslie's typing. She was nearing completion and wanted to be able to mail it off to New York before the award ceremony next week. After she got back from Los Angeles she would begin the script. Her mind still whirling through all she wanted to get done, she momentarily forgot whoever it was outside her door.

The knocking turned to pounding. Jamming the off button on her typewriter and angrily shoving her chair back, she stormed to the door. Her friends knew better than to disturb her now. She flung open the door and her storm-cloud expression instantly changed to one of shock and surprise.

"I guess you weren't expecting me," Eddie Chase joked as he took a step back from the door at the dark look on her face. When the look passed and changed into shock, he invited himself in. "Come in, Eddie. Oh, I'd love to. Thank you. How are you, Eddie? I'm great. How are you?" he continued with his monologue as he sat on her sofa and looked around. "So this is what Tom told me all about. Cute," he proclaimed and grinned broadly at her.

Leslie, silent through all of this, finally remembered to close the door. "This is a surprise, Eddie. Umm, how are you and...and everyone?"

"And...and everyone is fine, too," he replied looking steadily at her. "And...and everyone misses you a lot."

Leslie wasn't prepared for that. She nervously looked around, wishing she—or Eddie—was somewhere else and not having that conversation. "Can I get you something? Coffee? A sandwich? A taxi back to the airport?"

Eddie ignored her sarcasm and patted the cushion next to him. "No, I'm fine. Sit down, Leslie. Relax. I just wanted to talk to you."

Leslie reluctantly complied and bit back her retort that he could have used the phone. She gave him a small smile that did nothing to mask the hurt in her eyes. "It is good to see you. I've missed all of you," she admitted and then indicated her television set with a tilt of her chin. "I watch every week. The season went really well."

"We hoped to have another of your scripts to finish off the season."

Leslie frowned at that. "I don't understand why they used all three scripts so fast. I intended on them being strung out more."

"And most writers complain we don't use enough of their work," Eddie laughed, and then explained, "What you suggested would have been the normal procedure, but they wanted to get you established before the end of the year."

"Whatever for? What difference did that make?"

"Because of the award show. It is a big deal both for you and for the studio. You see, Leslie, everyone but you realized how good your work is. We all knew what the public reaction would be. Oh, by the way," he added, leaning over to kiss her cheek, "congratulations on the nomination. We're all proud of you."

She grinned and blushed. "Thanks. I won't win, of course, but it is still pretty exciting. For…for Tom and Phillip, too. You'll get yours next time," she added with a sly smile.

"What do you mean?"

She then indicated her kitchen table cluttered with papers. "That story is for you. Well, for Andrew, I should say. It answers the animosity questions between Andrew and Jane and also who the father of Jane's baby is—Jack or Rex."

Eddie looked impressed. "Sounds good. When does it go in?"

"To New York, next week. Then I'll start the script if Mr. Avery gives me the go-ahead. It will need a two-hour time slot, though."

He shrugged. "No problem. It's in your contract that Avery will do anything you say! Which tickles us to no end, by the way."

When he paused, Leslie looked at him expectantly. There had to be more of a reason than this for him to come all that way to see her.

He read her look. "So, I can see you are wondering why I'm really here. Isn't it enough that I miss your smiling face?"

Leslie laughed. "Yeah, right. Cut to the chase, Chase."

"Oh, clever. Can I use that?"

"You will anyway," she answered dryly.

"True," he admitted good-naturedly. "All right. Here's the deal. I'm here because of Tom.... Now, don't look like that! Hear me out. I'm serious. You really hurt him when you left like you did. He thought you would stay indefinitely."

"I never said I would," was her quiet, almost imperceptible response.

"I know. But we all thought you would. He just hasn't been the same, Les."

A jealous streak emerged that surprised Leslie when she found herself demanding, "Is that why he's dating Tina?"

Eddie noticed the edge to her question. "What did you expect? She looks just like you. She reads your lines on the show. Half the time she's called Leslie—which, by the way, *really* irritates her. Even Tom slips a lot. She slapped him one time when he did it.... Ah, I see that pleases you. So, you do care," he declared triumphantly.

Leslie looked away and let all that information sink in. So Tom calls Tina by her name. Her eyes smiled even though she wouldn't allow her lips to do the same. "Yeah, I care, Eddie. Are you happy now? But he sure took up with her awfully fast for being so broken up over me!" she pointed out, disgusted.

He looked at her closely again. "Ah, now you're jealous. Good.... Well, what did you think he would do? You vanish suddenly and leave your twin sister. You told him never to contact you. You don't understand men very well, do you?"

"I guess not," she answered shortly, turning red. "Thanks for pointing it out."

"Any time," he shot back at her. "That's not all I wanted to tell you. Who will be your escort next week?"

He was surprised when her expression turned humorous. "Oh, you'll love this. Mr. Avery," she announced with a grin. "He'll be there anyway for the costume and set design nominations."

"Ask Tom," Eddie suggested softly.

Leslie looked down. "I can't, Eddie. I'm only going to be there on the twelfth. If I see him again...." She left rest unsaid and shook her head.

"Listen," he sighed at her stubbornness. "There's going to be a big party after the ceremony no matter who wins. You deserve to be there. It was your scripts that got Phillip his nomination. You know that. We all want you there."

"It would be awkward with Tina," Leslie pointed out. "I'm just a writer, Eddie. She's one of the stars of the show now. She should be there with Tom. Not me."

Eddie glanced at his watch. He could tell he was getting nowhere with her. "I have to catch the next flight," he explained as he stood. "Will you at least think about it?"

She met his eyes. "Think about it?" she repeated with a catch in her voice she couldn't stop in time. "I live with this every day. I dread being even near L.A. because of the memories. It had gotten a little easier, Eddie. Now you've brought it out full force again," she told him frankly.

"Good. You belong with us, Leslie. We want you back," he said putting his hands on her arms. "Now, give me a hug and a kiss and promise me you'll seriously reconsider."

She gave him the hug and the kiss and a shrug.

"I'll see you on the twelfth," he told her as he waved and shut the door behind him.

"Thanks for stopping in," she muttered to the closed door and walked slowly back to the kitchen table to resume typing. Her finger was poised over the on/off switch, but her mind was far away in a beachfront house.


Leslie's parents, her ex-co-workers at the boutique, some local fans, and the photographer from the paper were on hand at the airport to see Leslie off. Everyone was confident she would win even though she was not so confident. Her black evening dress from Mona was carefully packed. It had a well-fitting bodice with full sleeves that narrowed down to the buttoned wrists. The waist was outlined by rows of black sequins and the skirt was full and would trail behind her as she walked. Tom's necklace would adorn her bare neck and she borrowed a pair of diamond studs for her ears.

After all the hugs and kisses and pictures, Leslie boarded the commuter jet and settled back for the one hour flight, her mouth dry, her palms damp, and her heart pounding. Her outfit in the box was held tightly on her lap.

She saw no one familiar at the terminal as she came down the ramp. She began to get panicky as the studio had said she was supposed to be met. Nervously glancing from face to face as she walked, a waving chauffeur caught her attention, holding up a sign that read Nelson. She sighed in relief when she saw him.

"Miss Nelson?" he asked pleasantly as he took her box. "I'm sorry I'm a little late. Traffic, you know. Mr. Avery is in the car. Please follow me."

He led her to the loading zone where a black stretch limo waited at the curb. The door was opened to reveal Richard Avery and Eddie Chase on the seat next to him, both men dressed in tuxedos. A passerby spotted Eddie, gave a short shriek and managed to wave before the door was closed.

"Surprise! Told you I would see you on the twelfth!" Eddie explained, all pleased with himself. "I couldn't let you go with Avery here. It just wasn't right. So I made the ultimate sacrifice."

"You draw the short straw?"

"No, lost best out of three in Rock, Paper, Scissors."

"Well, as long as you tried so hard," she kidded back, "how can I resist?" She looked around the car. "I do hope I'll have someplace to change other than in here."

"Oh, sure," Eddie piped up. "We'll stop at some gas station for you."

"Oh, goodie," was her flat reply.

Mr. Avery just shook his head and looked out the window. "Kids," he muttered. "I've arranged for a dressing room for you backstage since you had to fly in. We'll go straight to the Pavilion. The awards begin in two hours. After the ceremony, which will last forever, will be a dinner and then a photo session with the press. You will be back at the airport in time for your eleven o'-

clock flight."

"Unless you decide to stay," Eddie injected hopefully.

Richard looked puzzled by this comment but asked Leslie instead, "Do you have a speech memorized? I'd like to hear it before we get there."

"Speech?" Leslie echoed, her eyebrows going up. "Whatever for? I'm not going to win. Why do I need a speech?"

Mr. Avery rolled his eyes and rubbed a hand over his face. Eddie pursed his lips and looked out the window. Speaking very slowly, Mr. Avery said, "And what if you do win? You must be prepared, Miss Nelson."

A headache started throbbing behind her left eye. "Oh, I'll think of something if the impossible happens."

"It usually does, Les. It usually does," Eddie cryptically commented in an undertone.

She heard him and narrowed her eyes. "What do you know? What have you done?"

He was all innocence. "Nothing!"


There was no red carpet, no bleachers full of waving fans, no hosts from the news stations, no lines of photographers for that day's awards. The nominees quietly wandered in and were shown to their elaborately decorated tables.

Leslie emerged from her dressing room and was greeted by smiles from her two escorts.

"Very nice, Leslie," Mr. Avery commented. "Very tasteful."

"Eddie?" she asked as she turned a full circle.

"Ah, you're too short," was his remark.

She gave a laugh. "What?"

"Good," he nodded. "Keep *that* smile on your face, not the fake one we usually see."

Leslie took his offered arm and they emerged into the Ballroom. Leslie looked around and was confused. "This looks so different than the room they usually use. It's so...plain."

Mr. Avery explained, "The set you are used to seeing for the televised awards is in another room. This is the one they use for the technical awards. If we have time afterwards, I'll show you the other. We have to be seated now."

They were joined at their table by the costume designer and the set designer of the show whom Leslie had met them before. The show was up for a total of four awards that night, including Special Effects.

The lights dimmed and the ceremony began. It was handled in the same way as the more popular televised version. Well-known presenters would name the candidates and, in a lot of cases, clips from the shows were included on huge screens to the right of the stage.

Leslie looked at her program. Her category was about halfway into the evening. The others in their group were spread out somewhat evenly throughout the event.

Their first loss was Special Effects. Their first win was Set Design. Mr. Avery and the designer made their way onstage amid polite applause and made two short, appreciative speeches.

They came back to the table with the gold and crystal statue, grinning broadly. They both looked cool and calm. Leslie was a bundle of nerves.

Thirty minutes later the presenter, a late-night talk show host, read the names for the New Author of the Year division. Leslie's name was second of the five. A montage of each author's works was shown after the name was announced. Leslie had a tight grip on Eddie's arm as she stared at the stage. The men exchanged a worried glance. She was as pale as a ghost and didn't seem to be breathing.

"And the award for New Author of the Year goes to…Leslie Nelson! This is her first nomination and the first award for Miss Nelson."

The screens again flashed scenes from "The Time Police," yet Leslie didn't move. Richard and Eddie were about to nudge her when she suddenly stood from her chair and smiled warmly at the applause. The men looked puzzled but joined in the clapping.

Leslie walked steadily to the stairs of the platform and gracefully raised the hem of her dress to keep it out of the way of her heels. She received a hug from the presenter and was handed her statue which, had she noticed, had her name engraved on the front gold plate. The screens continued to show scenes from the series. When the clapping stopped, Leslie looked over the room.

"I was asked today," she began in a clear, smooth voice, "by Mr. Avery if I had prepared a speech. I hadn't because I am familiar with the competition and didn't figure I would win. But I would be a poor writer if I was to become speechless."

There was a small ripple of laughter that went through the audience.

Leslie smiled and continued. "So, I will be brief and thank those who have helped and encouraged me back home in Amherst and those wonderful people at Majestic who believed in my work and gave flesh and blood to the characters and ideas I put on paper. I share this award with all of you. Of course, I'm keeping it, but you can come by and see it any time. Thank you!"

She bowed her head briefly in a nod of thanks as more laughter and applause was heard, and she was escorted down the stairs by the talk-show host. Smiling, she returned to her table and was kissed and hugged by all her co-workers before she was allowed to sit.

"Very nice, my dear," Mr. Avery leaned over to take her hand. He was surprised to find it was cold and clammy and that she was shaking as she smiled back.

Eddie leaned over and whispered, "Now you can breathe, Les. Tom will be proud of you."

She averted her wide eyes from his as the next winner was announced.

Those were the only awards they won that night. Leslie could now relax and enjoy her dinner. Eddie knew she had tensed up again as he led her to the press conference. But, he also knew she would surprise him and come through as well as she always seemed to do.

There were numerous pictures being taken of the groups and of the individuals of each show represented. "The Time Police" group received their turn and Leslie faced her first camera interview. Fortunately, because of the number of awards and the shortage of time, the interview was general and brief. By ten o'-clock Leslie was on her way back to the airport.

At midnight the same group that had seen her off greeted

her with one question: "Well, what happened?"

When she opened the black box and held up the gold and crystal statue, her friends went crazy and showered her with champagne.

At two in the morning Leslie was back in her apartment alone, wearing her new black dress, staring at her first award, and mentally going over the entire day's events.

# CHAPTER 13

Long lines of cheering, waving fans greeted the elegantly dressed arrivals as they made their way up the red carpet to the gilded entrance of the Pavillion's Regal Ballroom. Overhead, the crystal chandeliers twinkled with hundreds of lights and prisms and played off of the sequins and beads and gemstones below. Tuxedoed waiters walked amongst the stars and offered drinks and hors d' oeuvres from silver platters.

Friends and co-workers, directors and producers, actors and dates all mingled in the spacious lobby before being escorted to their seats for the evening.

Phillip and Eddie arrived at the same time and went over to Tom and Tina, and Cindy and her escort. Eddie faintly shook his head at the question in Tom's eyes and then brightly asked, "Did you hear the news? Leslie won last night. You should have seen her in a black gown that swept along behind her! She looked great."

All were pleased by the announcement. Tina had glanced up sharply at Tom, but he had only a mild smile of his face. She couldn't see the flash in his eyes as he turned to Maxwell who had just arrived. She readjusted her arm as it rested in his and set her mouth in a determined smile.

Richard Avery and Ron Nickles joined the group and were introduced to Maxwell's date and to Cindy's. "We took two last night," Richard announced. "Let's do that again tonight!"

They all agreed and turned to enter the main auditorium. Phillip touched Eddie's arm and slowed his pace. Eddie did likewise.

"Tell me about Bunny," Phillip requested in a voice only Eddie could hear. "Was she nervous? How did she do?"

Eddie smiled to himself. Phillip still couldn't remember to call her by her real name. "She was so nervous that she forgot to breathe. She just sat there when her name was announced. We thought Richard would have to take over. Then, she rose like the phoenix, glided up to the stage, and winged a wonderful little speech. I was really proud of her. She, again, shocked Avery! He thought she was going to faint on him."

Phillip didn't reply in any way. He just smiled and nodded to Eddie as he followed the others to the row of seats designated for "The Time Police."


Phillip took the first award for the series that night in the Best Supporting Actor category. It was his first award ever. His broad smile enhanced his handsome face as he made a brief acceptance speech. The cameraman caught a glimpse of something shiny and zoomed in on a small bunny attached to the lapel of his tuxedo. The pin, however, was removed by the time he retook his chair in the audience.

He was pleased with his speech. He had thanked the ones who had voted for him and his co-workers. His special gratitude was for the writers of the show who gave his character so many dimensions, even love, he had added.

The show itself won the award for the most popular series. The two screens from the previous night's ceremony had been brought in and now clips from the series' four seasons ran. When Phillip had won, they played clips of the Professor in his love scenes with Jane. The clip that played now featured Jack, Sir Charles, Jane and Andrew. The group was deep in discussion:

Jane: Why can't you just go back in time and repeat the process that damaged the Professor? Then you could fix whatever went wrong.

Andrew (disgusted): Haven't you learned anything yet? Be-

*cause the same thing would happen again!*

*Jack: You see, Jane, history has already been made. Unless we knew exactly what went wrong with Rex, we can do nothing.*

*Jane: What if someone else went through the portal under the same circumstances? Then you could record and examine what happened.*

*Sir Charles: No! The risk is too great! I won't endanger any of my squad in that needless way!*

*Jack (thinking): Hmm. It is possible, Sir Charles. Under controlled circumstances we could benefit greatly by doing just that.*

*Andrew: Well, I'm not going to risk frying my brain on one of her hairball ideas! That's not the type of duty I signed up for. None of us did.*

*Sir Charles: You're correct, Andrew. We'll have to keep working on another way to help Rex.*

*Jane: I'll go. There's no other way. The Professor will just continue to hurt and destroy…. I'm expendable. None of you are.*

*Jack: No! I won't have it! You may consider yourself expendable, but I don't!*

The screen faded to black and the other four nominees were named and their clips were shown. Polite applause again followed each clip.

The presenter was obviously pleased as she read the winner. "And the award for Best Actor in a Dramatic Series…Tom Young!"

Tom made his way onstage amid clapping and wolf whistles from his friends. It took a while for the noise to abate.

He looked over the audience only to see Eddie smiling at him and thumbing his nose. Tom shook his head and began his speech with a grin. "This award means a lot to me because it is the Public Opinion Award. I'm privileged to be part of a wonderful cast of actors and writers. Without all their efforts there would be no 'Time Police' and no reason for me to be dressed like a penguin," as he tugged at his tight collar and the audience chuck-

led. "Thanks go to my friends and co-workers, to our fine director Ron Nickles (he paid me to say that) and to my girlfriend
L...uh, Tina who is a wonderful addition to the show." He coughed
and flushed at his slip. Tina's smile was frozen on her pleasant
face as the camera in the audience panned their row of faces
and stopped on hers. "So," Tom was finishing onstage, "thanks
again and be prepared for our best season ever!"

Tom was escorted to the stairs as the emcee returned to the
stage and concluded the evening. Tom bent to give Tina a kiss
and she offered her cheek, her smile still frozen. The smile faded
as the red light of the camera aimed at them went out and people began gathering their wraps.

The group headed backstage for the interviews and photographs that would air on the next day's news and entertainment
shows.

Phillip happily found himself surrounded for pictures and interviews. After watching Sarah do this for years he was enjoying
himself. The golden bunny pin reappeared briefly for the on-cam-
era interview.

Tina attached herself to Eddie's arm as Tom held his interview and didn't relinquish the arm when Tom had finished. Eddie
grinned gamely as he led her over to congratulate Phillip. When
she complained loudly of a splitting headache, Tom offered to
see her home. She thanked him but asked Ron for the favor.
Tina was smart enough to know she wouldn't see Tom again on
a social level, and she was professional enough to know she
wouldn't leave the show especially after the awards they won that
night. Hers and Tom's relationship instantly turned into a working relationship. Another thing she knew was that Tom wouldn't
follow her home. She had been called Leslie for the last time.


The fan mail that now came to Majestic Studio doubled in
volume after the award show aired. It had been steadily increas-
ing since the new season began in September, but now the accolades really arrived.

The most notable increase was the mail addressed to Phillip
Beck. Ever since the third show, CHATEAU REX, he was now

thought of as a romantic lead. This both surprised and tickled the actor. After sixteen years and countless appearances, he was being described as a sexy leading man.

His agent Bill recognized what had happened and was quickly arranging for scripts with renewed zeal. Within a month of the award, Zenith sent three scripts. North Star sent two. This time Phillip was wanted for the lead.

Public opinion was a strong force. If the public accepted Phillip as the lead, they would have him as the lead.

By May, Phillip was again overwhelmed with scripts, but he didn't mind. These were the ones he had been awaiting all those lost years.

He now found himself traveling to exotic locales for filming, and took the time to redecorate his mansion to resemble an English manor he had just visited that autumn. All of Sarah's white furniture was donated to charity, and all her clothes were packed into a rented storage shed and locked with one key. Davey's room was left as it was and the door shut and locked. He contacted his lawyer and sent him to Ireland where his wife Sarah was handed the divorce papers, a settlement for the house, a letter and documents for Davey in which she was demanded to deliver in due time, and a key and the bill for the storage locker. If she set foot in his house, she would be forcibly removed from the property. Appearances on "The Time Police" were limited to two a season and he agreed to one fan convention every other year. His face became a regular in celebrity magazines, and late night talk shows were now plugging his movies. More time was given to charities and the bookcase in his study began to be filled with more awards and commendations.

There was a special lock that was installed on the third drawer on the right side of his desk. This drawer held Bunny's letters, pictures, scripts, and the newspaper articles he had collected still remained. The last thing added was a shot of her in the black evening dress holding her award. The drawer was locked and the key, along with Davey's key, was added to his ring.

Phillip now had a private secretary and manager who worked closely with his agent Bill to keep all of Phillip's appearances and film dates organized. It pleased Phillip to no end that he could not longer keep track of everything himself.


In Ireland, Sarah and Marty were quietly married. Davey and his little sister walked down the aisle together in front of their parents, his steps were short to allow for Heather's small legs.

Sarah's career was stronger than ever. After Heather was born, she fanatically dieted and exercised and got back her beautiful figure. Heather would have her blond hair and Marty's dark eyes. The toddler received offers. Davey received offers. Sarah had more than she could handle. She and Marty decided they would never return to the United States.

When this was explained to Davey, he didn't seem to mind. Marty was now his daddy and that tall man had faded from his young memory. He was receiving an international education and could now speak four languages fluently. Sarah worked with him daily so he never lost what he had so easily acquired. What she never mentioned to Davey was Phillip.

Heather was the main delight in Davey's life. He adored his beautiful little sister. He wanted to teach her everything he knew and couldn't understand why she wanted to play so much. When he complained that Heather didn't seem very smart, his mother simply laughed and told him to be patient. "She's your sister for the rest of your life. You'll have plenty of time to teach her. Now go play and have some fun."

Sarah was feeling no regrets in taking Davey away from his father. She was selfishly pleased to know the deep loss Phillip suffered when he had come to France to see for himself that his dear son looked at him as a stranger. She now felt secure then that Phillip would do nothing more to get him back. She would honor the demands from the lawyer when Davey was old enough to know his past and understand her decisions. Then, and only then, would Davey be allowed to know about his real father.

The situation that caused Sarah the most worry was that of her private investigator, Wayne Fields. Long after she knew of her mistaken assumption she had continued to pay him in hopes of earning his doubtful loyalty. She had ordered him back and forth to Los Angeles in vain hope of finding some solid evidence she had craved—both against that nobody in Amherst and against her husband. Finally Wayne had rebelled and said he would no longer work for her. He was staying in that horrible little town in Northern California, and she hoped he would rot there with her dirty little secret. She had sent him a substantial final check with an unsigned letter requesting his silence, never hearing from him again.

As Sarah traveled around she heard bits and pieces of news out of Los Angeles. Only a few of her friends ever contacted her and they, too, told of a new rising star in the picture industry. She was shocked when she learned it was Phillip.

Having finished his filming in England and charming the British, he would be back next year to star in one of their biggest films along with newcomer Tina Rowan. "The Time Police" was hugely popular in England, and they liked the way Jane and Rex looked together.

Sarah found herself going through the movie magazines. Again and again she found articles about Phillip. Never once was she mentioned. He was now one of the most eligible bachelors in the industry and quickly becoming one of the most popular actors.

Staring at one gossip magazine's picture of his tanned, smiling, handsome face, Sarah thought grimly, *He did it. After all the years and all the lousy jobs, he did it*. He had done what he had always said he would do. She had never believed him after their initial move from New York. And he did it without her. It was a bitter pill for her to swallow.

It didn't help her mood, either, to see the current bestseller list out of New York. CHATEAU REX was still holding the number one position and ANDREW'S REVENGE was number six. The author? Leslie Nelson of Amherst, California.


**T**om Young found himself returning home to New York during the breaks from the series. His family was delighted to have him back so often, but, as time went on, their delight turned into worry. He just didn't same to be the same carefree, joking man who popped in occasionally to tease and torment them and then disappear as suddenly as he had come. Where he had been outspoken and charming, now he was quiet and morose. There was a cloud that dimmed the sparkle in his amber eyes.

None of his brothers or sisters could help their baby brother. They knew the problem wasn't professional since Tom's career was its highest ever. When they chided him for not bringing the Public Opinion award for them to see, he just quietly told them it didn't seem to matter so much any longer. This really surprised them. They were the ones that knew Tom's pride in his work, and his ongoing efforts to better his performance.

Any question put to Tom about his personal life went unanswered. Any joke or prank went unrevenged. Dinners and visits with old family friends were few and strangely uncomfortable. Where Tom was once the life of the party, he was now content to sit on the sofa and watch the other people enjoying themselves.

One day, after a strained two months, Tom announced he was leaving. No, not back to Los Angeles. Filming didn't start for another month. There was no point returning yet. No, he was going to the Caribbean for a while. Martinique would be nice.

His mother secretly smiled. Now this sounded more like the old Tommy. Going to some exotic spot on the spur of the moment. Staying for a while and then going off somewhere else. But she noticed the sparkle hadn't returned as it always had when he went on one of his other excursions.

She decided to approach him as he was packing to leave. Sitting on the edge of the bed, she refolded some of his rumpled clothes. "Will we see you again before the next season begins?"

Shaking his head slightly, Tom replied, "Probably not. I'm due on the set on the fifth."

She looked at him steadily. "That doesn't seem to please you. You're usually excited about the new seasons and scripts and all. Isn't it going well, son?"

"No, Mom, the show is great. It's getting better every season with the...the new writers and script ideas," he faltered and started packing faster. He knew what she was doing.

Diane Young smiled to herself. Her youngest son's movements and nervousness were quite familiar to her. Tommy always did things faster when he wanted to hurry through an un-pleasant conversation or situation. Now he was trying to leave faster because he was being questioned.

"Is she pretty, Tommy?" she asked with a knowing smile.

Tom abruptly stopped his movements and looked at her. There was no mocking or disapproval, only motherly concern in her soft face and brown eyes. He glanced around his old room before deciding to answer. His mother calmly refolded the clothes while she waited.

He gave a small sigh and a dry chuckle. "Well, to me, she is," he admitted as he stared off into space. "She's short and pe-tite. She has soft brown hair and big blue eyes. She's intelligent and funny and serious and self-conscious. She's not well-trav-eled yet, and doesn't speak any other languages. She's more like the girl-next-door." The sparkle was returning as Tom thought back and smiled. "When she's in an important situation and you think she's about to faint or run away, she squares her shoulders, lifts her chin, and you'd think she could face the Devil himself. Then, after it's all over, she begins to shake and you realize how much effort she just put in."

His mother saw the glimmer in his eyes. "Sounds like an in-teresting woman," she remarked. "And you love her a great deal, don't you?"

Tom relaxed and now sat next to her on the bed. The cloud was back as he gave his answer. "Yes, I do. It surprised me, too. I never knew what I had wanted in a wife. She never would have fit any description I could have attempted as to what I con-sidered ideal."

"Is it her looks or her social position that is holding you back?"

Tom looked confused by her question. "Holding me back?" he repeated as if he couldn't understand. "I...I asked her to marry me! I don't care that much about looks! How could I? Look at me,' he declared, gesturing all the while. "I know what I look like."

Diane took his face in her hands and told him, "To me you are the most handsome man in the world. And so are your broth-ers and your father. There are no women prettier than your sis-ters."

Tom smiled and looked down. "And Leslie is beautiful to me," he admitted.

Leslie. His mother mentally went quickly through all the names she knew were connected with the show. Ah, the new writer, Leslie Nelson. "Have you ever told her that, son?"

"No," he sighed. "It never came up. I ran out of time. She was gone and now I am bound by a promise I made to her."

"Promise?"

Tom hesitated, not wanting to bring up the rest of the painful memories by telling the whole story. He only told her, "When she suddenly decided to leave L.A., she made me promise not to contact her in any way. Even when she won her first writing award I couldn't let her know how proud I was of her. I guess she thought I would meet someone 'worthy of me' as she put it and forget her."

"Did you try and forget her?"

Tom gave a dry laugh. "I gave it a half-hearted attempt. I, unfortunately, picked someone who looked just like Leslie. When I called Tina by the wrong name one time too many, she, too, dumped me."

"Good for her," his mother declared. "I'm glad she dumped you! Don't look at me like that—you deserved it. You weren't being fair to either woman. Do you really love this Tina?"

"No. It's just that we're together on the show all the time and it seemed sort of natural to continue off-screen."

Diane Young shook her head. "I'm disappointed in you, Tom. You weren't raised to be a quitter or a moper. It's been misery having you around here these two months," she declared.

Tom looked stunned. His mother had never spoken to him that way before. She cut him off before he could say anything else. "Well, it has," she stated, folding her arms and setting her mouth. "Tell me this: Does Leslie love you in return, or were you just making a fool out of yourself chasing her around?"

"Well, the answer to both questions is yes, I guess. She said she loved me, and I apparently seem to be making a fool out of myself still."

"Well, you got that right," Diane muttered. "What are you going to do about it, Tom?"

"Do?" he echoed.

"Lands, you didn't used to be so dense," she sighed. "Didn't you read SPRING COMES TO THE VALLEY?"

"Leslie's fifth novel? Yeah, I read it. Maxwell is looking forward to having his own love interest on the show. At least until she gets killed off," he added with a small smile.

His mother didn't return the smile and continued looking steadily at Tom. "Do you really think Leslie wrote that for Maxwell Marlowe? That story is full of strong love and bitter parting. Tommy, you need to wake up," she declared. "She wrote that book for you, all the while thinking of you. After what you just told me it was written for no one else."

Tom couldn't reply. He had been touched by the whole story. It would be the most heart-wrenching episode they had ever filmed. After reading it, he thought Maxwell and Eddie would both be up for awards next time. But, now, he was being forced to view the novel in a different light—one that was written for, or actually about, *him*. Leslie must be as torn apart as he was.

With a smug smile, Diane rose from the bed. "Tom, she said, "go on to Martinique and spend the time thinking, not moping. I've never lied to your father or broken a promise in my life, but I heartily recommend you rethink your position on this one."

She walked over to her son and kissed him on his forehead. "How short is she, Tom?"

"Five feet four."

She shook her head. "You'll look funny dancing," she commented with a smile.

Tom grinned back. "Can I borrow your copy of the book? I'd like to read it again."

"Sure. And please ask the author to sign it for me," as she left the room to go to the library on the first floor.


**M**artinique was one of the most beautiful islands in the Caribbean. The white sand beaches, towering waterfalls, man-sized ferns, and an inviting harbor made it one of the popular stops for travelers. The dormant volcano was usually capped in clouds. Banana plantations dotted the countryside and colorful exotic flowers were found everywhere.

Tom sat on the porch of his quiet bungalow, far from the noisy cruise ship crowd. He had his own private beach and a rented car. All he could hear were the waves lapping on the shore just a stone's throw away and the palm trees rustling in the warm tropical breeze.

Having read through Leslie's novel twice, his mind raced as he pictured her sitting on her off-white sofa in her cluttered, homey little apartment, writing every word by hand and typing every page at her kitchen table. After that talk with his mother he could now see the love and the pain Leslie was, or had, gone through. Perhaps this book was her way of ridding her feelings and going on with her life. Or, perhaps Sir Charles' love being killed was her way of saying it was over for her. Perhaps Sir Charles' lingering sorrow was a reflection of her own.

> "Sir Charles sat listlessly in the laboratory. The calculations for the next journey had been set; the costumes were arranged; the door to the portal was open and awaiting the squad in readiness. He was alone in the room as the others had not yet arrived.
>
> He fingered something as he sat. Around and around he turned the object in his hand. He didn't look at it. He just knew it was there. It was a simple band of gold. If one had looked inside, the engraving would have been seen: 'To Andrea. My love. My life,' it read in clear, deep letters.
>
> Now that Andrea was gone he couldn't bring himself to part with the band he would have placed on her finger next month. It didn't seem right to bury it with her. Burying his hopes and aspirations had been enough. Now his fingers closed around the band until it left a deep, painful groove in the palm of his hand. The pain didn't begin to match the one in his heart.
>
> His glance fell upon the control computer. It was programmed to send them to 1929 to prevent a suicide after the crash of Wall Street. 1929. He didn't have to go so far back in time, he thought. Only three or four months would be enough for him. Andrea would be back in his arms once

*again.  He could prevent the terrible accident….*

*His thoughts were disrupted by the arrival of Jack and Jane Newby.  Their happiness together both pleased and saddened Sir Charles.  He was happy for them and sad that his own love was taken after so brief, so intense a time.*

*He again looked at the computer.  It was too late now, but their mission would only take three or four weeks.  He was needed now and he wouldn't let the squad down.  But when they returned…."*

Tom's eyes became dim in the fading light.  He looked out over the ocean as the sun sank lower and the clouds turned pink and orange.  Four hours passed when he realized he had beein sitting in that same position as he read Leslie's words.  Hearing her voice and sensing her touch, he thought about the aroma of her perfume and the shocked look on her face when she realized she had fallen asleep in his arms after the convention so long ago.  He smiled at the memory, for it was then that he realized she was someone special, and he really wanted her to stay.  But she didn't.  She simply said good-bye.  The last time she saw him she had made him promise to stay away.  Again she didn't look back.

What Tom didn't know was the uncontrolled tears that had been streaming down Leslie's face as she went up the stairs to board the airplane.  All he had seen was her straight back and her steady walk.  When she had finally settled into her seat the tears turned into inconsolable sobs, the other passengers around her in the commuter jet shifted uncomfortably in their seats.  No one disturbed her.  They stared out their little windows at the retreating Los Angeles basin as the plane headed for the valley.  He didn't realize how hard it was for her to watch the show each week and see him with Tina.  He never knew she had to wipe clean her glasses with shaking hands.

He only knew she that she said she loved him, but still made him promise to leave her alone.  As the sun disappeared into the ocean and the clouds faded into the dark sky, Tom stared out over the water, remembering another ocean and holding someone dear in his arms as the air had turned cold and she shivered.

# CHAPTER 14

**W**ayne Fields nervously paced the floor of his apartment. Asking Janice to come over and Leslie to come down for a few minutes, there was something he wanted to tell both of them before he and Janice exchanged their vows in two months. He was going to finally tell them the real reason he had come to Amherst. This was going to be a huge leap of faith. All of his sharpness and keen senses were pushed to the back of his personality. Sarah wouldn't have recognized him as the same man whose eyes bore right through her and understood her before she ever opened her mouth.

Now he really was an insurance salesman as his original cover story had painted him to be. He had gone to school during the day while the women were at work and lived off of Sarah's money. Her final check is what was going to finance the wedding and the honeymoon cruise he and Janice had been planning.

A few years ago he never would have even considered anything like this. Now was different, his conscience just wouldn't let it die. Wanting to be on even ground with both Janice and Leslie, he might even throw in the time he followed them to the convention and spent an angry, jealous night in his car when they never emerged from the hotel suites. He realized how shocking this would be to the two women. His knowledge about the convention was bound to be startling them because what had happened in those rooms had never been mentioned by either Leslie or the ever-informative Janice.

Wayne had mixed emotions about his friend Marty Thomas. On one hand, he was thankful Marty's job had sent him to Amherst where he met Janice. But, on the other hand, Marty was a slime bag, and Wayne was glad their paths would never cross again. It appeared that Marty had gotten everything he had ever wanted—beauty, fame and fortune—all at the hands of that ditzy blond model. But, Wayne wouldn't change places with Marty for anything in the world.

He looked around his small apartment and chuckled dryly. Like Marty would envy him! Sure, that would be the day.

Janice arrived first and called up the stairs for Leslie who could be heard banging away at her typewriter through the thin walls of the apartment.

Wayne greeted his fiancée at the door. "Hey, beautiful. What took you so long?" as he kissed her hello.

Leslie came down the stairs and pretended to be disgusted. "Oh, will you two knock it off, or go inside or something? Sheesh! Get a grip."

Motioning them in, Wayne immediately noticed the flash of humor was gone from Leslie's eyes when she tried to kid with them. To him she looked pale and listless and her smile seemed forced. He knew it wasn't because of him. That had ended long ago. She had been this way ever since her week on the set in Los Angeles when she had come home early and unannounced.

Janice was so busy being the boutique's new manager and planning their wedding that she hadn't seen the change come over her friend. Of all of Leslie's friends and family, only Wayne, who lived below her, knew how rarely Leslie got out any more. What he didn't know was what really happened in Los Angeles.

The ladies were looking at him to begin with the reason for their summons. Nerves coming back, he took a deep breath and began.

"I wanted to tell you both a little about myself that you don't know. I would like to ask that you let me just tell the whole story without either of you interrupting me. Knowing both of you as well as I do, I know that will be difficult for you," he added, trying to lighten the somber mood that had settled around him at his opening words.

Not realizing the emotions coming over him, Janice tried to protest and looked hurt. Leslie only gave a flicker of a smile as she settled back for whatever his revelation might be. Wayne saw Leslie's smile and figured she would view it all as a possible storyline. He just didn't know how true that would turn out to be.

"Well, ladies, here it is. Before I came here I was known as Wayne Fields, P.I. Private Investigator," he explained, barreling right in. "That means I would, basically, spy on anyone that the customer was willing to pay me to spy on and report what I found out. I did a lot of insurance fraud claims and a lot of spouse cheating cases. I was known to be one of the best in the business and I would take just about any case for the right fee.

"What brought me to Amherst was a job initiated by a celebrity's wife who is a well-known model. She was concerned about losing her property, or, in other words, her husband, to a woman she felt was a threat. It seems she found a pile of letters from a fan and realized her husband had gotten in touch with this fan."

Here he paused as Leslie had gone pale and her lips had parted, staring at him. Janice, too, looked shocked as the realization hit her.

"Married?" Leslie whispered, ignoring his request not to say anything. "I didn't know he was married. How could I have known?" A frown crossed her face as she thought back on what she had written in her letters to Phillip. "Wait a minute. There was nothing personal in those letters. Nothing. How could they have possibly considered me a threat?"

Wayne interrupted her interruption. "They didn't consider you a threat. The wife, Sarah, did...probably at the urging of her manager, an ex-friend of mine. I saw the letters, Leslie, all of them up to that time. I knew immediately that there was nothing wrong going on between you and Phillip."

"Wrong? Of course there wasn't! We never even met! We...we still haven't."

"Don't worry, Les. That's all in the past. Anyway, as I was saying, I was sent by Sarah to spy on you, Leslie, and report what you were doing, but mostly to see if you were after Phillip. I...I bugged your telephone and wired your apartment and searched it when I first got here. I was doing what was expected of me to earn my fee."

After speaking rapidly through that part, he paused again, hurt to see the disillusioned expressions on their faces. When they didn't say anything, he continued. "I knew you were okay. Anyone would have seen that. Well, anyone but that neurotic model who was jealous of what she didn't know. I would send her letters making it sound like there was a possibility of danger. That way she would keep paying me and not hire someone else who...who didn't know you or liked you and wanted to be near you like I did...someone who could have made your life miserable.

"At that point and time, you knew I liked you a lot, Leslie. I always hoped you would feel the same for me, but, as it turned out, you never did. You always seemed to be looking for something else. I don't even think you knew what it was. But I knew it wasn't me. As it turned out, you had a wonderful friend right there, so I turned to Janice as a friend. First it was to vent my hurt feelings and anger, and then I began to see her as more than just a friend and to see her wonderful, beautiful qualities. And, well, you know the rest."

He sat down opposite them as his explanation ended. He already felt better inside but knew the relief wouldn't be complete without their absolution.

"Are you still spying on me? Is my apartment still bugged?" a wide-eyed Leslie slowly asked.

Wayne threw up his hands. "No! I swear! I quit a long, long time ago. I kept sending fake letters and reports to placate Sarah, but I never watched you again. Not too long ago I received my final letter from her ending our business relationship and the request for me to keep my mouth shut. Now that she's had another baby by a different man, she doesn't need any negative press. It could possibly do her career a lot of harm."

"Then she's still married to Phillip Beck?" Janice asked.

"No, I think they're divorced now, and it's kinda ironic now that his career is taking off like a rocket. I wouldn't be at all surprised if she married her agent, Marty, my ex-friend. After all, he is the father of her second kid."

"Who...who else knows about my threatening correspondence, Wayne? My word! I never made it a secret that Phillip had called to encourage me." Leslie began to panic. "I could be really hurt by the press if they knew about you! What would the studio say? What will I do?"

Wayne went over to her and sat beside her. "Les, no one else knows what I just told you, not even Phillip. Only the three of us and Marty and Sarah know. And trust me, neither of them will ever talk about this. It would reflect badly on Sarah, not you," he insisted, trying to take her hand in a friendly gesture, which she didn't allow by pulling away. "You have to believe me. I didn't have to tell you any of this. I just wanted to start my life with Janice clean before the wedding. No more secrets."

"It's been years, Wayne, not weeks since you moved here. We accepted you and welcomed you and you repaid us by spying on me?" Leslie still couldn't understand it.

Wayne looked at Janice who had remained silent, because, thus far, the conversation had been between him and Leslie. "This has been bothering me for a long time! You both mean a great deal to me. If you want to know everything, by that I mean what I found out about you through my investigation, it only made me more interested in you. I'm so thrilled your work is getting the recognition it deserves. I only wish I could do something to help you personally."

Leslie dropped her eyes to the floor. She felt violated. "Are you sure no one else knows? No one in Los Angeles could ever find out what Sarah did?"

"I swear, Leslie, no. Not unless you tell them. I've burned all the tapes and notes, and I sold all my surveillance equipment. I now am an honest insurance salesman just as you know me," he said earnestly. "Now that I have a future with Janice, I want to keep it that way."

Janice thought of something else and asked, "What about all those times you went to L.A.? What were those for?"

Wayne shook his head. "That dizzy model thought Phillip was sleeping with some actress, so she sent me to find out who it was."

"Who was it?" Janice prodded, smiling and her eyes wide.

"There wasn't anyone. Beck had thrown a party—or, rather, Tom and Eddie threw a party at Beck's house—and a few of the guests had too much to drink and slept over. Apparently one of the women answered the phone when Sarah called and her nasty imagination took over," he explained.

"But that's just one time," Leslie pointed out.

"Yeah, but Sarah kept trying to find something to pin on Phillip so she could take him to the cleaners for all he had. Which wasn't much at that time," he added. "But, now with her new baby, she hasn't a leg to stand on. And Phillip's doing great, as we all know."

"Boy, what a lifestyle," whistled Janice, not even thinking about the fact that he had lied to her, too. "Did you see anything like that when you were there, Les?"

Leslie gave a brief smile. "No. Not at all. I guess I missed all the parties."

Wayne cleared his throat. "I need to know if you can forgive my lies, forget my past and accept me as I am now. Janice?" he asked his fiancée.

"Me? I thought this just concerned Leslie. You didn't spy on me, too, did you?"

"Not really. I followed both of you to that convention in the Silicon Valley, but I was angry at Leslie for not asking me to go along," he confided.

"I don't care about your past," she decided. "I love you as Wayne Fields, super insurance agent."

His load lifted a little, he smiled and turned back to Leslie. "And you, Les? Can you overlook my past?"

She met his eyes briefly. He couldn't tell how she felt. She still looked pale and shaken. When she did answer him, her voice was low. "I don't know, Wayne. All my life I've tried to be honest with people and I guess I'm naïve to expect the same in return from everyone. I kind of wish you hadn't told me."

"I had to. It's been bothering me a lot. And, honesty? Yeah, I do value honesty and that's why it's been eating me up. I don't want to lose your friendship," Wayne claimed and then added,

"Who knows? Maybe you could put it to good use as a plot in one of your next book."

Leslie gave a cold smile at that. "Yeah, a new squad member turns out to be a dirty double agent bent on destroying all the squad ever worked for."

Wayne flinched. "Well, you don't have to make it so graphic and evil. It isn't really that bad, is it?" he asked hopefully.

"Right now, yes, it is," was Leslie's honest reply. "Tomorrow or the next day? I don't know. Probably not." She arose from the sofa. "You'll excuse me if I don't stay for cocktails. I wouldn't want to think my hors d' oeuvres were bugged."

At their hurt expressions she sullenly added, "Sorry, but I'm very uncomfortable right now. I'll talk to you guys another time." Leslie left the apartment and slowly trudged up the stairs to her own rooms.

As her eyes traveled around the living room, her glance stopped on her shadowbox. She remembered that day, long ago it seemed, that the sheriff's badge had looked ready to fall over and the music box hadn't lined up with the dust marks. An involuntary shiver ran through Leslie as she attempted to get back to normal and went back to her typewriter to resume work on the script for SPRING COMES TO THE VALLEY.

Her fingers shook as she attempted to type, and after correcting four errors in one line, she angrily tore the sheet out of the typewriter and threw it across the room. She knew then it would be a while before she trusted or believed Wayne again. She reflected grimly on how her roster of friends seemed to be getting shorter and shorter.

There was a small crowd of fifty family members and friends gathered at the Amherst Gardens for the wedding of Wayne Fields and Janice Woods. Winding, grassy walkways led through flower beds of roses and azaleas and mums, past fern-lined waterfalls, and over wooden bridged streams. The white gazebo in which the ceremony was performed was overhung with fragrant lilac. A two-tiered birdbath and fountain tinkled nearby.

Wayne had gotten his way and wore a dark suit instead of

the hated tuxedo. Janice wore a tea-length white chiffon dress and a lovely brimmed hat. She carried a small bouquet of red roses and baby's breath. As a consideration to Leslie's feelings at the moment, they chose no attendants and stood alone in the gazebo with the minister and repeated their vows and promises with clear voices and happy faces.

Leslie stood with her parents amongst the guests with a calm smile on her face. As the ceremony progressed, feeling her mother's arm go through hers, she glanced over at Bonnie.

"Are you all right, honey?" her mom whispered.

"I'm fine, Mom."

Bonnie patted her arm and gave an inaudible sigh. "You know I'm happy for Janice, but I just can't help thinking that might have been you up there," she again whispered.

Leslie shook her head slightly as she looked at Wayne. "No, I never felt that way towards him. He was only a good friend. That's all."

Bonnie glanced at Leslie's face and saw the sad look in her eyes that had been present for many, many months. She patted her daughter's arm again and was silent. She didn't know whether to completely believe Leslie or not. She and Lou would have considered Wayne a fine son-in-law and they couldn't understand Leslie letting him get away like that. Now it was too late. They blamed a lot on Leslie's involvement and preoccupation with her writing for that silly television show. Leslie might have financial security, but she was still alone and obviously unhappy.

After the ceremony, they all pushed forward to congratulate the beaming couple. Then the crowd slowly worked their way to the clubhouse for the reception.

"Well, two more gone," Leslie abruptly stated to Bonnie as they carefully walked over the grass, their heels sinking into the soft turf.

Bonnie looked confused. "What do you mean?" she asked. "Gone where?"

Leslie's eyes indicated Wayne and Janice. "Now that they are married, I'm the last single one of the group. I'm the only one left," she stated as more of a dull fact than a startling revelation.

Bonnie tried to be hopeful. "Well, the next time a single man moves into the group he's all yours!"

Leslie smiled in spite of herself. "We all know how often that happens, Mom. Renee got married two years ago...."

"Three," Bonnie corrected quietly.

"Three?" Leslie became silent as they approached the clubhouse. She hadn't realized how quickly time had flown. Now that she no longer worked at the boutique, her time schedule revolved around television seasons and publishing dates. This would be the second time "The Time Police" would begin a season with one of her episodes, ANDREW'S REVENGE. She briefly wondered how Richard Avery liked her treatment of SPRING COMES TO THE VALLEY.

"Leslie?" Bonnie's voice and a tug on her arm startled Leslie. She then realized she was walking past the reception room.

She grinned sheepishly. "Sorry. My mind was elsewhere."

Her mother gave her a stern look. "Give it a rest for a while. Quit viewing everything as a possible plot. This is Jan's day. You've been friends since grade school."

Knowing her mother was right, Leslie put what she hoped was a pleasant smile on her face and joined the guests at the buffet table.

A little later Janice came over to her and they exchanged a tight hug.

"You look really great, Jan," Leslie smiled. "I love that dress."

"Forget me," Janice insisted as she led Leslie a ways off. "I worried about you. Wayne told me how hard you've been working and how rarely you get out."

Leslie glanced over at Wayne who was joking with Jan's parents. "Your beloved talks too much sometimes."

"Oh, you're not still mad at him, are you? I thought that was settled already," Janice stubbornly claimed, not waiting for an answer. "He's worried about you, too, you know. We'll be gone for two weeks on our cruise. Will you be all right?"

Leslie smiled indulgently, willing herself not to be touched by her friend's concern. "Oh, I think I can manage on my own. Did you want me to come with you?" she teased.

Janice didn't laugh. "I'm not trying to be funny, Les. I'm serious."

"Well, you shouldn't be!" Leslie declared, interrupting what she knew was coming. "This is your wedding day. You should be thinking only of Wayne and yourself."

"I'm going to say it anyway, Les, whether you want to hear it or not," Janice persisted. "Call Tom. You're miserable. I know it hasn't gotten any easier for you as you had hoped it would."

"I can't," Leslie sighed. "He's better off with one of his own. Not with me. I'll feel better.... Some day," she added wistfully.

Janice folded her arms in a most unbridelike fashion and frowned at her friend. "So, in the meantime you plan on sitting alone in that tiny apartment of yours, pining away and turn into a mopey recluse? You know, there aren't many people who know, but I know what you had to put up with with that lousy ex-husband of yours and how it affected you. And I think that is what is affecting your relationship with Tom. I'm sorry, but I don't want to see that ruin your life and a great opportunity with a great man. You used to be fun, Les. You've changed. Your smile, like that one, always looks phony."

"It is phony," Leslie admitted.

"If you weren't so stubborn you'd realize you could do something about it. But, you won't, and you won't let any of us help," Janice pointed out.

Leslie gave her a grin. "I'm sure this conversation isn't what you'll want to remember about your wedding day."

Wayne came over to claim Janice. "They want us to cut the bouquet and throw the cake or something, honey. You two have been gossiping long enough."

Leslie gave a small laugh. "Gossip?" she repeated. "Ha. Your wife here has been chewing me up one side and down the other."

Wayne met her eyes and gave her face a close scrutiny, not returning her laugh. "Good. I hope you listen," as he led Janice over to the three-tiered, rose covered wedding cake.


There was a pile of fax papers rolled on the floor when

Leslie returned home after the reception. The message from New York was that Wallace wanted her to attend a "Time Police" convention in October in Rancho Blanco. Eddie Chase and Cindy Sanders would also attend and Leslie would represent the writers. She smiled. Rancho Blanco was where she and Janice had attended their first convention.

The rest of the pile was from Richard Avery. He wanted rewrites on two scenes from SPRING COMES TO THE VALLEY, and he needed her to come to Los Angeles for some publicity shots. Since the series had won another award for its writing consistency, a group shot of all the writers was requested. He also wanted to know if she would be interested in appearing on a talk show with the entire cast that was dedicated to the series?

Leslie faxed back yes to the September date for the photo shoot and a no for the talk show. This hadn't been her first offer. Her agent recommended her accepting the appearances and had offered one there in New York. But Leslie was saying no to all of them. She agreed to the convention up north and let Wallace know. It would be nice to see Eddie again, she told herself.

Leslie looked over the scenes to be changed. Neither surprised her. One of the scenes was Jack and Jane's terrible argument that she had written when she was in a bad mood. The other was Sir Charles's over-long, inconsolable grief after the first news of the accident that killed his fiancée. Leslie knew she had rambled on and on. The publisher hadn't minded, but it was too much for the television show.

After spending four hours working on the rewrites and sending the pages back to Los Angeles, she was quite weary—both physically and mentally—when she finally crawled into bed. The only cure was the oblivion of sleep.


It felt odd for Leslie at the convention. She was on the other side now, but this time without her long-time cohort, Janice. Waiting backstage with Eddie and Cindy, they all sat at the same table as they fielded questions about the show, the scripts, and her books. She signed countless copies of her five novels and listened with interest to the compliments and the critiques. The fans asked what they could expect next and told her what changes she should make. Other than a little cramping in her hand from signing so many books, she enjoyed the first day.

Later that evening, Eddie invited Leslie and Cindy for dinner in his suite. Shortly after the meal ended, Cindy suddenly complained about travel fatigue and excused herself. Leslie gave Eddie a suspicious look as he went over to the sofa and settled in for the evening.

"I'm sure you planned that," she stated after Cindy left the room.

He grinned and shrugged. "Of course I did. I wanted to talk to you alone. Cindy understands and agrees."

Leslie looked over the rim of her wine glass. "Don't, Eddie. There's nothing left to say. Everybody else has already jumped all over me."

"Well," he claimed, putting his feet up on the coffee table, "it hasn't seemed to do any good. You've never been back to the set."

"Sure I have," she smiled smugly. "I was there last month to have my picture taken."

Eddie snorted. "Hmph. None of us were there."

"So write an episode and maybe you'll be invited to sit in next time."

He gave her a humorless grin. "Funny. You should do a comedy act. Actually you and Tom should do one together. You're two of the most stubborn people I have ever known!" he declared. At her silence he then bluntly asked, "Have you met someone else? Are you seeing anyone?"

Expecting to be told to mind his own business, he instead received a dry laugh. "My last admirer just married Janice a few months ago."

Eddie suddenly beamed. "Janice got married! That's great! Had I known, I would have sent something. I still can," he decided. "Linda and I'll send it through you, if that's all right."

"Janice would love it, Eddie. That's nice of you."

"Hey, I'm a terrific guy," he declared. "You know that."

"Yeah. I know that. I never did thank you for being there with me when I won that award. I did really appreciate it."

"Well, you'll probably be nominated again for this season, too. Especially after the SPRING script. It's good, Les," he told her.

She took a sip of her wine and narrowed her eyes as she stared at him. "What's wrong? Didn't you like ANDREW'S REVENGE?"

"I like this one better," he admitted seriously, not allowing her to bait him. "It betrays a deep passion within you. Who did you write it for?" he suddenly wanted to know, hoping to throw her off track.

She didn't let him. "Sir Charles."

"Yeah, right," he scoffed. "I don't buy that."

"Doesn't matter, Eddie," she sighed and looked at the picture bolted on the wall. "It's just a story."

He looked at her and frowned as he shook his head. "You're not going to give me a break here, are you? I know you wrote that for Tom. All of us do. He isn't dating Tina any more," he added. "Ever since that flub at the awards. Did you see what happened?"

Leslie just nodded as she looked at the glass in her hand. Her heart had jumped when Tom started to say her name instead of Tina's. "That was a long time ago," she mumbled in a monotone that revealed nothing.

She didn't fool Eddie. "Next time, you'll be there together," he predicted.

Leslie stood and set her glass down next to his feet. "It's late. I need to go to bed. I had to drive myself here, you know. Some of us lowly writers don't get the pampered treatment you stars get."

"Poor baby. If you lived down south where you belong you could have come with us," was his sharp reply as she was shutting the door to returned to her own room.

In the darkness Leslie stared up at the ceiling. She allowed one lone tear to roll down her cheek before she clamped down her emotions. "Why are you doing this to me, Eddie?" she whispered out loud. "It's hard enough as it is."

Wayne had winced when he read Leslie's sixth book DECPETIONS in which a rival of Andrew's over Maggie turns out to be a wicked agent from the future who tries to destroy the squad from the inside. Wayne had felt a barrier had arisen between him and Leslie ever since his confession, and this book, to him, proved it still existed. It wasn't her best work—there was too much anger throughout the writing—but it would make an interesting episode if she got the script finished in time for the end of the season.

Wayne and Janice had bought a house in one of the newer subdivisions in Amherst and settled into their domestic life. Leslie was an occasional visitor when she could be pried away from her typewriter. She smiled when they talked of travel and yard work, mortgages and babies, family reunions and picnics. They asked about her work and what was the news from Los Angeles and New York. Wayne asked if she could tone down her next script and change the character's name from Wain to something else.

"But, Wayne, no one else would know unless you told them," was her reply.

They never mentioned Tom or Phillip any longer. Soon the talk would center on the dinners and the nights out with other couples or the trip they would take with this or that family.

As had happened with Renee, Leslie felt uncomfortable as the only single one amongst the couples. She found convenient excuses for refusing the offers when they came and found she had more spare time on her hands and no one with whom to share it.

She knew being a single, successful businesswoman was an accomplishment and knew there wasn't any shame in being alone. A lot of people viewed this as a great time for her to travel and see the world.

Taking their advice, she began her climb out of her almost self-exile by booking a week-long cruise to the Mexican Riviera. Once onboard, and anticipating the myriad of fun activities the ship promised, she explored the ship from stem to stern before it sailed. After unpacking in her private cabin, she had gone up on deck just as they were setting sail, watching the festivities as the ship slowly pulled away from the dock. Streamers flying in the breeze, the ship's horn bellowing a parting blast, she smiled as she looked around.  However, what she saw were all the happy couples around her hugging and waving good-bye.  She was the only single person on that deck.  "I've just made an awful mistake," she mumbled to herself as the ship's band started playing and the couples started dancing around her on the deck.

The rest of the cruise was spent on the fantail, notebook in hand, writing the outlines for her next two books.

No, there wasn't any shame in being single.  It was just that, for the first time in her life, she realized she was incredibly lonely.

# CHAPTER 15

There were a few new, unexpected names at the Stargazer Awards that spring. The movie industry had a wider choice from which to choose their honorees for outstanding performances. Phillip Beck was up for Outstanding Actor and Tina Rowan for the Best Supporting Actress, both for their roles in the British film they had made together the previous year.

Phillip had appeared on "The Time Police" twice last season as he had agreed but was totally disappointed the scripts weren't from Bunny. He hadn't heard from or about her in quite a while. As his career flourished and he immersed himself into his new-found celebrity and charity work, his 'personal fan' seemed to be fading from his memory. He even forgot to ask Eddie about her.

Now, sitting there waiting for the highest honor an actor could receive, he found he was quite nervous as he and Tina waited together in the front row of the audience of their peers. Smiling, he clapped as the four other actor's names were announced and grinned when his own name was said last. A short clip from the movie was run, which, to Phillip, seemed to last forever.

The presenter, a prominent actress, opened the golden seal and nodded her head approvingly. "Phillip Beck!" she read aloud and smiled broadly.

Phillip found himself onstage holding the gold statue and facing an applauding group of fellow actors. It took him a few seconds to remember his speech. Clutching the award, he, in an emotion-filled voice, thanked all those who had helped and believed in him all those years. He was grateful to the industry for the recognition and thanked his agent and all the co-workers by name. He even thanked certain directors and writers. Deeply touched and appreciative, he exited to a standing ovation.

Three hundred miles away, Leslie watched the live broadcast alone in her apartment. She was thrilled when she first learned Phillip had been nominated and now impatiently watched the entire show to see if he would win.

She, too, clapped when his name was announced and she listened breathlessly to his speech. Even though she had not contacted him in such a long time, she still felt some kind of vague, indefinable bond between them. He had encouraged her, and she had written him two wonderful scripts. She noticed the close-up of the bunny pin he had worn at the Public Opinion Awards and knew, thanks to Eddie, that gesture was just for her.

Near at hand was a greeting card she had found for Phillip that had rabbits spelling out the word congratulations. It was addressed and ready to go. All Phillip had to do was win.

As the ovation followed Phillip offstage, a hand reached up and slowly clicked off the television. Leslie sat back in her chair and stared unseeing at the black screen, the joyful expression having faded from her face.

Phillip had thanked everyone Leslie knew from the series, even Russell the extra who was used in every episode. The only name he had left out was hers.

Backstage, after the ceremony had ended, was the kind of chaos in which actors and photographers often found themselves. All of those who had won the major categories were given first interviews and then led off to one of the parties filled with music, food, and friends.

Phillip was trying to juggle a plate of food and a drink as he worked his way through the crowd acknowledging the accolades and greeting his friends as he went. He was approached by a well-known reporter who snapped a picture and asked for a private interview.

Phillip smiled as he replied, "I'd love to, but you'll have to contact my agent to set up the time. Let me get you his card."

They went to a quiet corner where Phillip set down his plate and goblet and reached for his wallet. As he fumbled through the cards a beat-up snapshot fell out and onto the floor. The reporter retrieved it and handed it back as he took the offered business card. Not looking at the agent's card, he was now curious as he watched Phillip. Because of the confused look on the actor's face, it was obvious he didn't remember there had been a photo in his wallet.

Phillip temporarily forgot the reporter and the loud party going on around him as he opened the folded picture. His perplexed expression turned to one of surprised recognition as he looked at the shot. A six-foot tall amusement park rabbit was hugging a brown-haired woman. A pleased smile crossed his face as he leaned back against the wall and continued to stare at the crumpled snapshot. All this time he had somehow overlooked it.

He remembered the day he first saw this particular picture and the letter that had accompanied it. All the memories returned that he had pushed to the back of his mind and eventually forgot. His special fan who had liked his work. The fan who wrote CHATEAU REX which had really put him in the public's eye. She had known what he could do.

Smiling, he silently thanked Bunny as he refolded the picture and carefully returned it to his wallet. When someone jostled against him he was mentally brought back to the party and his surroundings. As he stood there, his pleasant smile froze and then slowly began to fade, the only observer being the reporter silently watching his face.

Phillip looked around the room at all the people talking and laughing and dancing. He knew almost all of them and was friends with the majority. However, he realized, two years ago he wouldn't have been invited as a guest, let alone as a nominee. Now he had just won the highest honor. And he had forgotten the one person who had been there in spirit and had given him that one script for which he had waited. It was then that he realized he never even mentioned her.

Phillip's eyes closed briefly and he leaned his head back against the wall. Whispering in a soft voice that only the reporter heard, he murmured, "Sorry, Bunny."

Against her wishes, Leslie found herself on the commuter jet and on her way to Los Angeles again. Richard Avery told her it was imperative that she come to the studio that afternoon. There were problems with her last script that required her attention. They were finishing the season with her DECEPTIONS story, and he refused to use the fax machine. Leslie was needed, and her contract stipulated her final authorization. He said he sympathized with her reasons for not wanting to come and agreed to work with her even though, in his own mind, he thought she was being unprofessional and silly.

The same driver met her at the airport with a smile of recognition on both their faces. The limousine was all hers. Leslie rested her head back against the plush seat. She was weary. After working so hard on the last script to meet the studio's deadline, they had abruptly changed the filming date. Now it would be the final episode and apparently they were unhappy with her work.

Leslie had already decided to take some time off before beginning her next book. Her fans wanted another Professor Rex story. The studio was interested in a story that featured the Maggie Rush character. Eddie had blatantly hinted about a story that would send them back to the days of pirates so he could show off his swordsmanship, but Leslie just wanted to rest for a while. She had her own ideas for her next projects but now lacked the necessary ambition and drive. Instead of following up on her idea of going abroad to a spa and being pampered for two or three weeks, she was now on her way to Majestic Studio. Once again there was the need to confront Richard and Ron, while trying to avoid the actual set and the actors. It was a toil more than her tired mind and spirit could deal with at the moment.

The car was waved through the security checkpoint and wound its way through the lot to the main offices. The driver informed Leslie he would wait with her baggage to take her to the hotel when she was through inside.

Grabbing her briefcase and entering the building, the first receptionist recognized and welcomed her. Mr. Avery wanted the author on the set in the production booth as soon as she arrived and she was handed her security pass badge.

Inwardly groaning, she thanked the woman and went back to the car. As the limo headed for the building that housed "The Time Police" set, Leslie attached the badge to her dress pocket and fought down her nerves. She hoped she could get to the booth unseen by any of the cast.

The guard was expecting her as he called for an aide to escort Leslie. She smiled as she walked past some props she had described in her book that would be used by the enemy agent.

She was left at the stairs and climbed up to the booth, knocking as she opened the door. All inside turned as she entered to greet her. Mr. Avery left the window to come over and Ron briefly nodded as he returned to the script. The actors were doing a walk-through guided by the assistant director. By turning her back to it, Leslie avoided the window as she was motioned over by Nickles. The position was observed by the two men who exchanged a brief look.

"Miss Nelson, we understand your reluctance to be here, but we require your cooperation to get this handled speedily. Then you can run and hide or do whatever you think you should," Ron briefly stated as he indicated which script page was being rehearsed.

Leslie shot him an embarrassed, angry look as she opened her briefcase to remove her script. Biting back the sharp retort on her tongue, she concentrated on the scene. She was immediately familiar with where they were and forced herself to look at the set on the soundstage below. All the regulars were there along with the guest star portraying Wain. Her eyes couldn't help it and strayed to Tom. He looked the same as ever.

Richard handed her a set of headphones. "Put these on and we'll run through the scene again. I'm sure you'll be able to immediately identify the problem." He touched a button on the console to tell the assistant director to begin again.

When the announcement was given the whole cast looked up at the production window. Leslie took an involuntary step back even though she knew she couldn't be seen over the glare of the lights.

All in the booth followed along as the cast went through the confrontation scene between Wain and the squad. The dialogue abruptly ended where the fight scene would be put in.

Leslie could see nothing wrong. "I don't see what the problem is," she admitted. "Does it run too long or what?"

Mr. Avery shook his head. "You thought that sounded fine? Ron, have them do it again."

The actors repeated the scene. Their reactions and their responses were just as they had been written. To Leslie it sounded feasible for the tense situation. She removed her headphones and patted down her hair. "I still think it sounds good. If you'll tell me what you don't like about it, I'll try to see if from your angle," she offered with a helpless shrug.

Richard and Ron discussed this between themselves in low voices. Ron then left the booth and went down to the set. The cameras were positioned and everyone took their marks. As Leslie watched, the scene was repeated and filmed. Half of the actors left the set and those remaining did some close-ups and reaction shots.

A confused Leslie alternated between watching the action and listening on the headphones while comparing the script. Mr. Avery was busy with the proceedings and ignored her.

In an hour the seven minute scene had been shot and reshot. At a signal from Ron, Avery glanced at the technicians who nodded at him. He hit a button on one of the consoles. "Okay, people, that's a wrap. Good job. Five o'clock at The Pier," he announced as everyone cleared the set and disappeared.

Leslie was staring at him with her mouth slightly open. "What was the big problem?" she wanted to know. "Where's everyone going?"

Richard gave her a smug smile. "We wanted to make sure you were happy with the final scene."

"Final?" she echoed, bewildered by this strangeness. "That's not the end of the story. No wonder you don't understand...."

"No, no," he interrupted. "I know that's not the final scene of the show. It's just the final scene we had to shoot. All the others were done. We needed your approval."

For a moment Leslie was dumbfounded. When she found her voice again she managed to control the anger that had arisen. "You mean to tell me I came all this way for nothing?" she quietly demanded. "This was a trick? Why, pray tell?"

Ron came back into the booth at that moment and saw the writer's red face. "Oooh," he grinned. "Somebody's not happy."

"This isn't funny, Ron," Leslie stated as she slammed shut her script and stuffed it into her briefcase. "I would like to know what you wanted that was so important that I approve it."

Ron shrugged and pushed his glasses up on top of his head. "Didn't want you to miss the party."

Leslie looked back out the window. Some of the props were already being carried away. "I don't want to go to a party. You seem to know why. I'd like to go home since I'm not really needed here."

Mr. Avery shook his head, unconcerned by her outburst. "No can do, Les. There's not another flight until tomorrow night."

"That's ridiculous!" Leslie averred. "There's always flights. There should be one at eleven."

"Booked solid," Ron told her, leaning back on the console.

The anger flooded out of Leslie. She sank down into a chair. She was tired of fighting and she was tired of explaining. "You're going to make me go whether I want to or not, is that it?" she resignedly asked.

Richard motioned her to the door. "I usually expect more enthusiasm at my parties," he grumbled as they walked down the stairs. Only some technicians were left working about the set. "Leslie, let me tell you something I don't ever tell the writers. I probably should tell them, but I don't. They tend to get swelled heads and demand more money. You've done good work for this show. We were already in the Top Ten, but you helped keep us there. We've even picked up more awards because of your scripts. And you know what CHATEAU REX did for Beck." He paused and glanced at her face, expecting some indication of how she was reacting so far. She was unreadable. *She's doing it to me again!* he grumbled to himself. Continuing out loud, he said, "You deserve to be at this celebration as much as anyone here. I know your personal reasons behind all your refusals, and I think they are ridiculous!" he declared with feeling as he opened the outer door. Before he allowed her to get into the car, he finished what he had to say. "I like you, Leslie. Whenever we've disagreed on some point with your stories, sometimes you were wrong and you were gracious in your corrections. But, you've usually been right. However, this time you're wrong. You probably think I don't have any right to talk to you this way. But I know how Tom has been affected this past year and I can see how you've changed, too. You're obviously not happy. Tom's miserable when he's not working. Something has to be done. This is my studio, so I'm doing something," he stated and removed his arm that had been blocking the car door. "Now, get in the blasted car."

Leslie silently climbed in the back and set her briefcase on the floorboard. She was desperately trying not to cry and didn't trust her voice just then. Of all the people who had told her this same speech over the years since her unexpected divorce, Richard's had just touched her the most, and she had no idea why she was so affected.

"Who knows I am here?" she managed to ask after a few moments of expected silence.

"Only Ron, Eddie, Linda, and I. She's in town for the summer."

Leslie gave a small smile. Eddie. Of course he was in on this. "Where's the restaurant?"

"It's a club, actually," Avery explained as they drove along, heading towards the ocean. "We've rented the whole shebang for tonight. There'll be dinner and dancing and a wonderful view of the ocean."

Leslie removed her security badge and looked at it. "I guess I won't be needing this," was her comment as she tossed it on the floor next to her briefcase.

He glanced at her face. "Are you going to pout the whole night, or are you going to enjoy being with your friends again?"

Leslie looked out the window as they sped along the freeway. All she could picture was Tom's face as she had said goodbye.

At her silence, Avery added, "Phillip was invited to attend. He's leaving for a movie in New York early tomorrow morning, so I don't know how long he can stay. He's interested in his next script for the series."

"So am I," Leslie commented with a ghost of a smile. "After my rest I'll probably do another Rex story."

"Good. He'll be pleased to hear that."

Leslie returned her eyes to the cityscape, and Richard lapsed into silence.


Leslie now in the midst of a happy, mingling crowd, was being welcomed by the other writers and introduced to some of the crew she hadn't met yet. Everyone was in a party mood. The season had ended on a high note, everyone was renewed for the fall and signed on for the next season.

Eddie and Linda Chase warmly hugged her with Eddie commenting that he was glad she decided to come after all.

"Hmph," Leslie sniffed. "I was kidnapped and you know it!"

"Whatever," Eddie waved her off as he took Linda's arm and led her over to meet someone.

Leslie turned to go to the picture window overlooking the Pacific Ocean. She ran into Tina who crossed her path. They had an awkward moment until Leslie said, "I think you're doing a wonderful job with Jane. You've made her just what I wanted her to be."

Tina smiled warmly at the unexpected praise. "Thanks, Leslie." She paused and then added, "I was a little apprehensive earlier when Eddie told me you might be here. But he reminded me that we're all working towards the same goal of an excellent show. I do like your scripts. But, I admit I was afraid you'd make Jane into some evil shrew."

Leslie laughed at that. "No, I'd never do that!" she admitted.

"After all, she's very dear to me."

Tina looked away for a moment and waved to one of the guests. He came over and gave her a kiss on the cheek. "Leslie, this is my boyfriend, Mike Barnes."

Leslie shook his hand. "Yes, I recognize you from the Sunday News Events Show. It's nice to finally meet you. I don't watch your show nearly as often as I should," she admitted with a laugh, feeling more at ease by the moment.

There was a huge commotion over by the front door of the club. All eyes turned to see what was happening.

Tom and Maxwell made a grand entrance wearing gold crowns and red cloaks borrowed from Costumes. They were good-naturedly cheered and applauded as a path was made for them to enter. Maxwell regally waved and bestowed blessings on the little people around them.

When Tina turned back to Leslie to continue their conversation, all she could see was Leslie's back as she hurried out the back door and onto the terrace where canopied tables stood waiting for guests. Leslie almost ran down the wooden stairs that led to the private beach. There would be dancing down there later, but now the colorful lanterns swayed over empty sand.

Tina glanced up at Mike. "Oh, dear. That's not the reaction Eddie was hoping for. I'd better go tell him what happened with our reluctant guest."

Eddie was busy trying on Tom's crown. "I really should be wearing this," he was reasoning, "since you and Maxwell robbed me of my much-deserved award these two years.... Tina!" he called as she approached. "Don't you think this fits me better?"

She grinned at all three of them. "I think you all look silly," she declared, "but then, what do I know? I'm new. Eddie, I wanted you to meet someone, my friend Mike Barnes," as she clamped onto his arm and led him away from the group.

Eddie tossed the crown back to Tom as he was drug away. "I already know Mike. I was the one who introduced you," he started to protest.

"I know," Tina replied and then lowered her voice when they had walked a ways from the group. "Leslie just ran out the back door towards the beach. We were chatting when Maxwell and

Tom came in. Next thing I knew she was gone. I thought you should know."

Eddie made a disgusted noise as he looked out the window. "Boy, she's still being stubborn! And after all this time, too. Well," he thought out loud, "looks like Uncle Eddie will have to try another approach."

"What are you going to do?"

"Heck if I know," he admitted. "I'll see if I can get Tom to go to her. I was hoping their eyes would meet across the crowded room and all that stuff."

Tina gave him a lovely smile. "Why, Mr. Chase, you are the hopeless romantic, aren't you?"

Eddie grinned back. "Yeah. Linda loves it!"

He left Tina and headed back to find Tom. After a private whisper, "Leslie is down on the beach," he was surprised when Tom immediately hurried to the door, his face a mixture of hope and hesitancy. Eddie looked fairly stunned. "Gosh, didn't realize it would be that easy."

A murmur went through all those in attendance as they saw Tom leave. Within a few minutes all had glanced towards the oceanview windows before resuming their conversations. They all as one had the same knowing smile on their lips as they silently wished their friends success.

A latecomer entered the private party and towered over most of the guests. He was enthusiastically welcomed and greeted as he made his way over to the head of the studio.

"Phillip," Richard offered his hand. "Glad you could make it."

"Thanks for the invitation, Richard. Unfortunately I can only stay about an hour or I won't get enough sleep tonight. I hate five a.m. flights. Nice turnout," he commented, accepting a shrimp cocktail from a passing waiter.

"Hey, old man!" Eddie exclaimed, slapping him on the back. "About time you put in an appearance."

"Edward. Linda, how nice to see you again. It seems we're exchanging coasts. I'm on my way to New York," Phillip told her.

"Which movie did you get, Phil?"

"SECRET HEARTS, SECRET LIES. It's a mystery and love

story. A. T. Enright is directing," he added as he glanced over the room. "Where's Tom? I wanted to say hello."

Avery looked to Eddie to respond. "Um, he's here. He's down at the beach."

"Beach?" Phillip echoed. "That's odd. He has enough of that at his place."

"He's out there talking to Leslie. Well," he hesitated, "we're hoping they're talking."

"Bun...Leslie's here, too? Wonderful!" Phillip exclaimed. "I was hoping she would be. I have something for her. It's about time we finally get to meet each other face to face."

Phillip strode off towards the door before the others could say anything.

"Bad timing, Beck" Eddie muttered after him.

Phillip walked out on the terrace and looked for Leslie and Tom, not understanding the possible meaning of their being together. Walking to the railed edge he looked down and saw them. He silently watched for a moment, his face going blank. For a moment or two he fingered a small gold box he had taken out of his pocket. Bringing it up to his lips, he tapped it a few times, deep in thought as he stared unseeing at the ocean. When he turned to reenter the club, he found Eddie just inside the door watching him.

Tried as he might, Phillip's smile still sagged a little and his eyes lost a little of their gleam. "It doesn't appear to be a very good time to meet Bunny," he commented quietly as he looked at the little box in his hand. "I need to get home and get some sleep, Edward. Would you give this to our Madame Author for me, please? Tell her.... No. Just tell her I'm sorry our paths never crossed. Perhaps next time."

Eddie accepted the golden box and nodded as Phillip headed towards the front door. As he disappeared, Eddie wondered if it had been a look of disappointment he had seen or something deeper. He had never fully understood the ifs or the whats that had passed between Leslie and Phillip. That chance fan letter he had received so long ago had touched all their lives. Phillip's life had changed dramatically as had Leslie's. Now Phillip was gone for an extended filming in New York. It appeared as if he had just received a silent reply to an unanswered question he had had a long time.

Eddie's curiosity overcame him. He casually backed into a quiet corner so he would be unobserved by the others. He opened the hinged box to see what Phillip had left behind. A smile erased his furrowed brow. It was the solid gold bunny lapel pin with the Ceylon blue sapphire eyes that Phillip had worn when he won his first award.


**W**hat of Leslie and Tom, though? What had Phillip seen when he looked over the railing?

Not that many moments earlier, a dry-mouthed, nervous Tom Young had spotted Leslie sitting on the bottom step of the landing staring fixedly at the incoming waves. She was holding her arms close to her body, shivering.

Giving himself an Irish accent like one of the sound technicians, he remarked casually, "Well, Miss, you be lookin' a might cold. Would ya be needin' a coat now?"

"No, thanks, Sean. I'm not cold really. I...." She glanced up and saw Tom standing there. Whatever she had planned on saying was never uttered.

As she shakily stood, Tom descended the rest of the steps. He put his hands on her arms. "You're shaking like a leaf," he exclaimed. "You should be inside."

"The...the breeze is warm. I'm...I..." she stammered. She looked into his amber eyes and could see the love and the hope in them. All the years of self-doubt dropped away. Her shaking stopped. Reaching up, she put a steady hand on his cheek. As he leaned his face into the caress, she smiled. "You really do care, don't you?" and her hand dropped.

"I always have. You just never believed me." He dropped his hands from her arms and picked her hand up again. "Let's go back inside and tell everyone you've changed your mind about moving down here. With me."

Leslie pulled back on her hand to bring him closer. Her other hand went behind his neck, her eyes resting on his lips. "We'll tell them...in a minute or so," she barely whispered as he encircled her with his arms and sealed the promise with a long awaited, passionate kiss.

# Epilogue

Legend has it that if you quietly crawl through the rickety chain link fence that surrounds the deserted studio and if you can find the dilapidated building that once housed "The Time Police," you must stand very still. If you are patient enough and wait long enough you will see the rabbits that live in the creaking, weather-blown ruins. Don't bother bringing carrots or lettuce for the two residents of the old Majestic lot. They aren't interested in the outside world. It's said they have their own portal hidden in the ruins through which they come and go and take care of each other.

The children who venture in to search for the rabbits believe in the portal for they can never tell where the mysterious pair is hiding. Those who attempt to find the hidden lair never return to the studio again.

There are those people who don't believe in legends. They claim the two rabbits were just creatures that wandered out of the surrounding hills and lived in peaceful isolation. These people are aware of the many love stories—both true and make-believe—that came out of the studio so many years ago. They could even provide names to the more well-known loves, like Bob and Laura, Steve and Carol, Tom and Leslie, Sir Charles and Andrea, or Doug and Marcy. They might confuse fact with fiction, but the stories and the movies and the names remained long after the people and the studio had dissolved into dust.

But the children and the romantics believe. They even gave names to the elusive rabbits. The brown rabbit with the amber eyes they call Jack and the lighter brown rabbit with the big blue eyes they call Jane.

—The End—

Thanks and Acknowledgements:

THANKS TO MY PROOFREADERS AND EDITORS:
JOEY KITZMAN
KARLA GALLAGHER, ENGLISH B.A.

# ABOUT THE AUTHOR

## NANCY TEMPLE RODRIGUE

Nancy lives in the small town of Lompoc, California, where she writes her novels, in addition to operating two online businesses. Besides writing, Nancy is an avid reader and also enjoys knitting and crocheting. Her award-winning 1957 T- Bird (as seen on the back cover of the first novel in her Hidden Mickey series Hidden Mickey: Sometimes Dead Men DO Tell Tales!) is regularly shown at local car shows, along with her husband's beautiful 1923 Ford T-Bucket roadster. Living in the beautiful Santa Rita wine region she also enjoys visiting the beautiful vineyards nearby and tasting the wonderful wines they produce.

The Fan Letter was authored during the late 1980's to early 1990's, the time period where Nancy authored several Science Fiction Fantasy novels. The Fan Letter was her last novel in that time period, a romantic fantasy about a popular television series fan writing to her favorite actor, and the way their lives intertwine when her letter sets off a chain of events that affect both her life as well as this actor's life and career.

In her writing of the second novel in her Hidden Mickey series Hidden Mickey 2: It All Started… Nancy once again added the fantasy element with a new mysterious character, Wolf. She gives this character the uncanny ability to embody a different form as he moves through the fabric of time with a mysterious pendant. Wolf then becomes a primary character in her third novel of the series, Hidden Mickey 3 Wolf!: The Legend of Tom Sawyer's Island, and the fourth book in the series Hidden Mickey 4 Wolf!: Happily Ever After?. Nancy's novels show her admiration and respect for the man of fantasy who started it all–Walt Disney.

Nancy actively participates in book signings and speaking events, and she loves talking to people who enjoy her novels. Fans can go to www.Double-Rbooks.com to follow Nancy's blog and learn where book signing event dates and locations are posted.